PRAISE FOR

HELENKAY DIMON

"She's a delight."

—*New York Times* bestselling author Christina Dodd

"Sharp writing and plenty of sexy romantic sizzle."

—*Chicago Tribune*

"HelenKay Dimon is a genius."

—*Joyfully Reviewed*

"So smart, sexy and fast-paced, I devour her stories."

—*New York Times* bestselling author Lori Foster

"Sexy, emotional, funny . . . Dimon gives it all to her readers . . . [This] shouldn't be missed."

—*New York Times* bestselling author Jill Shalvis

"Dimon's fresh new series is enjoyable, and the plot will appeal to many different readers. By turns funny and romantic, the sexual tension between the main characters is portrayed perfectly."

—*RT Book Reviews*

"The sex is steamy. The repartee is witty. There are some things in life you can just depend on, thank goodness."   —*Dear Author*

"I didn't want to stop reading."   —*Smart Bitches, Trashy Books*

MERCY

HelenKay Dimon

HEAT | NEW YORK

THE BERKLEY PUBLISHING GROUP
Published by the Penguin Group
Penguin Group (USA) LLC
375 Hudson Street, New York, New York 10014

USA • Canada • UK • Ireland • Australia • New Zealand • India • South Africa • China

penguin.com

A Penguin Random House Company

This book is an original publication of The Berkley Publishing Group.

Library of Congress Cataloging-in-Publication Data

Dimon, HelenKay.
Mercy / HelenKay Dimon.—Heat trade Paperback edition.
pages cm
ISBN 978-0-425-27073-8
1. Women soldiers—Fiction.   2. Special forces (Military science)—Fiction.
3. Disappeared persons—Fiction.   4. Soldiers—Fiction.   I. Title.
PS3604.I467M47 2014
813'.6—dc23
2013037037

PUBLISHING HISTORY
Heat trade paperback edition / May 2014

PRINTED IN THE UNITED STATES OF AMERICA

10   9   8   7   6   5   4   3   2

Cove image: Woman in man's shirt © Yeko Photo Studio / Shutterstock.
Cover design by Diana Kolsky.
Text design by Kristin del Rosario.

For Jill Shalvis,
who believes even when I don't

ACKNOWLEDGMENTS

Thank you, first and always, to my husband. You make every day better and never complain about my deadline stress. Every writer needs a spouse like you.

To Leis Pederson, for being a great editor and taking a chance on this one, and to my agent, Laura Bradford, for making every part of my career run smoother.

To Anne Calhoun, for reading the first three chapters and offering invaluable insights, and to Vivian Arend and Jill Shalvis, for reading the final draft and giving me confidence. You're amazing authors and I am lucky to have all three of you in my life.

To Alison Kent, Wendy Duren, Kassia Krozser, Jill Monroe and Stephanie Feagan, for listening and making every day brighter with your emails and support. Thank you for everything.

To the readers and reviewers out there who support the romance genre. None of this can happen without you. Thank you!

ONE

Becca Ford ducked into the alley running next to Holton Woods, the exclusive members-only supper club perched at the end of the cul-de-sac on the edge of Washington, D.C.'s Dupont Circle neighborhood. With quiet steps, she edged along the side, her back skimming the wall as she scanned the area for cameras. For once, the plan depended on being caught by security instead of dodging it.

In any other city alley the smell of stale beer and a sharp smack of vomit would have hit her the second she turned the corner and stepped behind the three-story brick building. Not here. The members—politicians, powerful businessmen and foreign dignitaries—didn't go through the intensive membership process and pay the hefty initiation fees and monthly dues to come to just any club. No, Holton Woods once housed a private boys' school and it retained its exclusive attitude even now.

Her gun pressed against her lower back as she stared at the double doors and obvious alarm system and lock securing this side of the property. She'd skipped the most logical choice of knocking on the front door, knowing she'd never get past the bruising body-guard to reach the boss. The only answer was to get "caught" and dragged inside. Let the men think they'd won the round. That they were in charge. But she'd know the truth.

Still, she thought about the very lethal man on the other side of the door and calculated her chances of living through the next five minutes and put the probability around twenty percent. Not great, but the possibility of survival hovered around zero if she didn't get inside. She'd pissed him off and he could just as easily destroy her as help her. But she didn't have another option.

After one final sweeping glance above for cameras, she stepped closer and sensed a presence in the alley matching her step-for-step. Bright sunshine pounded down as the punishing humidity drenched the back of her thin black tank top. She kept her head forward, but her gaze traveled. On her third step she heard a distinctive click, and a shadow danced on the pavement to her right.

With all her training, standing still proved difficult. Her instincts screamed to duck or punch before someone closed in. This someone was smart enough to grab her arm and close the distance between them to keep her from lashing out or performing a back kick to his balls.

And this one definitely had balls. The attacker was a man. His broad shoulders gave his shadow a menacing look and blocked the sun streaming behind her. She could smell a subtle scent that reminded her of Earl Grey tea.

Metal pressed against the back of her head, and not with a gentle touch. This was the push of a gun by a guy prepared to shoot her then dump her body well before the club opened, hours from now. The waistband of her olive cargo pants pulled tight against her stomach as her weapon scraped against bare skin, then was gone.

She was about to turn around when the gun was shoved hard enough to knock her head forward. "Hands up, sunshine."

She knew the voice, all rough and angry. Wade Royer, club manager, six-foot-three enforcer to the boss and a suspected criminal. To her, more than suspected, which was why she had worked to have this guy arrested eight months ago. Worked and succeeded. She'd brought him in, despite the odds. She'd done her job. The prosecutors failed to do theirs . . . or collected big checks not to. Either way, she took the fall, or that's what seemed to be happening to her life right now.

With her hair in a ponytail, his hot breath blew across her exposed neck. "The boss has been watching you skulk around out here and wants to see your pretty face up-close."

She fought off a tremble, but not from Wade's closeness. With the scruff over his chin and dark stare, he screamed scary, and terrified men twice his size, but she could handle him. She'd shot, stabbed and outrun men like him for years. The phone would buzz with an assignment and she'd go wherever the order said and do whatever she was told. If caught, she was on her own. If killed, no one would care. That was the job.

But the idea of seeing Wade's boss again rattled her resolve. The memory of his piercing eyes had her stomach bouncing, partly from unwanted excitement but mostly from a churning dread of his power over her. Even though it had been the plan to confront him, just knowing he'd been watching her roam around outside his building trapped the air in her lungs like a giant, choking fist. She coughed to find her breath but nothing came.

The image of the boss's face had barely rumbled in her brain before one of the back doors swung open. An eerie blackness loomed in the opening right before a figure filled the space.

Jarrett Holt, tall, dark and so deadly his competitors literally disappeared. He stood there in a black suit that matched his black heart and an ocean-blue tie that highlighted the eyes he once told her he'd inherited from his whore of a mother. Not prostitute. No, Jarrett referred to the woman who gave birth to him as a whore, as if the rough word condemned her more than Jarrett's harsh upbringing.

In some respects he looked like any other serious D.C. business owner fresh from a conference with a list of wealthy contacts on speed dial. But Jarrett was not like any man she'd ever known. Black hair he wore longer than was fashionable, until it grazed his collar, and a permanent shadow of stubble low on his cheeks and chin. He hid his millionaire status as well as he hid the secrets of how he amassed his fortune and gained his power.

He possessed the toned build of a long-distance runner, which he was. He had broad shoulders and loomed over her by a few inches, even though she stood just shy of five-ten. But his strong hands grabbed her attention. They could bring a woman to shuddering orgasm after only a few knowing touches.

He'd wielded a hold over her that straddled the thin line between pleasure and panic, never physically hurting her, but all too willing to shake her equilibrium until she fell at his feet. He'd enjoyed dominance and demanded full control over her body. And he was her only chance at staying alive long enough to figure out how to convince her former employer to leave her alone.

"Rebecca." Jarrett was the only man who ever used her full name, though he usually saved it for their time alone, in bed, right before he entered her.

She blinked away the memory before it sidetracked her or he read a hint of it on her face. "I need to talk to you."

"Last time we talked you were on your knees with my dick in your mouth while your team broke in and arrested me." Before she could say anything his cold gaze flicked to Wade. "Did you check her for weapons?"

"I have her gun."

"She'll have others." Jarrett stepped back and tipped his head for Wade to bring her inside. "To my office."

As Jarrett reset the lock on the back door, she walked through a storage room filled with stacked boxes and down the dark hallway to the door she recognized at the far end. No light filtered through. That's how Jarrett liked it. He moved in shadows and did most of his business at night.

The backrooms of the club would be the perfect place for him to unleash the vengeance he'd promised as Elijah Sterling dragged him away in handcuffs that day eight months ago. Out of spite, Elijah had refused to let Jarrett zip his pants before opening the front door and letting the media come crashing in. Cameras flashed and the headlines branded Jarrett as a sick pervert who ran drugs on the side of his legitimate but secretive business, all while Elijah ducked out of sight to maintain his cover.

Then a few days later the bad press stopped as fast as it started, and the headlines talked of a setup and Jarrett walked free, pants zipped this time. The doors to Holton Woods reopened to members that very night and had been open every night since.

Members didn't get to see the inner workings or parade through the back hallways, but that's what was happening to her. Wade had both of her hands clamped in one beefy fist and the gun trained on her skull with the other, but Becca didn't try to run. This was exactly where she needed to be, inside and behind the protective wall of Jarrett's security team and expertly wired building.

Thanks to a series of cameras and the attentive service of the mostly female staff, he had information on every man who walked through the club's doors. No matter how much Jarrett denied it, Becca suspected the club's services extended past food, cigar smoking and business talk. There were private rooms for gambling and meetings, with personal female attendants assigned to each door.

Not that any of the twentysomething women looked like they conducted lap dances on the side. No, Jarrett carefully chose his female employees and each possessed the intelligence and language skills one would expect from MBA candidates. He kept their uniforms sexy rather than sleazy. Slim black skirts, spiky heels and stockings with seams up the back. White shirts unbuttoned to show the lacy black bras underneath.

Thanks to the services he provided and the manner in which he did it, his tentacles extended and grew every day, touching bankers and businessmen, politicians and police. In a city filled with powerful people, he sat at the center of it all.

Wade passed Jarrett's office door and jerked her to a stop while Jarrett opened it. He walked inside without looking back, showing the calm assurance of a man who commands loyalty and knows he's protected.

Her gaze traveled over the room. Little had changed. The big desk and leather chair that telegraphed he was in charge sat dead center of the room. Thick drapes hid large windows, keeping the light out. Piles of papers covered his workspace and flat-screen monitors lined the walls, showing scenes from the club floor and the outside areas around the building. Those last ones were new but explained her quicker-than-expected capture.

Jarrett waved his second-in-command off without even glancing up from the piece of paper he'd picked up from his chair. "You can go."

Wade hesitated at her back. His large form didn't move, but the grip on her wrist eased. "Do you want me to search her first?"

Jarrett looked up with his gaze touring her body from head to foot then back again, stripping her bare without touching her. "I'll take care of it."

With a grunt Wade left. The door clicked shut as Jarrett lowered the document that had snagged his attention only a moment before. With slow, sure steps he walked around to the front of his desk and leaned against it. He folded his arms across his chest as he stared her down. The move pulled the material of his shirt tight across his biceps.

Her gaze lingered on his impressive arms then slid up to that face. She'd churned through every other possibility in her mind. She was on the run without an identity or any funds. Movies that showed operatives moving here and there without trouble, all while finding hidden bank accounts and weapons stashes, were pure Hollywood. When your black-ops employer wanted you terminated, it created a firestorm. Nothing survived, not a single scrap of paper. The people at the top left nothing behind, not even the decaying bodies.

She was determined not to end that way.

Since her hands shook, something that hadn't happened to her since her initial training outside Berlin years ago, she clasped them together behind her. "I need—"

"Take your clothes off."

The hollow words echoed through the quiet room and skidded into her. "What?"

But she knew. In some ways this wasn't even a surprise. This was a power play, one of many he'd likely subject her to before he decided whether to kill her or help her.

"I want everything off." He didn't move. Didn't even blink.

Blood rushed through her veins and thundered in her ears. "Why?"

"Weapons."

With her hands in the air, she bent down. Careful not to spook him, she slid a knife out of the side of her ankle boot and dropped it on the floor in front of him. The small gun tucked by her opposite ankle came next. Metal clanked against the hardwood. She usually carried more, but most of her stash sat in an apartment she couldn't return to.

She stood up with her hands raised. "That's all I have."

Still, he didn't move. "You'll understand if I don't trust you."

"You did before."

"Back when we were fucking?" The only sign the meeting affected him at all came in the way he clenched his hands into fists then relaxed them only to do it again. "Every last piece of clothing comes off right now or I put you back on the street without the weapons."

That would mean her death. Humiliation she could handle. She'd signed up for that in coming here, and he could do so much worse to break her spirit.

She'd push down her pride and swallow it back. But something else ate at her gut. The idea of being naked with him filled her with a confusing mix of dread and yearning. In their months apart she'd tried to stamp out any stray bits of attraction to him by repeatedly reading his case file, burning the reports of his sins in her mind. None of it worked to fully erase the memory of his hands and mouth sweeping over her skin.

"Now, Rebecca."

The rough edge to his voice had her reaching for the hem of her tank. With a tug she pulled it out of her pants and whipped it over her head. She started on the pants next. Her belt buckle clanked as she undid it. The rip of her zipper streaked through the room.

As she kicked her boots off, she glanced over at him. His laser-like stare focused on her hands. He'd loosened his arms and let them fall to his sides. When she stripped her pants down and off her legs, he gripped the edge of the desk on either side of his thighs.

She stood up again, facing him in a simple white bra and panties. The sheer fabric, soft a second ago, now scratched her skin as his gaze swept over her, lingering on her breasts then dipping below. They'd slept together for months, but she never felt so raw, so exposed.

"Keep going." His voice stayed even, but in an almost imperceptible move his jaw tightened and his knuckles whitened from the force of his hold on the desk.

"I'm clearly not hiding anything."

"And you're clearly not understanding me. I want you naked."

Dragging as much air into her lungs as possible, she centered her mind again, swiping it blank for survival. With a weight pounding on her chest, she reached around and unhooked her bra. Her breasts spilled over the edge then were free. Without looking at him, she leaned over and skimmed the panties down her legs, forcing them off inch-by-inch.

She stepped out of them as soon as they hit the floor, but refused to cower. He'd seen it all before and was just testing her now. She needed to live through this to have a chance.

She lifted her head and met his glare with one of her own. "Satisfied?"

"Come here."

After all the terror of the adrenaline-pounding last twenty-four hours, she didn't think she'd find more fear. She'd tucked it all away in that dark corner of her brain, but it raged now, wild and out of control.

Her bare feet slapped against the floor while she closed the short space separating them. His muscles stretched as he stood up and shifted to the side.

"Put your hands on the desk," he said.

Her heartbeat hammered through every bone, every cell, making her dizzy. With her body shaking, she rested her palms flat against the desk and bent over. She pressed her arms tight against her sides and locked her elbows in a vain attempt to cover a portion of her C-cup breasts, but her ass was in the air.

When he stepped behind her, she braced for anything. He'd never hit her, but that was before she'd brought law enforcement down on his head. No matter what he had done, he would see that as the ultimate betrayal.

Her stomach leapt the second before he touched her. Even in her confused haze, she sensed it coming, wanting it and denying it. Firm hands pressed against her skin, low on her thighs. She expected the grip of his fingers to mirror the thread of anger in his voice. Instead, his fingertips brushed and caressed as they moved up.

The rhythmic sound of his breathing fell around her. When his hands reached her ass and his fingers danced along the seam, her knees buckled. But he was there. He brought his body in closer, wedging her between the desk in front and his firm thighs behind.

One finger slid down the crease between her cheeks and kept going until it rolled around her clit. Then it slipped deep inside her. Uncontrollable shivers had her arms bending. She wanted to believe the emotions battering her from every direction stemmed from adrenaline and the will to survive, but she honestly didn't know.

"You're wet." A tremor played in his voice this time.

She nodded because she didn't think she could form words. While one hand covered her, with his middle finger now plunging in and out, the other went to her head and tugged on the ponytail holder. It fell to the floor as her long hair cascaded over her shoulders and across the tips of her breasts.

"Tell me what you need, Rebecca."

The word "you" was right there on her next breath, but she bit it back. Letting him use her body would tear at her soul and further mix the black-and-white layers of her life until all she saw was gray.

But she'd forfeit that piece of her if it meant survival.

It was the desperate wanting she feared. Giving in to the side of her that waited in the darkness, craving what he could give her, had the potential to irrevocably shatter something inside her. He could take so much that there wouldn't be anything left, so she had to separate and watch from outside with a forced detachment.

He was a criminal. She repeated the mantra until it beat in time with the movement of his fingers. But even as the letters flashed in her brain, she wondered what the word truly meant. The people she worked for and trusted had tried to kill her, so she couldn't tag them as the good guys while saddling Jarrett with the enemy title.

As common sense waged a battle inside her, she inhaled a deep breath, ignoring the rough sound, and focused on saying the words. "Help. I need your help."

"To come?"

"Jarrett . . ." Her voice trailed off before she could beg since she had no idea what she would ask for. Thoughts and warnings bombarded her brain.

"Say it."

She shook her head. "To survive."

"Meaning?"

"There are people who want me dead."

His fingers stilled for a second then pressed inside her again before he pulled in closer and rubbed his rising cock against her through his pants. "That's the inevitable end of your job."

"People I trusted are after me this time."

"Interesting." He grunted in what could only be described as a male version of I told you so. "So, now you need me."

"Yes."

"You know what I'll demand in return."

Her eyes closed. The feel of his body over hers, of his hands caressing her until her speech stumbled . . . She wondered if she'd be safer on the streets, away from him and the spell he wound around her.

"Rebecca?" His fingertips brushed against the dead center of her back right before his tongue licked the spot. "In return for protection, I get you. All of you, however I want you."

The last gasp of air hiccupped in her lungs and suddenly she didn't care if anyone came in or the police burst through the door. "I don't—"

"If you want my help, I demand the words."

His lips skimmed up her spine and the last of her defenses crumbled. "I'm yours."

TWO

The words rang in Jarrett's ears. Rebecca had claimed she belonged to him once before. This time she would, but on his terms. She'd be his to conquer. His to use and discard. His to fuck as he pleased, without any regard for what she wanted or needed.

He didn't even care why she was really here. Her reasons didn't matter because he would not cede any emotional ground.

But he would touch her, as often as and in any way he wanted. Her body always intrigued him. Long and lean, so sleek and trim. The perfectly round breasts at least a size larger than should be natural for her frame. When they first met she tried to hide them by smashing them under stiff exercise bras. He bought her lacy feminine ones and felt a surge of satisfaction when she smiled over them.

He generally didn't care what a woman wore, but he realized he preferred her straight brown hair falling over her shoulders like it was now. The same hair she liked to wrap around his cock as she used her hand to get him off. Add in those intelligent moss-green eyes and it was a wonder he ever let her climb out of bed.

He skimmed his fingers over the smooth skin of her back to that shallow dip right before her ass. He'd kissed that sexy softness so many times, loving how her body shook as he pushed into her from behind. As his fingers slid over her ass cheek now, he was torn between the stark need to fuck her and the urge to spank her. Not a sexy love tap either. A blow intended to bring pain.

He'd never hit a woman in his life, but there was a time when he'd seriously considered killing this one. Trapped in a blanket of red fury, sitting in a jail cell then later waiting out the days for a meaningless trial that never came, Jarrett had dreamed up ways to do it. Spent time imagining his revenge, and only backed off when the dark dreams began to consume every hour.

He refused to give her that much power over him again.

She'd lied and betrayed him. She twisted him up until he lowered his defenses, then she handed him over to the very people who sought to destroy him. Thanks to her, he'd entered into a sick bargain to regain his freedom. One he still regretted.

Every rage-filled second of the last eight months came rushing back to him as her body clenched and soaked his fingers. She spoke of survival like she knew a damn thing about the concept. She believed being used as a pawn long ago in a parental kidnapping scheme gave her the right to separate from society and kill for a living. Oh, she prettied it up with talk of special operations and service to country, but at base she was a hired gun.

Now she'd work for him as a sex toy he'd play with or ignore as he pleased.

Starting right this second.

His palm continued to explore every curve. The more he touched, the more his upper arm shook. It took all of his concentration to keep the tremor from traveling down to his hand. He called up his fury and let it wrap around him as he plunged his fingers in deeper, harder, and tried not to get sucked back into her sensual web.

A shudder ran through her as her arms went slack. It had always been this way. When he didn't know how to handle her in the past, he'd used her body's reaction against her. On this level they communicated. Or so he thought right up until her team broke down his club's front door.

"Do you want me to fuck you, Rebecca?"

Her head fell down between her arms and her hair spread over his paperwork. "Jarrett, please."

That husky growl. It once lured him to the cusp of doom. "Answer me."

She stayed silent but her body began to rock against his fingers. She was right on the edge, every line and muscle primed.

"Or maybe I have my answer."

When a small groan escaped her lips, he shut his eyes and blocked out the delicious sound of capitulation. After a shaky, pained countdown from five, he slipped his fingers out of her. It took him another few seconds to trail his other hand across her ass and finally break all physical contact. Blood pounded in his cock as he clamped his teeth down on the inside of his bottom lip and stepped back.

Her body slumped against the desk as her gaze flew to his. "What are you doing?"

He would not fall for that breathy tone a second time. Would not believe the sensual craving he read in her eyes. She killed for a living and even now could be setting him up for a second round in hell.

She would not know what she cost him.

Calling on his formidable will, he brought the shields crashing down again, careful to drain any show of interest from his face. With a thin-lipped frown back in place and the mental reel of her past treachery playing in his head, his control clicked together like a series of lock tumblers.

"Stand up."

She blinked several times. "Wha . . . what?"

"You heard me." He walked around to his desk chair, honing his skills on increasing her shame as he paged through the documents on his desk. The words blurred, but he pretended to read, anything to let her know she meant nothing to him.

"At least let me explain," she said in a shaky voice.

He glanced at the monitors and saw the clear hallway. "We're going upstairs."

She slowly straightened. "Why?"

At full height, her body was on beautiful display. He could see the miles of fair skin and the three-inch scar where a man long dead once sliced a knife between her ribs. There was a time when seeing the visible memory of that near-fatal injury started Jarrett's heart thundering and made him wish he'd been the one to kill her attacker.

This time Jarrett refused to feel anything. Even as his gaze traveled over the peeks of flesh not shielded by her hair and across those stiff nipples, his cock pressed hard against the back of his zipper. But he fought off every urge.

"Your job is to agree with what I say and right now I say we're leaving my office." When she opened her mouth he raised an eyebrow and her words cut off.

With an exaggerated sigh she bent down as if to reach for her panties. "Fine."

"Leave those on the floor."

Her body shot up straight again, with those fantastic breasts on full view this time. "I'm naked."

"No one will even notice." Her eyes closed and he knew his words stung. He refused to care and silently berated himself for even seeing the flash of pain.

"Can I just—"

"You want another favor already?"

This wouldn't work if she begged. He would not let her sneak under his defenses and chip away like she had before. He'd altered his life for her once, gave up long-held beliefs and even confided in her like some lovesick pathetic boy. And it had all been a fucking game to her.

The memories ignited his rage all over again.

"Let me wear my shirt." This time anger spilled into her voice.

That fast, the equilibrium shifted. He could handle her fire, tunnel that straight into the bedroom and use it to fuel their sex without ever letting an ounce of emotion drip in.

"No." He walked to the door and opened it. Ignoring her stunned expression, he motioned for her to lead. "Now, Rebecca."

Her eyes narrowed slightly as she performed a quick visual tour of the room. When she started moving he guessed she didn't find what she wanted, whatever that was.

"If you plan to kill me, you should do it now."

That quick, he had his answer. A weapon. She still expected him to cut her down like she deserved. No, he'd decided to play with her instead, at least until he knew her plans this time.

He shook his head. Threw in that condescending *tsk-tsk*ing sound he knew pissed her off. "So dramatic."

"That happens when your house catches fire and your car gets run off the road." She stood right in front of him at the edge of the doorway with legs wide and hair streaming down her back.

"If I wanted you dead, you'd be dead." And that wasn't an exaggeration. He'd never been saddled with society's notions of right and wrong when it came to killing. Some people deserved to die and he performed a service when he did the dispatching.

Her chin lifted even higher. "Others have tried and failed."

"I would succeed." He pointed toward the hall. "Go."

Her shoulders fell a fraction as she tiptoed the last steps to the doorway and craned her neck to look down the hall. The low rumble of voices echoed from behind the wall separating the office space from the public areas of the club.

She slipped into the hall without looking back and turned to the right. He didn't rush to take the lead because she knew where to go. The private elevator to the top two floors sat a few feet away. Just long enough for him to watch her graceful walk and see that high, tight ass swish in long steps. They were angry steps. He could tell from the straight backbone and the way her hands balled into fists at her sides.

Naked and seemingly resigned to her nudity, she stopped at the elevator doors, keeping her gaze straight ahead. He could see her swallow and watch her shoulders dip then square again, probably as she fought off the urge to hide her body from him. If he wasn't so hell-bent on hating her, he'd admire her spirit.

He'd just pressed his palm against the security reader and turned the key he kept on him at all times, when she whispered something. He had to duck, leaning in to hear her. "What did you say?"

"Tell me you're not behind this."

He didn't want the particulars of her life now, but curiosity ate at him. "This?"

The doors opened but she didn't move. "My team is dead."

Not news. Up until a month ago he'd tracked her every move. After the charges were dropped, he'd called in favors and used all of his resources to uncover as much information about her undercover team as possible. Knowing what at least two of them looked like made that easier, so did his improper access to top secret files.

Watching her travel and live her life like she'd never fucked up his drove him mad with a mix of rage and unspent sexual frustration, so he'd shifted his focus. He followed every other member of the four-person team, plus its leader. Oh, yes. Todd Rivers couldn't take a piss without Jarrett knowing. Through a series of questionable accidents and odd crimes, most of the team was dead. Todd was very much alive, but his day would come.

"You'll excuse me if I don't weep for the people who planted evidence to have me arrested," Jarrett said.

She faced him then. Her eyes narrowed as her mouth fell into a grim line. "That's not true."

"Lying won't help your position with me." He put a hand against her back and ushered her inside.

The mirrors highlighted her bare body from every angle. She appeared too busy staring at him to notice the show she put on. He slid the key into the elevator lock and pressed number three.

She waited until he stood beside her, shoulder pressed to her arm, before talking again. "You're trying to tell me you were innocent of the charges?"

"I've never sold drugs in my life." That she would think otherwise after their months together pissed him off the most. When the accusations flew, he'd waited for her to step up and deny. Her silence from back then still pounded in his brain. "Not that I could ever figure out why a CIA front group would be involved with domestic drug running."

"You aren't supposed to know anything about our group. No one is. Disbanded or not, it's black-ops and falls squarely in the plausible deniability realm."

He smiled at her. "Yet, I do know about your now-former team."

"Then you also should know we weren't originally here for a drug raid."

"So, I was being tracked for something else then. Interesting." But not surprising. He'd always figured he'd collected the wrong bit of information about the right person, and that had put him and the club in the bull's-eye.

Now he knew the truth. Faked drug charges gave them the in. Becca or someone on her team came up with the idea and ran with it. He'd barely left her side for months, spent his nights kissing her, touching her, fucking her. It's true the line between right and wrong didn't exist for him. Nothing was ever that easy. But dealing drugs—hell, even trying them—was not something anyone could honestly lay at his door. He knew too much about where that destructive road led.

She turned to face him. "I saw the drugs, Jarrett."

Not possible. The words punched him and he fought off a flinch. Forced his expression to stay blank.

The doors opened straight into a small entry foyer outside his front door, the only one on this floor.

"If that's true, and I'm not convinced it is, you saw what someone wanted you to see." He packed away every word she said, every phrase of the conversation for later dissection. "This discussion is over."

He repeated the security procedures at his door and pushed it open right after the lock cleared. He was halfway into the foyer, his dress shoes clicking against the inlaid marble, when he stopped and glanced around.

She stood in the doorway, not moving. "Elijah is dead."

Looked like she didn't know everything after all. "I am aware of his status."

"And?"

"And what?" Jarrett dropped the keys in his suit jacket pocket.

"Did you kill him?"

Jarrett wondered what it took for her to hold back the question this long. Not that he intended to answer it or prove to her how wrong her assumptions were. "Come inside, Rebecca."

Still she didn't move. "I know you hated him."

"A vast understatement." When his phone buzzed, Jarrett ignored it. "You, him, everyone who built a phony case against me."

His phone buzzed a second time, and this round he grabbed it out of his pocket. While he checked the screen, she came inside. He glanced up and watched as her gaze touched every surface and hesitated on the fireplace mantel, where the few photographs he'd ever allowed of them together once rested. Only a clock sat there now.

Her chest expanded as she blew out a long breath and headed to the left. His room.

"Stop," he called out.

"Why?"

"You're on the right."

She glanced in the direction of his bedroom door. "Since when?"

"My bedroom is off-limits to you."

Her head fell to the side and frustration showed in her expression. "Is this necessary?"

"Why don't I tell you about my short but very real time in jail, then you can decide how serious I am." His fingers tightened around the phone and the plastic case cracked under his hold. "Go into your assigned bedroom."

Her gaze bounced to the erection that still hadn't abated. She nodded then started walking.

He followed her inside but leaned against the doorjamb as she brushed her hand over the comforter then sat on the bed. Seeing her there, legs partly open and body bared to his gaze, shook his resolve.

"You will stay in here unless and until I allow you to leave. So that we're clear, I will fuck you in here and not my room."

"Are you going to chain me to the bed?" Her voice carried a whip of sarcasm. The look on her face suggested she was a few seconds away from losing her calm reserve.

"If necessary."

"I didn't sign up to be your prisoner."

"I think we both know you did."

She shook her head. "What about eating and the bathroom?"

"You may go into any part of my apartment except my bedroom and private office." His phone buzzed for a third time.

"I used to live here. I slept in that bedroom every single night." She put her hands on the edge of the mattress and tucked her legs as close to the mattress as possible, hiding her bare feet underneath the bed.

The shift caught his attention and had his gaze roaming. "You were my girlfriend then. Whatever rights you had are gone."

"What am I now?"

His eyes met hers. "At my mercy."

She stared at her lap and his gaze followed her there. Waxed bare and so damn hot. His brain battled with his dick. He wanted to slide into her mouth, but Wade clearly needed him downstairs or he wouldn't keep calling.

After a lifetime of putting his needs last, Jarrett followed suit again this time. "I expect you to be here when I get back. Right here, just as you are now."

He buttoned his jacket and ignored the way it gaped over his pants. By the time he reached the downstairs floor he needed his body back in control.

"Where are you going?"

The more familiar she became, the harder he pushed back. Some internal switch in his brain ticked on, ensuring she understood her place. "Not your business."

He got the whole way back to the door before she spoke again. "Don't you want to know why I'm here and what I really need from you other than a place to hide?"

He glanced over his shoulder. "I'm still trying to figure out why you thought you'd be safe with me."

She nibbled on her bottom lip. "I am, aren't I?"

"For now."

THREE

When his determined footsteps receded and the front door slammed, Becca blew out the breath she'd been holding. The confrontation had been rocky, bordering on humiliating, as expected, but she wasn't dead. She wouldn't have been surprised if he pulled out a knife or gun and made her beg for her life. Not after he promised to destroy her all those months ago.

His claims about not dealing drugs hit harder. He'd always denied the charges, but didn't they all. Seeing a rich man's lawyer cry to the media about falsified charges had become such an eye-rolling event that it no longer even registered in her brain.

Face-to-face with the sharp snap of Jarrett's voice and piercing gaze right there where she couldn't look away or ignore proved different. He'd almost willed her to believe. He acted like he didn't care about one syllable she uttered as he vibrated with indignation over the old charges.

It was an impressive display, but she'd seen the drugs right downstairs in one of the storage rooms and found more in the office in this apartment. As part of her assignment she posed as an employee of Spectrum Industries, a small satellite communications company that served as cover for her black-ops team. The cover gave her the in at Holton Woods, but her sales meeting with Jarrett had turned very personal, very fast.

She'd lied to him and led him down a path that never felt right to her. But she didn't plant evidence. No member of her team had. Not possible since, as the one on the inside with the greatest access and the most to lose, she'd insisted she be the only one allowed in the apartment. Even if someone "helped" the investigation along downstairs, that didn't explain what she'd seen here, in Jarrett's private sanctuary.

She chewed on her lower lip as she stared out the open door and into the hallway. Minutes passed but the questions refused to leave her brain no matter how hard she tried to kick them out. Checking the old drug-hiding place now wouldn't prove anything and she wasn't in the apartment for that anyway. She needed access to his computers and information, and a place to hide. Plus, he could have changed where he stashed the drugs or finally stopped dealing for real.

It shouldn't matter how he earned his money . . . but if he really had been set up, if getting out of jail amounted to more than a simple case of applying the right pressure to the right powerful person, then everything about the last few months of her life was a lie. And what she did to him . . . she shook her head to block out the thought.

Still, it took a second to make the decision. Her innate need to investigate and uncover kicked in. Not knowing when he'd be back, she moved as fast as possible. She slipped into the bathroom connected to what she supposed would be her temporary room and grabbed a pristine white towel off the rod. As if Jarrett would have anything other than white towels. The entire apartment was a shrine of white and gray.

Unless something had changed, and she doubted it had, his decorating world consisted of black hardwood floors and a monotone color scheme of streamlined gray sofa cushions in the living room and a matching comforter on the bed. No knickknacks. No clutter, not even a stray newspaper.

Even the few photographs on the walls were black-and-white prints of places she doubted he'd ever visited. He had plenty of money but rarely ventured outside the club's walls. When they were together his only view of the actual sky came with his regular runs and a dinner out every now and then.

With the plush cotton wrapped around her, she walked back to the door, enjoying the constant blast of air conditioning that chilled the place. Jarrett hated heat, which always amused her since he'd settled in a city known for its unrelenting summer humidity. He combated the problem by running the air in the hot months and barely turning the heat on during the winter.

She stared across the hall at the closed door. The knob turned under her hand without trouble. Not a surprise. Jarrett lived a closed-down life outside of his apartment, but inside there wasn't a single lock.

She flicked the switch, and bright lights bounced off the wall of mirrors and every shiny surface of the workout equipment. This was where he honed that body into pure muscular perfection. She'd long ago figured out his regimen had more to do with clearing his head than a true dedication to exercise.

After a brief scan of the room she turned off the light and closed the door. No, what she wanted would be at the other end of the spacious apartment. She crossed through the open living room, only sparing a glance at the kitchen and dining area, neither of which looked like anyone had stepped in there in the months since she'd been gone.

She hesitated at the short hallway on the opposite end of the large living space. The doors to the office and his bedroom were partially open. The temptation to push the door and peek into his private bedroom, to see if anything had changed, if there was even a hint of her past presence, pulled at her. Shutting down the instinct, she focused on the office and stepped inside before common sense clobbered her.

The only light in the room came from the one on the desk. This one, like the one downstairs, was framed by computer monitors. Two this time. Unless things had changed, one provided him with a constant stream from the security feed and the other was for work.

Papers were stacked in neat piles on the exact center of the top. Not as much as a pen mark marred the calendar blotter.

Her gaze skipped over the two black leather chairs and bold geometric gray-and-white patterned rug to the wall of closets on the far wall. She'd found the drugs there last time, behind boxes. The police found more in a secret but unlocked compartment in the wall. No way would he be stupid enough to repeat that . . . but the lure proved too great. She'd been investigating and searching for so long as part of her work life that she couldn't break the habit.

She opened the double doors with a click and dropped to her knees. The boxes that used to line the floor were gone. With the back wall cast in shadows, she couldn't see a thing. She fought back a flood of dread as she balanced one hand against the doorframe and strained to reach into the deep closet and the space behind.

Her fingertips brushed against the smooth wall, checking for a seam. She knocked and smacked, slapped her hand against every inch, but nothing. Not even a hollow thud.

She sat back on her heels. Whatever was once there was now gone. With her eyes closed, she silently berated herself for flipping into operative mode. His crimes were no longer her business. Going after him would not solve any of her problems. The exact opposite, actually.

When her eyes opened again her gaze landed back on the computer monitors. That fast, the training revved up again. Something had him rushing out of there. For all she knew, he was behind the attacks on her team and setting her up for the biggest fall of all.

She repeated the excuse as she got to her feet and sank into his desk chair. Never mind she wanted to know what he was doing right now.

As she hit the space bar to turn on the screen she tricked her brain into thinking she *needed* to know.

FOUR

Jarrett exited the elevator on the first floor and ran straight into Wade. Since the guy had the body of a professional football player, getting clipped in the stomach by his elbow wasn't something you could laugh off. Not that Jarrett felt much like laughing at the moment anyway. "What the hell are you doing lurking around out here?"

Wade looked like he was fighting off a smile as he rubbed a hand over his beard. "Waiting for you to finish."

Since he'd rather be upstairs doing anything but talking, Jarrett ignored the verbal jab. The incessant messaging gave him little choice but to come downstairs. Now that he stood in the dark back hallway of his club, his temper sparked. "How about telling me what's so damn urgent."

Wade leaned back against the wall. The shift highlighted the gun clipped to his side. "I guess I interrupted."

Weapon or not, if the smirk didn't disappear soon, Jarrett would remind Wade that the boss-employee part of their relationship meant he wanted a straight answer without having to demand it. "I'm still waiting on a response, preferably one that doesn't piss me off."

Wade's expression sobered as he stood up straight again. "Natalie Udall."

"I guess you didn't hear the 'no pissing me off' part." At the mention of the woman's name, a nerve in the back of Jarrett's neck pinched. He rubbed the muscle to ease the sudden cramp. "What about her?"

"She's here."

At least the woman upstairs had a use. Natalie was nothing but trouble. "Why?"

"Not sure, but she seemed mighty interested in you being in your apartment instead of in your office. Apparently, people think you spend all of your time working."

Jarrett didn't intend to provide details of his working hours to anyone. What he had with Becca once was over. Whatever they had now, no matter how complicated and infuriating, would be private. And shallow. Emotionless. He promised himself that much.

In all the thinking about Becca, Jarrett missed an important detail. That wasn't like him, but it had always been that way with her. He stopped mid-step and put out a hand to bring Wade to a halt beside him. "One more thing—"

Wade smiled. "I was wondering when you'd remember our guest hidden away upstairs. The one who's not Becca."

"I've tried forgetting about him and how I let him stay. Believe me." Jarrett shook his head. "And, for the record, I consider him our *unwanted* guest."

Wade's expression went blank. "You know how I feel on that score."

Only too well, and it jabbed at Jarrett at times. When everything blew up, and it would, he'd have to take the blame for opening the front door and letting the danger inside. "As of today, we'll have two unexpected guests."

"So, Becca is staying?"

"For now."

"He's not going to like Becca being here. Their history is . . . let's say complicated."

"Not the word I'd use, but message received." Jarrett stared at the ceiling and blew out a long breath. "Okay, main rule here is no one but me goes near the third floor."

"Of course."

Jarrett tried to imagine Becca's reaction if she walked onto the second floor, where Wade lived. "The last thing I need right now is that confrontation."

Speaking of which, Jarrett's mind wandered back to Natalie as he started walking again. It was just like her to show up at the wrong time. Made him wonder just how closely the CIA watched his business these days. "Nosy bitch."

"You mean Natalie? Yeah, I'm sure she's been called worse."

"Sometimes by me." He exhaled, because what he hoped would be a short visit downstairs to his office had turned into a full-blown nuisance.

Becca sat in his apartment, naked and likely doing something he'd warned her not to, and he was down here. Having her roam free, without supervision, made him twitchy. That woman could find trouble. Not that he kept anything important up there. He wasn't stupid. But that hadn't stopped her from framing him last time.

Then there was the naked part. This time he vowed to fuck her and not care. Their time together would be hot and dirty and completely commanded by him. She'd leave and he wouldn't so much as glance at the door as it slammed shut behind her. But none of that lessened his need to thrust inside her now.

First he had to get through what promised to be an irritating few minutes of government-speak. "Where is Natalie?"

"In the bar. Waiting."

"Right." Jarrett checked his suit jacket and flooded his brain with memories of Becca's betrayal in an attempt to calm his pounding erection. "Stick with me."

"Afraid to be alone with Natalie?" Wade chuckled. "I'm guessing Becca is more dangerous."

"I need you in case I get struck with the urge to strangle her." They walked in unison, their dress shoes clicking against the shiny hardwood floors.

"Which woman are you talking about?"

"Yes," Jarrett said and Wade chuckled.

Both women pushed Jarrett and tried to manipulate him, but in very different ways. Natalie assumed she could best him. Win. As if he'd ever let that happen.

With Becca a nonstop movie ran in his head. Her naked and sprawled across his bed with her arms over her head and her legs spread wide. Him between her slim thighs. His taste on her tongue and her moans echoing in his ears.

The image snapped off when Wade crossed in front of Jarrett, pushing open the door to the main bar seating area and stepped inside. A steady beat of music thumped in the background as it did whenever the club was closed and Wade picked the playlist.

Jarrett glanced around the velvet-lined booths and nodded with approval at the empty room. Wade clearly had shooed the attendants off the floor and the few male cleaning staff who were still there to set up scurried out of the open space when Jarrett pointed toward the kitchen door.

The place would open in about four hours and everything had to be set up and perfect by then. Every piece of crystal cleaned and sparkling. The room polished and primed for the men who demanded the highest quality when they filed into their claimed bar seats.

Jarrett learned long ago men would pay for better service. How when the customers were happy they spent more, drank more . . . talked more. Which gave him the perfect excuse to cut this unwanted meeting short. Not that he'd ever let Natalie linger.

Even in the dim lighting he could see her perched on a barstool with her impressive legs crossed and business suit tidy, this one trimmed close to her body in boring navy because she always picked monotone drab colors. She had a clenched government-worker-bee look to her, complete with blond hair coiled on her head in some intricate style that gave him a headache.

A practiced chill radiated off of her, but even with the harsh façade he could make out the woman underneath. The photographs in her employment file showed a much more informal Natalie, one that even managed to smile now and then. Not his type, but objectively attractive in a from-the-South, had-to-hide-her-sexuality-to-compete-in-a-male-dominated-career way.

Even now that soft North Carolina drawl would seep into her voice when her defenses dropped. He knew because his very presence on the earth seemed to prick her temper. He doubted this conversation would be any different.

She hated that he knew about the Spectrum shell company and the operatives behind it, as well as about her position at the CIA.

Things he wasn't supposed to know, that almost no one knew. He only obtained access because her bosses, men higher up who lacked her smarts, needed him for information and their usual tactics in lying, planting evidence and destroying lives had failed.

Lucky for him he had stockpiled information that made him relevant to those men in suits at Langley. When he decided to bargain for his freedom he made sure the deal came at a cost to those who wanted to destroy him. It had to be that way because he had almost lost his fucking mind when he lost Becca, and someone had to pay for that.

"Natalie." He slid onto the stool next to hers while Wade took up his regular position behind the bar, only a few feet away.

"I've asked you to call me Ms. Udall."

Jarrett nodded. "And I've declined."

She glanced at Wade then back to Jarrett. "I need to speak with you privately."

Wade cleaned a glass. "I think she's talking about me."

This was nonnegotiable. Jarrett had learned about trust the hard way at Becca's hands and before. Wade still enjoyed privileges few had. Their relationship transcended that of employer-employee.

"Wade stays." He always stayed, except for the plans Jarrett had for Becca upstairs. Plans he intended to implement within the next fifteen minutes.

Natalie swirled the water in her glass, letting the ice cubes clink against the side. "This is business."

"Wade knows about your job and a whole host of items buried in folders in safes somewhere that you'd likely rather neither of us know. That was the deal I made with your bosses at the CIA. That's always been the deal, and you know that."

Her gaze narrowed. "You continue to be confused about how our relationship works and your very limited role in any agency operation."

"Admittedly we have a communications issue." Jarrett leaned his elbows against the intricately carved bar and stared at the perfect lines of bottles on the shelves behind. "For reasons that are not clear, you think you own me."

"I do."

"I assure you, you don't." He faced her then. "Why are you here?"

"Spectrum."

That was the second time in an hour that particular topic came up. First Becca stumbled up to his door and now Natalie came poking around. "Not my favorite subject."

"We finally found something we agree on."

"And if what goes on behind Spectrum's doors is such a big secret, why do you people keep talking about the place?" Jarrett never wanted to utter the word again.

"As you point out, only very few people know the truth about Spectrum, and almost all of them who remain alive are in this room right now."

His thoughts bounced to the woman upstairs and how she seemed to bring nothing but disaster into his life. "Get to it."

"The business closed."

"I saw the fake bankruptcy filing for Spectrum in the paper. Almost looked like the company really existed."

"Several members of the team are dead, but I think you know that as well." Natalie took the file from under her elbow and slid it across the top of the bar to him.

He resisted the urge to grab it. It was unlikely she'd provide any real intel anyway. He'd been tagged as the enemy, someone they *had* to deal with thanks to their agreement. "I read the newspaper. Saw the obituaries, complete with made-up histories and families. Must be hard to dump carefully crafted identities after you spend so much time and money creating them."

"And do the real families ever know the truth?" Wade asked.

Jarrett guessed, just as with him, there would be no one to tell when the end came. "Good question. Natalie, care to take that one or is the answer classified as well?"

From the frozen features to the flat mouth, her look telegraphed her hatred. "I'm wondering if you, Jarrett, are the one pulling the strings, arranging for everyone who harmed you to disappear."

"Interesting theory."

"It's as if you decided to eliminate Spectrum and everyone behind it."

There was a time he considered it, but the CIA could not lay that sin on his door now. "I sense you question my subtlety."

"But not your thirst for revenge."

He had officially had enough of this game. He shifted in his seat, inching closer so she wouldn't miss a word. "You closed up Spectrum, not me. I had nothing to do with that business decision."

"We disbanded the cover for reasons that are none of your concern." She trailed a finger around the rim of her glass. "But someone, I'm thinking you, is going a step further and taking out the people who worked under it."

Jarrett glanced at Wade. Jarrett read the same thoughts bouncing around in his head in his second-in-command's eyes. Either they were being played or the CIA had not pulled the trigger on Spectrum's operatives. According to Becca and everything Jarrett had figured out on his own, someone had, which raised a lot of questions. None of which he planned to ask Natalie.

"There's no need for me to do anything. I was cleared of the trumped-up drug charges and your bosses assured me Spectrum would no longer be a problem, which is clearly the case." But Jarrett trusted the CIA's promises as far as he could drop-kick Wade. Danger lurked and Jarrett never dropped his guard.

"I find it hard to believe you wouldn't seek revenge on the people who destroyed your reputation." A smile curled at the edges of Natalie's lips. "After all, a woman, an operative, one of Spectrum's team, slipped into your life and bed and made herself at home in your world. That has to eat away at a man like you."

This was a dangerous game. Natalie sat right next to him, poking at still-gaping wounds and not understanding her peril or how the fury over Becca's betrayal still raged in his brain until it wiped out every reasonable thought.

He masked all of those ricocheting emotions under a tone of bland disinterest when he spoke again. "I'll ask again. Why are you really here, Natalie?"

"Becca."

"What about her?" On cue, the alarm on his phone went off. A simple code of four short buzzes followed by a second round. When Wade jerked and reached for the phone in his pocket, Jarrett knew he'd gotten the message, too.

That meant one thing—Becca was wandering around upstairs, stepping exactly where she shouldn't be. She'd either breached the doorway to his bedroom or private office. Either option cast doubt on her "someone is trying to kill me" claims.

Wade glanced in the direction of the back hall and raised an eyebrow. Jarrett shook his head. He didn't want anyone seeing

Becca naked but him, though she could be dressed and scaling a wall to the outside by now for all he knew.

Still, she'd come to the club for a reason. Maybe she found what she wanted or planted something new to screw him over. Either way, the damage was done. Rushing up there wouldn't fix it, regardless of how much he itched to do it. His sole focus switched to getting Natalie out the door so he could get upstairs faster.

When his gaze clashed with hers again, the intensity of her anger nearly swamped him.

"Do you have somewhere more important to be?" Natalie's chill had morphed into an icy drip in her voice.

"Actually, yes."

Her annoying smirk of satisfaction wavered. "You're telling me you don't care about the information I have on your former lover?"

"The key word is 'former.' I stopped caring about Becca a long time ago." He refused to let that be a lie. Even ignored the way Wade's eyebrow lifted.

Natalie finished her drink and dropped the glass against the bar with a thud. "I don't believe you."

"I don't care." That much was true. He never cared what anyone at the CIA or with the police, or even Spectrum, thought about him. He'd abdicated a small portion of control in order to stay out of prison, sure. He laid the blame for that on Becca, but he was no one's bitch. No one's.

"Then I guess you don't mind that Becca either is in danger or *is* the danger." Natalie said it as a comment, but it was clear from the slow emphasis of each word she didn't believe the sentiment.

At least they'd finally hit on a topic that did interest him. Not that he let that show. He steeled his body to remain still and forced his mouth into a thin line. "You obviously want to tell me something, so why not just go ahead and say whatever you came here to say."

"She is the prime suspect."

The news kicked him in the gut. Not what he expected at all. Wade frowned. "Suspect in what?"

Natalie ignored Wade like he was beneath her. Just the help. Her focus remained on Jarrett. "Eliminating her team."

"Why exactly would she do that?" Jarrett asked, unable to conjure up an explanation that made any sense.

"Power gone wild. Thirst for revenge. Lost her mind." Natalie held both hands up in the air as she ticked through the possibilities with all the enthusiasm of someone reading from a grocery list. "The reason doesn't really matter. The point is that she'll be put down like a rabid dog."

The description set a flame to Jarrett's brewing fury, but he refused to even flinch. "And why are you telling me?"

"I thought you should know in case you got the wild idea of trying to help her." Natalie finally glanced at Wade. "If she comes here—"

"Which she wouldn't." Jarrett said it like an order, basically commanding Natalie to speak to him again.

It worked. The explosive fury behind those brown eyes burned into him. "You are to contact me immediately if you hear from Becca."

He'd hand over the keys to the club before he took directions from Natalie or anyone in her office. And no one was touching Becca but him. "Again, Natalie, I don't work for you."

"I know you think that."

"You seem to forget our deal." Not that he ever could. It proved to be the ultimate case of sleeping with the enemy. "I gave you information you needed—"

"To stay out of prison."

Jarrett bit back a sharp response, one that pointed out how much he hated it when people interrupted him. But that would give her power. If she knew his weak points, those things that grated and prodded at him, she'd use them against him daily. Hell, he'd do the same thing in her position.

"You were desperate to have it and I acquiesced." The same information he'd painstakingly collected and portions of which he continued to hold back for his protection and the safety of a select few others. "We both know the drug charges were bogus. The concerns about what I knew from customers, those from outside of the country and those in power positions in D.C., led your office to admit Spectrum had exceeded its authority coming after me."

"I don't believe we admitted any such thing."

Maybe not directly, but it happened at some level or he wouldn't be free. He had ferreted out that much. "The team wasn't supposed to plant drugs or have me arrested. Because, as we both know, the CIA isn't in the domestic drug-crime-fighting business. But I'm thinking someone at Spectrum went rogue. When you realized, you terminated the team and the operation. Then you got into bed, metaphorically of course, with me."

Natalie spun her seat around to face him with her smirk back in place. "I never would have made the deal with you."

"Then it's a good thing you're not in charge at the CIA." Jarrett slid off the seat and stood next to the bar. "Next time make sure you have an appointment before you come over. I am no longer available for drop-in visits."

Her feet hit the floor as she reached out for his sleeve, her hand catching only air. "We're not done."

He thought about the silent alarm and the woman upstairs and all he wanted to do to her, and kept walking toward the hall. With his final step in the room, he glanced over his shoulder and shot Natalie a look that made most men wither. "Yes, we are."

FIVE

The leather chair squeaked as Becca leaned forward and stared at the sign-in on the screen. Figuring out Jarrett's convoluted password would be impossible without an intricate computer program, a tech expert and hours to analyze.

Not that she truly cared, whatever his current crimes, except to the extent she needed him out of jail for now. That was all. She wouldn't let any other attachment or concern grow. She absolutely refused to worry about him. She'd wasted far too many hours on that useless task already.

Being back in the condo, up on the third floor and locked behind a wall of security, the rush of adrenaline that had been flowing through her and fueling all those fears bubbling in her mind slowed. Jarrett walked her into the building. He didn't reach for a weapon or call his old contacts from the streets and have her hauled away. He put her in his most private space and bossed her around, but stopped before unleashing his fury with more than words.

An attack could still come. The waiting and quiet could be a game, and she'd mentally prepared for that possibility, but the panic that assailed her the second she stepped in the alley had disappeared. At the realization her heartbeat eased back to a normal rate.

Jarrett had to be in control and liked to deliver each sentence with a harsh bite to his words. She'd deal with that. The whip of need she experienced around him proved to be the bigger problem. Which was why she needed to get to work and get out of there as soon as possible.

Even knowing he wouldn't be dumb enough to write down a password, she eased the chair back and opened the top desk drawer. The sound almost drowned out the soft click of the front door closing in the other room. Almost.

She shot to her feet with one hand clutched on the knot holding the towel together. The other reached for the desk lamp and yanked the cord from the wall. Not much of a weapon, but something in case a trained killer, and not Jarrett, lingered out there.

With her back to the wall, she peeked around the hall corner and spied Jarrett right by the front door. Tall, angry and frowning in her exact direction. He excelled at that sort of thing.

With the towel clutched tight against her chest and the lamp hanging loose in her other hand, she stepped out into the open living room. "It's you."

The frown deepened. "Who else would it be?"

"I don't know. That's kind of the point of me having this." She held up her makeshift weapon, letting the plug scrape against the floor.

"I see we have some confusion."

"About what?" But she knew. He was a man accustomed to having his rules followed and she'd violated quite a few since he walked out the door, including the asinine no-clothing one. She wasn't clear what he knew or how, but she guessed something tipped him off or he wouldn't be back so soon.

"I thought I made my expectations clear." The anger vibrating in his voice didn't leave much room for mystery about his mood.

She rushed to jump in before the anger festered. "I can explain."

His hands remained behind his back but his gaze narrowed at her interruption. "You have either developed a hearing issue or the entire purpose of your trip here has been a ruse."

The man's paranoia was running in its usually high gear. "How do you figure that?"

"One could see this little visit of yours, along with the claims of being chased and in danger, as a second attempt at a setup."

The lamp touched against her thigh as she lowered it. "You had me strip. You know I didn't bring anything in with me."

Tension continued to pulse off of him. "Is that a denial?"

"It's the reality. I'm here to help *me*, not to hurt *you*."

His eyebrow lifted. "You were in my bedroom, a place I specifically prohibited you from going."

"Wrong."

"Excuse me?"

She remembered the deadly soft tone. When he spoke like that, the unbending Jarrett appeared right after. Not that he bent all that much to begin with, but when threatened he downshifted into scary mode. She used to hear the monotone clip while he talked business and wonder about the life expectancy of the person on the other end of all that ire.

The file she had on him back then referenced a list of people from his past who mysteriously disappeared, but the idea of him as a killer never matched up with the man who rained kisses over every inch of her bare flesh. Of course, neither did the drug running. Tough and haunted, yes. Unreadable at times and ice cold at others. But a cold-blooded murderer she could never see.

"I was in your office. But I think you knew that before you even got up here." An odd thought crept into her brain. She visually scanned the mantel and ceiling for potential hidden cameras, wondering how a man who coveted his privacy so much could open his life up to such unending security scrutiny. "Did you wire the place?"

"I give you points for not lying about being in the office." He still hadn't moved. Had barely blinked.

Her gaze shot to his arms as she tried to figure out what he hid in his hands. "Not really possible to do since I'm holding your desk lamp."

The severe frown slipped for a second then shifted back into place. "Do you care to tell me why you were in a room where I ordered you not to go?"

He phrased it like a question, but she knew from the steel thread in his voice that he wasn't expecting an answer. She gave him one anyway. "Technically, you told me to stay out of your bedroom."

"No, I—"

She wanted to scream at his stubbornness. "Okay. Fine."

"You would be wise to stop stalling."

On that he was right. There was no reason to lie. "I wanted to see if I could tap into the security system and see what you were doing downstairs."

"Why?"

"I'm showing a lot of faith in coming here. You could do anything to me. Turn me over to the very people who want me dead." The fear burning a hole through her stomach gave rise to her voice. "Hell, you could be the person behind all of the team killings."

"Put the lamp down."

The base suddenly weighted her down on one side. "You're not going to respond to that accusation or ask me anything else?"

"I don't ask. I tell."

"Right. Silly me." She put the lamp on the floor and stood up, feeling his heated gaze roam over her as she moved.

"I don't remember giving you permission to wear a towel."

Whatever happened downstairs hadn't eased his fury. Quite possibly it enhanced it, which made her even more curious about the last fifteen minutes.

She bit back a sigh as she mentally debated the best way to soothe the beast roaring to life within him and otherwise making her life more difficult than it needed to be. "We're back to that?"

"The rules remain the same, Rebecca. You have my temporary protection and in exchange—"

"You get me." She said it before he could utter some awful word that made her cringe. One that reminded her of how little she meant and of the hatred brewing right beneath the surface.

"Remove the towel."

Amazing how something as flimsy as a fluffy piece of cotton could provide an emotional barrier. Could shield and protect. The idea of being without it sent a strange hollowness rolling over her. With it on, her old life came rushing back, shoring up her strength long enough for the confidence she took for granted to peek through.

She needed something from him and sensed that ran both ways. His likely grew out of an unsatisfied wish for revenge, and part of her believed he was entitled to it. But there were limits to what she would do to beat back the clawing inside him. She'd willingly give her body in exchange for protection and the use of his valuable resources. She'd hold back the rest so he couldn't emotionally stomp her into pieces.

But one of them had to give in this battle. She'd showed up on his doorstep pleading for help and then agreed to his terms, so she'd already lost. Her gaze went from his stiff shoulders to the nerve twitching in his cheek. No matter what she said he wouldn't back down. That wasn't his style.

She could actually see her chest rise and fall as her fingers fumbled with the tight knot. The towel slipped away in a whoosh and the cool air-conditioned breeze brushed over her skin. Fighting off the urge to cover her body, a waste since there wasn't an inch he hadn't already touched and kissed, she faced him head-on.

Not glancing away when his stare swept over her. "Satisfied?" she asked when his visual tour showed no signs of stopping.

"I will be soon." His shoes tapped against the hardwood as he shifted his weight and brought his hands in front of him. His keys rattled in a glass bowl a second later. "Go lie across the bed. Hands above your head. Legs open and feet against the mattress. I want to see all of you when I walk in the door."

The words shot a shiver straight through her.

"Now, Rebecca."

She didn't hesitate a second time. Retracing her earlier path, she headed toward the extra bedroom. With every move she heard Jarrett's shoes thud behind her. When his fingers slid down her spine in a firm touch that sent her stomach tumbling, her steps faltered.

She reached the doorway and clung to the frame as she forced air back into her lungs. After a deep inhale her muscles stopped shaking. Just as she pushed off and stood up straight, ready to take her position on the bed, he slipped his hand over her ass cheek, caressing her even as he lit her nerve endings on fire.

She bit back his name, refusing to give him the satisfaction of saying it.

Lips pressed against her hair and a hand flattened against her stomach pulling her body back tight against his. He palmed her breasts and nuzzled the side of her neck. The room spun and the hammering need she'd pushed out of her memory came whizzing back.

His closeness blocked out everything else. Her body melted against his and he'd barely touched her.

She shifted her head to the side as her hand traveled over the outside of his muscular thigh. Over the silky material of his expensive suit as the heat from his body pounded into her.

"Get on the bed." He whispered the order into the dip between her shoulder blades.

She nodded, unable to say anything while she climbed onto the mattress. Lowering her back to the bed, she stretched her arms over her head. The instructions played in her head as her legs fell open.

Forcing her eyes to stay open even as a kick of lust blurred her vision, she glanced around, but he hovered just out of sight. Only the bright white ceiling greeted her. Desperate to watch him, she grabbed a pillow from the top of the bed and stuffed it under her head, propping her shoulders up.

There he was.

He stood at the end of the bed, staring down at her. Despite her wish to hold on to the briefest ties of control, her body grew wet and her hips rose in invitation for him to touch her. The sudden shock of intimacy sent her insecurities flaring. One of her legs fell closed but he touched her knee and pushed it back open again.

"I want every part of you to belong to me." He slipped his jacket off and his hands went to his tie.

In a few tugs, the material loosened and he unbuttoned the top of his crisp white dress shirt. A few more and he uncovered that amazing chest and the sprinkling of rich dark hair that once tickled her nose and smoothed through her fingers.

Through it all, his gaze never wavered.

The mattress dipped under his weight as he put a knee between her open thighs. His hands skimmed down the inside of her legs and his mouth followed a beat behind. A nibble then a brush.

When his two middle fingers finally slipped inside her, pumping and rubbing, she closed her eyes. The deep presses sent her insides dancing in a wild frenzy. Expert caresses from a man totally in tune with her body.

She wanted to hold something back, to not give him the satisfaction of taking her to the place where she would chant his name, but she knew that wouldn't be possible. The months apart only made the yearning spiral tighter.

Then his mouth touched against her. That tongue licked up inside her until he found her clit. He sucked until a breath hiccupped in her lungs. This time she couldn't fight off the sensations. Light and dark exploded as she dug her heels into the bed. She shifted her hips, trying to bring his fingers deeper inside. But he toyed with her, making her slick but not giving her the touch she needed to send her careening over the edge.

With one final lick, her inner thighs pressed against his shoulders as she tried to tighten the tiny muscles inside her. He picked that moment to sit back then stand. Heavy breaths caught in her throat as she forced her eyes to stay open and watch him. She bit back the call to bring him back.

Need clouded her mind as she saw his shirt open and untucked. When his hand went to his belt, she sat up and slid to the edge of the bed. Her hands pushed his aside as she pressed her lips to the bulge under his dress pants. His cock jerked under her mouth and through the material. Loving the reaction, she did it again, rubbing the heel of her hand over his length until every inch was outlined and straining.

"Damn." The breathy word sounded like it had been pulled out of him.

His hands went to her shoulders as her fingers went to work. She opened the belt, letting the buckle drop open as she abandoned it for the zipper. A rasp echoed through the room when she ticked it down in careful beats.

With his fly open and his hands in her hair, she slid her fingers inside and took out his cock. Long and smooth, heavy and warm.

The punch of desire nearly knocked her backward.

Unable to stop, she licked her tongue along his length. When his hips shifted, she slipped the head into her mouth and sucked. Her hand pumped, her lips moved up and down. Heavy breathing filled her ears and she didn't know if it came from her, or him, or both.

When his hips bucked a second time, he slipped a hand under her chin and lifted her head. "Not in your mouth this time."

She flicked her tongue over his top. "Yes."

"I said no, and I decide how to use your body." He pushed her back against the mattress. His body followed hers. She'd barely adjusted to the secure sensation of his weight anchored over her when she heard the crinkle of a wrapper. Her gaze followed the sound to the condom in his hand.

He was prepared and she was ready. She turned to tell him so, to whisper the words against his lips, but he moved his head and her kiss landed on his cheek. His body froze.

"Jarrett?"

The silence stretched. When he did speak, the words came out as a husky growl. "Turn over."

The rough order didn't match his caresses. "What?"

"Now." With the corner of the wrapper in his mouth, the rip sounded all around her.

Before she could adjust or analyze the changes in him from the sharp crack of his voice to the angry stiffness across his shoulders, his hands went to her hips and he flipped her to her stomach. Her palms flattened against the mattress as the breath stammered out of her.

With jerky movements, he lifted her legs and put her on her knees. When she tried to push up with her elbows, his hand clamped around her neck, not tight but with enough force to hold her still.

"Like this." His hand went to the space between her shoulder blades, pressing her upper body against the bed as her ass hung in the air.

Then his cock pressed against her entrance. He rubbed it over her, just inside of her.

She didn't know what he wanted her to say, if he wanted her to say anything. Gone were the sensual touches and nip of his teeth. This was about power and command.

He loved the rawness of this position. Months ago he'd bend her over a chair or have her drop her hands to the bed while he stepped up behind her. But this felt different. It *was* different.

The few words she could manage died on her lips when he

shoved her legs farther apart. The move left her open, totally at the mercy of his thrusts.

And he didn't hold back. He plunged inside her in a long, steady push, before retreating then starting again. Her nerves tingled as her body adjusted to his girth. She'd just regained her equilibrium when he began pumping into her and she lost it again. The steady rhythm pounded her into the mattress. Her body slid across the comforter as she turned her head to the side and gasped in a rush of air.

She wanted to hate him for using her body, for turning their sex into nothing more than a release mixed with a power play. But the heat of his body over hers and the clench of his hands against her bare hips touched off something base and wild in her.

She wanted this, wanted him. She came to this place knowing they would have sex and secretly waiting for the moment to arrive. Raunchy, hot, it didn't matter. He wasn't forcing her. He was separating his emotions from his body and she envied that skill.

She closed her mind to what used to be and settled for the sensations of now.

Fire burned through her nerve endings as his body rubbed and pressed against hers, steady and deep. Every muscle inside her pulled tight. The spinning sensation took over. Blood pounded in her ears as her brain shut down. The need to explode, to find release and let her body break into pieces, raced through her.

Her hands curled into the comforter. Their bodies turned slick with sweat as his cock plunged into her and the soft knock of the headboard against the wall filled the air. Rather than move away, she pushed back into him. The need to beg, with the words sitting right there on her tongue, had her biting the inside of her cheek.

She clamped down on every sensation except the rough feel of his body sliding in and out of hers. The act. The grind.

When his thrusts sped up, she sat back even harder, bringing her ass tighter against him. His response came in his deep grunt and the firm stroke of his cock inside her. The press matched the thunder of blood through her veins. Everything began to spin as her head pressed against the pillow next to her hand.

She was just about to shout for him to go faster when her orgasm slammed into her. The churning broke free and her muscles clenched. Her body began to buck as he pressed deep one last time.

Her eyes slid closed as the sensations pounded through her. She could feel him above her, around her. It wasn't until his orgasm ended and the thrusts died down that the full force of his actions hit her. He turned her away and denied her his mouth and the joy of seeing that sexy look on his face. She'd always treasured that moment when he lost control, but all that was denied to her this time.

She became just another body to him and he made sure that's all she amounted to.

Her mind spun as all the thoughts she held back during sex bombarded her now. The emotional wall between them hadn't cracked at all. The sex was hot and spontaneous, echoing back to their daily lovemaking sessions, but this time wasn't about lovemaking. It was sex. Hot sex, but just that.

After a few seconds, he rolled off of her and onto his back. One arm crossed over his eyes and a hand rested on his chest.

She faced him, watching the practiced detachment and wanting to reach out and touch his shoulder. To explain what happened months ago and plead her case. If he'd shown any interest in anything more than keeping her naked and primed for his use, she might have.

He half lifted the arm from his eyes and pinned her with a one-eyed gaze. "Now tell me why you're really here."

SIX

Wade slid his security card through the reader and heard the lock to his second-floor industrial loft apartment click. He had about an hour before the staff started assembling downstairs, looking for final directions for the evening shift. But his phone would keep buzzing all night if he didn't make this side trip upstairs. Personal errands weren't his thing, but nothing about his life could be considered normal right now.

He opened the door and blinked when the combination of a lean but lethal build and the barrel of a gun blocked the view of the wide-open space inside. It looked as if their upstairs guest was just as pissed off as Wade predicted he'd be.

Elijah Sterling didn't move. Didn't say a word.

The weapon stayed steady on Wade as he followed the muscled line of the arm holding it. He took in the slim-fitting gray tee and straight coal-black hair Elijah inherited from his Japanese mother. The scar trailing along his jawline and severe frown promised he wouldn't think twice about firing if needed. Wade really hoped it didn't come to that.

He put his hand on Elijah's wrist and pushed on his arm until the weapon aimed at the wall instead of vital body parts. "Lower that."

Elijah's chest rose and fell on harsh breaths. "I thought you might be her."

"Becca?"

"Is another one of my former Spectrum team here?" He had worked himself into a killing state.

Wade had seen the look before. The crazed wide eyes. The erratic breathing and tremble that suggested he balanced right on the edge. "I think they're all dead except for you two and Todd, though I can see you might not find that comforting."

The last time Wade had seen Elijah this frantic and out of it was the night he landed on the Holton Woods doorstep, bleeding and ranting, half unconscious but still spouting nonsense about cover-ups and death squads. After everything he'd done to fuck up Jarrett's life, Elijah should have hit the road and kept running. But he'd been dumped in the alley next to the club, likely to set Jarrett up for a murder, and it almost succeeded since Elijah was half delirious and hovered near death. When he finally stammered out that he had information Jarrett needed, he got a ticket inside.

Wade never thought Elijah would survive that night, but he had. After a few days in lockdown, he'd made promises and offered a deal—he'd hand over certain documents and connect a few dots to take the heat out of the continuing threats from the CIA. In return, Jarrett gave Elijah a place to hide and medical care. He didn't need focus or a purpose. He had one—revenge for the termination of his team.

And Becca was one of his targets.

Which led them right back around to the one woman who seemed to ruin everything simply by existing. Wade wished Jarrett would see her destructive force before it knocked him down a second time.

Wade threw his keys and everything else in his hand on the small glass table next to the front door. "She can't come on this floor without a security card or alarm code. She doesn't have either and she thinks you're dead."

Elijah glanced at the keys before looking at Wade again. Those near-black eyes sparked with fire as Elijah spoke. "But she'll get the codes and go searching. It's part of who she is."

"Who you both are."

"Yes, it comes with the training. If you survive it, you're forever changed and ready to hunt down clues and information, no matter the trouble you cause."

Wade wondered if Elijah was describing his own obsession or guessing at hers. "I'm going to hope you're wrong about that."

With the cavernous open room right there, Elijah paced the few feet of concrete directly in front of Wade. Back and forth, with his black sneakers making only a whisper of sound against the floor.

Wade was about to ask for some breathing room when Elijah came to a halt in front of him. "Where is she right now?"

"With Jarrett, and that should stop this conversation." Wade shifted to pivot around Elijah and head for the kitchen.

Elijah caught his arm. "Fuck that."

This rage had the potential to blow loud and huge. Eli and Jarrett, two men who demanded control and absolute obedience locked in a power play. Wade couldn't think of a worse scenario.

"Jarrett is in charge and decides who comes inside his building, from the clients to the staff to the visitors. That includes you, so I wouldn't push him."

"She's different." The gun stayed in Elijah's hand even though it now pointed at the floor.

"Yeah, well, we don't get a say in who he screws or if he lets her back in his life."

A red fury covered Elijah's face. "Becca Ford destroys everything." The words ripped out of him as if he struggled not to scream his insight.

And Wade couldn't disagree with either the fury or the words. "That's what history suggests, yes."

"Why are you so calm about this? You don't want her here either." Elijah was waving the gun now.

Gone was the steady black-ops genius who broke in the club door with his team eight months ago and started Jarrett's legal nightmares. This Elijah had been hunted and beaten by the very people he once trusted. He had nothing left to lose. With his training and emotional blankness, he could only be described as scary dangerous.

Wade didn't want to fire the guy up any more, but he wasn't exactly thrilled with Jarrett's decision-making today either. His boss's usually firm grip on control slipped when Becca's face popped up on the security cameras. After nearly ten years as Jarrett's sidekick, Wade could count the number of times something shook Jarrett's resolve. All but one grew out of his relationship with Becca.

Wade wanted her gone. "She fucks with Jarrett's head. So, no, I don't want her here. He has an almost inexplicable weakness for her and—"

"She will get me killed."

"Then I guess it's good people think you're already dead."

Elijah spun around. The gun arced through the air as if it were part of his body now. "You think this situation is fucking funny?"

"Not even a little," Wade said. The only thing less funny would be getting shot at the front door to his own damn apartment. He left those days when he threw in with Jarrett.

"Now, step back." Wade was prepared to use the weapon tucked into his belt to make the point if he had to and started a mental countdown.

After a heartbeat of silence, punctuated only by Elijah's sharp breathing, he turned around and headed for the family room. The gun clinked against the coffee table as Elijah set it down. He sat down hard in the middle of the sleek gray sectional a second later.

For one brief beat, the mask fell and Wade got a peek at the rolling panic underneath. A dark shadow moved behind Elijah's eyes and his throat bobbled. For a guy who never flinched, any sign of worry signaled a catastrophe, and this went well beyond worry.

As it always did when Elijah exposed a glimpse into the real man underneath, Wade's control broke. "Eli—"

His head dropped back against the cushions. "This is unbelievable."

The whisper broke through the last of the tension whipping around Wade. "Hey, listen to me. It's going to be okay."

"Why is she here?" Elijah lifted his head. His eyes darkened as he let out a long exhale. "She should be running or in CIA custody. Anywhere except in the place where this whole shitstorm started. I'm here, in part, because of her. To figure out her role in all of this and make it all stop."

With the emotional surge over, Wade shut the door to the private floor and walked over to the couch. "I don't know what's going on with her."

"You had to overhear something."

Not enough, which was why he made the call to the one other person Jarrett would listen to and could not ignore. The other person Jarrett considered a friend. Wade knew he needed reinforcements to convince the boss on this one and didn't hesitate.

"Jarrett rushed her into his office and kicked me out." Wade said as he sat down next to Elijah. Not across from him or in another chair. Next to, close enough to feel the furious heat radiate off the other man's body.

"I watched it all on the internal security feed. They came out of his office and he took her upstairs." Elijah wiped a hand down his face. "Paraded her through the halls naked."

Wade swore under his breath. So much for all those calls for revenge and promises to destroy her if she ever walked across the D.C. border again. In those early days after the arrest and as the scandal hit the papers, Jarrett had lived for the scenarios he created to go after her. Now, within ten minutes of seeing her, he already had it bad for the woman again.

"Not his most subtle move, but probably not a surprise." Wade shifted and turned until he faced Elijah with their knees touching. "I told you, when it comes to her, Jarrett thinks with his dick."

"Jarrett Holt, one of the few men *I* view as dangerous, and I'm a trained killer." Elijah touched a hand to his chest. "This guy has a brain misfire over pussy?"

Wade winced over the new round of fury rising in Elijah's voice. "You might not want to say it that way to him."

"Fucking women."

Wade barked out a laugh. "Don't ask me. They're not my thing."

He balanced his elbows on his knees and stared at the thick black rug in the center of the room under his feet. He tried to reason this through, figure out the right words to say to Jarrett to get him to give Becca some money and send her away. The public viewed Jarrett as ruthless and cold, until someone wanted something, then all of a sudden he was the only man in town worth talking to. But Wade knew better. Jarrett rose from a pile of crap and created something. Then Becca broke him.

The arguments stopped screaming in Wade's head long enough for him to notice the dragging quiet. He glanced up and caught Elijah staring. The heated anger had left his face and his gaze roamed now.

His fists unclenched and he spread his fingers on the thighs of his khaki cargo pants. "What is your thing, Wade?"

The change in the mood, the new type of tension swirling in the room, had Wade's mouth going dry. "I think you know."

"I know what worked for you last night. How you begged for my mouth as you grabbed the headboard."

Images flashed in his head. Elijah between his legs, sucking as he worked a hand up and down on his cock. Wade had to swallow twice to get the words out. "The club opens soon."

Elijah sat up, shifting to the front of the cushion and dipping his head until only inches separated them. "You saying no?"

Looked like Jarrett wasn't the only one having trouble hanging on to an ounce of control. Wade wondered if the weakness for sex was contagious. Something circulating through the building's air vents. "Have I said no since you got here?"

A small smile played on the corner of Elijah's mouth. "Not once."

"Then you have my answer."

He pointed at the carpet. "Get on your knees."

Wade wanted to say no this time. Wanted to keep the conversation, the pent-up anger, aimed at Becca and exhaust it so Eli could move on. Wanted to but failed when Elijah reached over and cupped his hand over the zipper of Wade's pants.

His cock jumped to life under Eli's palm. When his fingers traced the length and gave a squeeze, Wade forgot all about the other people in the building.

It had been this way from the beginning. Eli lay in bed for days as he recuperated. His fury against the CIA festered. Wade would visit and stand by the bed and listen, hoping to hear something that would help Jarrett's case. Then one day Eli's hand knocked against Wade's leg. He ignored it, wrote it off as a strange gesture, until the next day when Eli's palm rested against the outside of Wade's thigh for more than a passing second.

Every offhanded brush had burned through Wade and shaken his up-until-then solid hatred for Eli, but Wade tried not to let the break in his defenses show. He lasted until the day, a week after those initial stray touches, when Eli stared him down. With their gazes locked, he'd skimmed his fingers over Wade's fly then caressed the erection he kicked to life underneath.

The first day Eli was well enough to stand and move around without help, he walked across the second-floor hallway and climbed into Wade's bed. He'd been there every night since.

Sliding off the couch now, Wade's knees hit the floor. His hands traveled up and down Eli's firm thighs, outlining every muscle and pressing his legs farther apart to make room between them.

"I need this." Elijah's hands were everywhere. Over Wade's shoulders and chest, curling down until they stopped at the button to his pants. "I need you."

Wade knew. He felt it in the steady thrum of excitement moving through Eli's muscles and in the way his stare turned hot. The readiness touched off Wade's.

"Let me take away some of that stress," he said as he cupped the bulge tightening the material behind Eli's zipper.

Wade closed his eyes as Eli tunneled fingers through his hair. "Damn, I always want you," Eli said.

The words chipped away at the walls Wade built as protection against caring too much. The fevered words, the quiet way Eli would run his fingers over Wade's cheek and across his collarbone in the dark of the bedroom and long after they'd gone to bed. It all combined to mean something. More than once Wade had pretended to be asleep to savor the touches.

"That's how I want you—wound up and ready." Wade popped the button on Eli's pants. "Now you tell me what you want."

Eli slid a hand under Wade's chin and lifted his head until they stared at each other. "Your mouth. On me, over me."

"I'm going to suck you off."

"Yes." The word came out on a groan as Eli pushed Wade's head down.

Wade traced Elijah's cock through his pants, felt the ridge and saw the distinct outline. He rubbed his hand over it, squeezed and tightened his grip until Elijah shifted his hips forward. The zipper ticked as Wade slowly lowered it, unveiling inch after inch of Elijah's impressive cock where it pressed against his underwear.

From the first time together, they'd established a pattern. Elijah led but Wade set the rhythm. He decided if they went slow or fast. When they used their mouths and how Eli entered him.

Wade slipped Elijah's cock through the slit in the boxer briefs. Pumped his hand up and down until it swelled to life. He drew the head into his mouth and licked his tongue over the tip. The smell, the hardness, touched off a wild frenzy inside Wade.

His mouth slid down, taking Eli deeper as his moan echoed through the cavernous room. Loving the husky sound, Wade pushed the cock to the back of his throat then slowly drew it out again.

"Wade . . ." His voice cut off. "That feels so damn good."

Wade licked a line up Eli's cock. "I love the way you taste."

Elijah's head fell forward as he whispered into Wade's hair. "Then make me come."

SEVEN

Jarrett propped his back against the stacked pillows of the guest bed and watched Becca. Slow and steady, she sat up. Facing him with her legs crossed in front of her, she picked up a stray pillow and tucked it in her lap, between her legs, covering all but her shoulders and thighs to his view.

He would have ordered her to put it down and show him everything, but the sex clouded his head. Even now need pounded him. He fought back the urge to roll her under him and slip inside her again.

It had taken only the barest touch of her skin to transport him back to the time before her betrayal. His tongue licked inside her and he forgot about her lies and willingness to hand him over to people who wanted to destroy him and all he'd built. That body, that mind. She wove a spell around him, dragging him in deeper. If she hadn't tried to kiss him, he'd probably be drooling like a pathetic dog at her feet.

His lack of control pissed him off. Made him long to hate her.

Maybe hearing whatever tale she wanted to sell him would restoke his rage. He didn't even bother to pull up his pants. He just lay there, bare assed with his pants shoved down to his upper thighs. Ready to laugh off whatever bullshit line she planned to feed him.

"I'm listening," he said as he forced his mind off her body and back to her lying words.

"This isn't a secret." Her hair drifted over her shoulder. "I need somewhere to hide while I figure this out."

"So, I'm your landlord and we're trading sex for rent." He should want that, demand it even. Yet he hated the thought of being used by her for nothing more than a release and a roof.

She clenched the pillow tighter against her bare chest. "I didn't say that."

"While I admit I don't know you—you proved that eight months ago—I did learn something living with you."

"Like?"

"You aren't the hang-around-the-house type." Now he knew she'd been too busy snooping and reporting back to her superiors.

"Maybe I am now."

He scoffed. "Sure."

"I'm tired of running, Jarrett. It started as a kid and I still haven't stopped."

Jarrett knew her history. The custody case that blew up into a kidnapping and international race. Years of hiding, changing names and moving around. It all ended with her father dying at the end of a police officer's gun and Becca blaming her mother.

The fact that Becca dealt with the upheaval by picking a career that put her on the run fascinated Jarrett. When he first found out her life was a lie he expected her childhood history to be part of the concocted cover, but the file he collected on her backed it all up. It was quite possible her upbringing was the one truth she'd told him.

But no way would he let the sad story or the exhaustion in her voice pull at him. This was all about acting for her. About carefully throwing out a word for maximum impact and getting what she wanted, regardless of what that did to him. "I'm betting you have a safe house and stored money. Yet here you are with not even an extra shirt to your name."

She rolled her eyes. "You wouldn't let me wear it if I did."

Seemed the wariness that followed her when she first arrived was now gone, and sarcasm moved into its place. Wasn't that just fucking great? "Tell me about the safe house."

She fiddled with the bottom edge of the pillow, rubbing it between two fingers. "Exactly why would you think I have one?"

"Humor me."

"I kind of am."

His temper flared and he had to clamp down hard to keep his back against the pillows and his indifference in place. "Rebecca."

"The safe house was a rendezvous spot for the team. Since most of the team members are now dead, *hanging out* there seemed like a bad idea."

"Probably a good call."

"Someone cleaned out two of the drops where I kept money and identification documents." She exhaled, letting her head drop back and treating him to the enticing length of her neck. "The crash pad I had on my own could be compromised because I have no idea who knows what or how."

"I'm betting there's more to this story."

"I know everyone thinks operatives have passports hidden in

every country, but I don't." She lowered her head and faced him again. "And what I do have hidden I have to be able to get to without being shot or set on fire, so there's that."

He ignored the fire part. "So you came to me."

She shook her head and her mouth moved, all before her shoulders fell. "Okay, yes."

"The man you betrayed." This time he moved. He couldn't stand to sit still one more second.

The point was to reduce their interaction to sex, distant yet satisfying. In-depth conversations and unaccounted for time together would only lead to trouble. He unbuttoned the cuffs of his shirt and the bottom two holding his shirt closed.

"Again, not how I would phrase it." Her words came out slowly as her gaze followed his hands.

"I'm stating a fact." He shrugged out of his shirt and threw it in a heap on the chair next to the bed.

"It's a matter of perception. From where I sit you were the liar."

"I'm not going to argue with you about the drugs, because they were not mine." Rather than dwell on her words, he shoved his pants the rest of the way down his legs.

"So you say."

"Put the pillow down." He spared her a glance as he kicked off the last of his clothes. When he noticed she hadn't moved, he tried to make his command clearer. "Now."

"Jarrett, you don't need to order me around." The pillow moved against her as her breathing grew heavier. "I'm not fighting you about having sex. I said I was yours and I meant it."

"Happy to hear it." He took off the condom and wrapped a hand around his cock. "Move the pillow."

She eased her hold on it. "You need to know you can't break me."

"An interesting concept." He watched her as she eased her legs apart. "Why do you think I want to?"

"Experience."

"While we're on that subject, you know what I like." Her mouth over him until his cock slid down her throat. Her riding him. Him sucking those nipples. He planned to run through every mind-blowing step then go downstairs and not let it touch him. Pretend it never happened.

"Does that mean the interrogation is over?" she asked.

"Come over here and we'll see."

He expected a battle. It wasn't until she dropped the pillow on the mattress and showed him those breasts that he realized he was not the only one using sex to his advantage. She avoided his question. Expertly.

Damn her.

When she sprawled against his thighs and her fingers skimmed down his cock, he fought off the sensations rippling through him. With a hand under her chin he lifted her head. "Tell me the rest."

She blinked several times. "What?"

"Why do you need *me* specifically and not some other guy you fucked on the job?" He cupped her cheek and didn't let her turn away. "If you want to be treated as more than a sex toy, you might want to try the truth."

"Sex toy?"

"Is there a term you'd prefer?"

When he let go, she dropped her head to the side, sending her hair falling over his bare thighs. Seeing that, feeling the gentle touch, had the air punching against the walls of his chest. She started talking a second before he forgot his plan and dragged her up to straddle him.

"Your computer system," she said.

His mind rushed to catch up with his dick. "Excuse me?"

"I need access to your computer system with its rotating IP addresses and bouncing signal through proxy servers and whatever else you have that will ensure no one backtracks the snooping to me."

He framed her face with his hands and forced her to give him full eye contact again. Not that she couldn't lie without blinking, but he wanted to make the task difficult at least. "You think I'm handing you my passwords?"

She nodded. "And opening your Rolodex, or whatever electronic version you have of one. Might be I need your contacts to dig deep enough to figure out why everything went sideways on Spectrum and who placed the order to kill off the team."

He wasn't sure if he should be impressed by her hubris or stunned by her insanity. "Ignoring the fact none of that is ever going to happen, if you do manage to get to ground zero on this fact-finding mission, what then?"

"I convince the person doing the attacking to leave me alone."

He snapped his fingers. "Just like that, huh?" But he knew she wasn't talking about a friendly chat. She was a survivor and would take down whoever got in the way.

"Yes."

Looks like insanity won the day. "No way any of that is going to happen."

"We can set up any parameters you want." She crawled up his body, stopping when her knees touched the outside of his hips. "But I need the power circles you move in to make this work."

He tried not to touch her, but she wasn't making that easy. With all the sifting and bouncing, her breast brushed against his cheek and now pressed against his chest.

He cleared his throat, but it didn't do anything to stop the erotic dance playing in his head or the swelling of his cock right beneath her. "You mean you want my Holton Woods client list."

With her hands planted on the headboard she leaned in closer. "Possibly."

Sweet hell. Her scent wrapped around him, and his body jerked when her wetness pressed against his thigh.

"You've lost your mind." And he was two seconds away from losing his.

"I'm desperate."

His hands went to her hips. He had to slow this down, if only to grab a second condom. "Apparently."

"And I am willing to give you whatever you need to help me." She said the words while trailing a line of kisses down his throat.

"You mentioned my need for revenge. What do you do if all investigative roads lead to me?"

She lifted her head, slipped her fingers through his hair. "Are you trying to kill me, Jarrett?"

He was a fucking dead man. "You aren't going to control this situation or me."

She pushed up on her knees. With a hand on the back of his head, she brought her nipple to his mouth. "We'll see."

Wade groaned as he rolled over and sat up on the edge of the bed. His head spun, so he grabbed on to the mattress to keep from tipping back over.

Eli had drained every ounce of energy from his body. Even now Wade looked down to where his limp cock lay against his thigh and tried to remember when his pants came off. Eli's mouth and hands. The sex was a wild ride that had Wade hooked.

"One more round." Elijah's sleepy voice echoed through the room with his favorite refrain.

Wade already expected his legs to wobble when he stood up. "Another round and you'll have to carry me downstairs."

Eli laughed, something he rarely did. "That would be interesting."

"I'm trying to imagine what the club patrons would say." Wade didn't hide his sexuality, but he didn't advertise it either. Once or twice club members had come on to him and he shut that down fast. No way was he screwing with the folks he served.

When he leaned forward, thinking he'd get up, Eli stopped him with a hand on the arm. "Don't leave yet."

A second later his palm skimmed over Wade's back. Fingers traveled down his spine to the top of his ass. Then lips pressed against his bare hip.

The man had the stamina of a boy half his age.

Wade twisted around to look at his lover. Eli rested on his side as his tongue licked over Wade's skin. The exhaustion so prevalent when he tried to sit up less than a minute ago vanished. His body revved to life and he had to smile at how quickly his mind turned from *I can't move* to *I want him again*.

Still, he held on to common sense this time. Knowing Jarrett didn't accept "having good sex with Eli" as an excuse for being late opening the club helped. "I can't."

Eli leaned back and stared up at Wade. "Are you too sore?"

He rubbed his palm over Eli's upper arm, tracing the line of his muscle with his finger. "I'm good."

"You're fucking great, but that's not news." Eli dropped back against the pillows in a sprawl.

"You're talking about the sex, I'm assuming."

Eli's dark-eyed gaze toured Wade's face. "In part."

Defining their time together as something more than sex? That was new. "Really?"

"I know I can be a shit."

"True."

"Thinking about Becca being in the same building makes me crazed and this situation . . ." Eli exhaled long and loud as his hand fell back against the pillow. "I'm just saying you're the one good thing I have going now."

Wade hated that the words meant so much, but Eli rarely opened up. Only in bed did he lower his defenses. He stayed in black-ops shutdown mode most of the time. He'd made clear at the start the relationship would revolve around sex, then end when he no longer needed to hide out in the building.

And now this. Leave it to Eli to open the door to real emotion when Wade had to get downstairs to work.

He balanced a palm against the bed and leaned over Elijah. "I know this situation, being hunted, sucks for you."

"My temper tends to rage even without being threatened, but it's true bucking death isn't helping."

"You're getting better about the outbursts." And Wade welcomed the change.

At first Eli slammed around like a caged animal, only finding any sort of peace when they had sex. Now he could relax enough to study files and not need to pace around mumbling.

"Because of you." Eli's hand trailed down Wade's chest.

Wariness warred with pounding excitement inside Wade. "What brought this on?"

Eli frowned. "Things are going to get bad. While she's here, I mean."

Wade feared the same thing. "Okay."

"Well, I want you to know when I lose it, and I will, it's not about you."

His cock jerked to life when Eli's fingers slipped down and around him.

Wade tried to clear his throat but whatever was stuck in there wouldn't budge. "You could try not losing control."

Eli leaned forward and ran his tongue over Wade's nipple. "Not possible around you."

This time words tripped in Wade's brain. "I meant the anger."

"I'm talking about us." Eli cupped the back of Wade's neck and brought his head down until their lips almost touched. "So, stop talking and get back into bed."

EIGHT

Two hours later Jarrett stood in the doorway to the main lounge area as the club's energy ramped up for the night. Silverware clanked and the murmur of conversation flowed from the first wave of casual diners and business dinners.

Jarrett surveyed it all as a surge of satisfaction roared through him. Not bad for a son of a whore who spent most of his elementary school years eating stale chips for dinner because that's all there was. He'd fought and crawled and done nasty things he'd sooner forget, but those days were behind him. Even after the near-killing blow from Becca. He'd picked up and gotten back to work, rebuilding trust and ensuring his clientele the charges amounted to nothing more than a rogue police operation.

Having clients in high places helped to sell that story. So did the information he turned over to the CIA in exchange for his freedom. It was the ultimate deal with the devil, but he'd survived the flashover when there was no way he should have.

He watched Wade step out from behind the bar and walk over.

He smiled and made small talk with a few of the members. Jarrett wondered if some of these elites had any idea the man who served them drinks once worked as an enforcer for some very nasty criminal types. Those days were long gone, but Jarrett suspected the instincts were as sharp as ever.

Wade stopped next to Jarrett and joined in scanning the crowd. "Elijah is worried."

Which reminded Jarrett how crowded the top two floors of his building had become. "He should be grateful he's not dead."

"He was watching on the surveillance monitors. He saw Becca come in. Saw you walk her through the hall." Wade grinned. "I believe he mentioned something about her being naked."

That was enough to kill of the last of Jarrett's sexual high. "Fuck me."

"I'm guessing that's what happened upstairs this afternoon." Wade returned a nodding greeting to a congressman who walked by before slipping into a back booth. "Guess you forgot about Elijah being in the building and tapped into the security feed."

Jarrett hadn't bothered reasoning out the issue of the conflicting endgames at work in the minds of the two people upstairs. Now he would. "I should have shot him two months ago when he crawled up to the door and begged for help."

"Technically, you did. Took out the gun and nailed him in the shoulder."

Another voice broke in. "Don't admit to doing that."

Jarrett hadn't even heard him step up, but Sebastian Jameson stood on the other side of him. Well over six feet with brown hair and glasses, he looked every inch the proper prep school boy, Ivy League–educated lawyer type he was.

Of course, the reputation about his wild private life didn't match the influential business life. At thirty-four, his bedroom scorecard put most men in town to shame. Jarrett was only a few months older and had gone round with many women, but Bast trumped it all because a book by his ex-wife forever memorialized his antics.

The poor bastard.

"Bast?" They shook hands. "What are you doing here?"

"Decided to stop by for dinner."

Jarrett noticed Bast didn't even try to make the excuse sound convincing. "Since when do you leave the office and eat before eight?"

"I'm a member here. Do I need a reason to stop by?"

Jarrett let out a loud exhale. "So, Wade called you."

"To be fair, I texted," Wade said.

Bast looked around Jarrett and nodded to Wade. "He may have mentioned some trouble and you needing a keeper."

Jarrett couldn't find the energy to get pissed off. Not when Wade's call was probably the right move. "I'll fire you later."

"That should be interesting."

Bast laughed. "I advise against that course of action as well. Some days Wade is the only thing standing between you and oblivion."

"True." Jarrett debated putting off the conversation to come. Faking a work emergency and excusing himself. But none of that was his style. He motioned Bast in the direction of the back office. "Come with me."

They walked to the door leading to the private space. Neither spoke. Conversations and music whirled around them, but no one tried to stop them. Likely had to do with their matching frowns and dark in-charge suits.

Jarrett opened the lock and walked in. He stopped when he saw the pile of abandoned clothes in the middle of the floor. The bra was tough to miss since it sat on top.

And Bast being Bast, he didn't ignore the lingerie. He glanced down with an obvious smile. "Interesting."

Bending down, Jarrett scooped it all up and dumped the stack on the floor by his feet behind his desk. "I'm clearly off my game today."

"Speaking of which, what did you do that has Ward calling me during the middle of the day, insisting I stop by?" Bast didn't bother sitting down in one of the chairs. He slid a thigh on the edge of the desk and leaned there, looming over Jarrett.

"Becca Ford."

Bast's grin faded. "I thought you stopped doing her eight months ago."

"Do you have to phrase it that way?"

"I'm thinking yes."

Not one to share, Jarrett hadn't confided much with other people about those lost tense months. Wade knew about what unfolded because he had a front-row seat and landed in the cell beside his boss. But Bast knew because Jarrett unloaded on him as a friend and hired him for his expertise. They'd shared a lot over the years, but the emotional dump was new, and Bast took it like he did everything else, without even one "I told you so."

Jarrett figured after spending weeks living in Bast's guest room because he couldn't stand being in the bed he once shared with Becca, and having him to thank for being free, he owed his friend the truth. "She contacted me."

"About?"

"Someone wiped out her black-ops team."

Bast didn't flinch. The guy was rock solid and not easy to ruffle. "Except for her."

"Exactly." And that part still didn't make a lick of sense to Jarrett.

"Convenient. Is she blaming you?"

At one time Jarrett would have deserved the doubt. In those early days, he ran different kinds of clubs. He offered women and protection and didn't ask questions, all under the umbrella of low-class strip clubs. He didn't worry about the people who worked for him back then, except to make sure they weren't screwing him.

But that was in a different city and another time. He was a different man those days. One who remembered what it meant to be hungry and not have a bed to sleep in each night. He fought like hell not to get dragged down there again, and those fights sometimes took him to nasty places.

Which led him to . . . "I notice you didn't ask if I committed the Spectrum killings."

Bast tipped his head as if in silent salute. "This isn't my first day on the job."

"She wants my help to figure out what happened and why."

"Give her a few hundred dollars, tell her how lucky she is she didn't fuck you over ten years ago, when you handled problems with more permanent solutions, and send her away."

Typical Bast advice—rip the problem out of your life and get rid of it. If only it were that easy.

"Can't do any of that," Jarrett said.

"You mean you didn't do that." Bast's body froze as his gaze toured the room. "Shit, Jarrett. Is she here?"

"As a lawyer, don't you need plausible deniability or something?"

"Lawyer by training but a negotiator in fact. The guy who kept your ass out of prison and wherever else the pricks at the CIA planned to stash you."

To Jarrett those skills were far more valuable than anything a litigator could have done for him in a courtroom. "Much appreciated, which is why I insisted on paying you despite your protests."

Bast held up a finger. "At a significantly discounted friend rate."

The comment sidetracked Jarrett even further. "That wasn't full price?"

"You only got charged for actual expenses and partial staff time. My extremely high rate wasn't included."

Jarrett mentally calculated the bills and thought about the condo he could buy in D.C. with that money. "Jesus, really?"

"You didn't read the bill before you paid it?"

"I would have handed you a million dollars and not asked any questions. God knows what you did was worth even more than that." Keeping the government's eyes off Jarrett's past and negotiating a deal that bordered on bribery could have landed Bast in prison as well.

"Good to know for the future, but for the record, I'm not looking for more work. I don't want to do this dance with you again. I'd rather you be free."

"That makes two of us."

Bast shrugged. "After all, if you go away and the club closes, then where would I eat and conduct after-hours business?"

Jarrett knew his friend of more than a decade was kidding, but still . . . "That's moving, really."

"I'm here for you."

"But I know what I'm dealing with this time."

Bast groaned. "Cut the bullshit."

He was one of the few people on the earth who could utter those words and remain standing. Jarrett didn't take shit. Despite the expensive suits and command he exercised over the floor of his club, underneath he still could drop a man to his knees without guilt. "Excuse me?"

"This woman left you in pieces last round."

Jarrett shook it off because the memory shoved him back in the dark hole he struggled and fought to break free from . . . with Bast's help. "That's an overstatement."

"Is it?" Bast stood up and rebuttoned his suit jacket. "Jarrett, we've been friends a long time. Back before you were respectable—"

"Am I now?"

"—and before my private life got paraded around every bookstore."

"I don't like where this conversation is going." When Bast whipped out the "we've been friends" speech, a lecture usually followed.

"You are not alone in that." Bast rolled his shoulders back, stretching to his towering height. "You want me to tell Richard to be on call and get the law firm ready to do courtroom battle because this time it could go the distance, fine. You want me to step in and get you out of trouble, and with Becca around trouble *is* coming, my friend, I'll do that, too. But maybe we can cut this off before you have to rebuild your life again and just kick her the hell out."

All good options. Jarrett didn't plan to follow any of them. "Let's say I don't send her away."

Bast blew out a pained breath. "There has to be another woman in the D.C. metro area you can fuck."

The word slammed into Jarrett. Mindless fucking mixed with a touch of revenge had been the plan when he first saw Becca standing in the alley. But something inside him rebelled at the thought of hearing the label now. He'd engaged in that behavior back when he got out of jail. Nights with women he barely knew, names he couldn't remember, all while trying to screw Becca out of his head for good. So, he recognized the concept. He just couldn't get it to work for him when it came to her.

Bast held up his cell phone. "Hell, I can call four women right now and set you up for the night of your life."

And he was a guy with that kind of access. "This isn't about sex."

"Are you sure?"

"I know what I'm doing." But since he just made the sex comment, Jarrett wondered if that were true. This was supposed to be sex only, and now he denied it. Becca had him spinning in circles.

Bast rolled his eyes. "Oh, yeah. Clearly."

"Have you ever known me to be out of control?" Jarrett regretted the words as soon as they were out because Bast actually did.

"You don't want me to answer that." Whatever he was going to say next cut off when his cell rang. After a brief check he glanced at Jarrett again. "Just promise you'll keep me on speed dial."

"I'm not stupid." Jarrett put it out there. Now he'd have to hope to hell that was true.

Becca spent some time after he left the condo searching the place. The move wasn't about setting him up or violating his privacy. It was more about taking an inventory and seeing what tools, if any, were at her disposal to hunt down the CIA information she needed.

For some reason she couldn't bring herself to open his bedroom door, the same bedroom they once shared. She knew he could hide documents and files in there. She also understood how tight a rein he held on his anger when he touched her. He might think she couldn't feel the tremble in his fingers, but she did.

The initial fears about him hurting her dissipated with each passing moment but crossing the threshold to his private space might be the one push too far. So, for now, even though skipping that room nearly killed her, she fought the impulse to storm inside. She tried to focus on something she sucked at almost as much as waiting—taking a few minutes to relax and not strategize.

After ten minutes of fiddling, Becca finally figured out the expensive new stereo system he'd installed since she moved out. One last button and music filled the condo. The steady beat bounced off the white walls and high ceiling. She hummed as she walked back to the kitchen because humming helped her think, and no matter how hard she tried she couldn't help but think about her life now and what it could become.

Part of her couldn't believe less than twelve hours had passed since she showed up in the alley. Being in the safety of the condo helped settle the jumping in her stomach and the constant racing of her mind. For the first time in months, maybe years, she wasn't looking around corners or waiting for the next gunshot or random fire.

She'd escaped the last attack, but only by inches. They—whoever they were—set off a flash bomb in her kitchen, blocking her path to the front door. Good thing she always had a second and third way out. She didn't hesitate to throw the emergency rope out the bedroom window and climb down three floors. She'd hit the ground before they started firing into the street.

She'd been ducking and hiding ever since.

But right now her biggest concern was her wavering control. Once she fought through the humiliation and harsh whip of Jarrett's voice, she found her equilibrium. He wanted to use sex to control her, but truth was she had the same weapon at her disposal. She enjoyed sex with him, craved it even. The way she could make him react gave her an advantage.

It all sounded simple. She could find her release, work off tension and be safe. Or so she thought until her needs and his response burrowed under her skin. She never should have straddled him. Something about the intimacy of that position had her remembering the days when she fell fully into her cover and longed for her relationship with him to be real.

Attuned to every sound, when she picked up the soft click of the door, she yanked open the top drawer and grabbed a knife. With her back shoved into the corner of the kitchen cabinets, she crouched down, ready to spring.

Jarrett walked in and came to a sudden stop. His gaze zoomed right in on her, and the corner of his mouth twitched. "Not the usual welcome home."

Words tumbled out of her in relief. "Maybe not for you, but this is my life lately."

"What's with the attack mode?'

She forced her fingers to ease up on the death grip on the knife handle. "I'm a bit vulnerable up here all day."

"Ah, I see." He nodded as he closed the door behind him. "But what you aren't right now is naked."

That again. She set the knife on the counter and picked up the coffeepot. "I didn't want to burn myself."

"Does that happen to you a lot?" As he walked toward her, he draped his suit jacket across the back of the sectional and loosened his tie. "You, the woman who blows up buildings and can carve up a man three times her size in ten seconds."

Forget walking. The man was stalking her. She put the pot down and held on to the counter behind her for support. "You forgot to mention my sniper-like shooting skills."

His gaze traveled along the length of her open shirt—his shirt—and the significant slip of skin open to his view. "The shirt comes off now."

Something about his hands mesmerized her. Always had. Lean fingers, nice clean nails but hints of calluses on his palms from the harder life he once lived. He wore a stainless steel watch. Nothing fancy. Just practical, expensive but subtle like he was.

Her fingers clenched against the cool marble countertop. "Why are you upstairs?"

One of his eyebrows lifted as he undid the top button of his dress shirt. "Why do you think?"

A ball of desire whipped around inside her. "Afraid I'm digging through your drawers?"

"I could probably say something crass, but I'll refrain." Still, he did smile. "The shirt. Remove it."

She looked down. Thanks to her stance, the opening between the edges of her shirt now reached down to her stomach and one of her nipples peeked out. "It's basically unbuttoned."

"That's not the same thing, now is it?"

A thought whispered through her mind. She glanced up at the clock above the mantel. "It's only eleven. The club is in full swing, yet you're here with me."

"Making sure you're not causing trouble." But his voice turned husky as his gaze dipped, skimming over her exposed breasts then lower.

Her body, so in tune with him, reacted to the rich sound and visual caress. Her heart rate ticked up and she struggled to keep her breathing steady. "That's not what you want? Me being naughty so you have to control me?"

"Your mood changed, grew less cautious and certainly less submissive, since you were hanging out in front of my security cameras." He leaned against the counter, facing her.

"Maybe I've decided if I'm going to be here and be your sex toy, I'd really play the role." No, she needed the desire to run both ways. If she was going to be vulnerable and needy, so was he, damn it.

"That's not exactly what we agreed to." He pushed off from the counter and stood up.

In a long, leisurely sweep, she ran her palms down the front of his shirt. From his shoulders to his stomach his heated skin burned under her hands. "Are you complaining about me enjoying my assigned role too much?"

He swallowed visibly. "Enjoying and controlling are two different things."

"You're in charge."

"Yes, I am."

She leaned in and placed a kiss at the base of that sexy throat. The thumping beat she felt there made her smile. He might act indifferent, but his body signaled something else. Something primal and hot and ready to bend her over.

Pulling back, her hands went to her shirt. "Then you tell me. Should I be naked for this part?"

His knuckles turned white where he curled his hands into fists. "For every part, actually."

She let the oversized shirt fall to the tile with a whoosh. "Better?"

Before he could say anything, she closed in and slowly, with aching precision, opened one button after the other, revealing miles of his sleek skin underneath. "And you need less clothing, too."

His hands found her hips as she stripped the shirt open and down his shoulders. When she tugged, he let go of her but only long enough to let his shirt fall.

Something about seeing his chest and tracing a line along the scar under his collarbone made her pulse race at sprint speed. He could wear his pants if he wanted, but she loved having this part of him open to her view. Like this, she could forget about the past with its cycle of lies, drugs and rumors. Seeing the mix of his new business legitimacy and the reminders of the harsh existence he'd overcome got her hot every single time.

"Tell me what you want." She whispered the question as she undid the buckle on his pants.

"Your mouth sucking my cock."

He always did give good naughty talk. "That was the plan." She pressed her lips to his bare skin, caressing and licking over his flat nipples. Savoring his taste as she traced a line between his developed pecs. She dragged her mouth over him, tasting every inch as she moved lower. She didn't rush. Every exposed bit of flesh enjoyed her attention. And when she kissed his stomach and it dipped on a harsh intake of breath, she did it again.

By the time she dropped to her knees and she reached the top of his pants, his hands were tunneled in her hair and his harsh breathing hammered in her ears. As she lowered his zipper, he pushed her hair to the side and off her neck. She could feel his heated gaze burning into her from above.

Still, she didn't skip one luscious step. She slid her fingers inside his pants and past the waistband of his black briefs. With her palms brushing over his ass, she stripped everything off and down his legs. When his belt buckle clanked against the cool floor, she started a trail of kisses back up his firm thighs.

She could smell him, feel the energy vibrate off of him. She watched him open his legs as much as the dropped pants would allow and smiled when he swore about the confining material.

Not that she planned to free him. Oh, no. She had him where she wanted him.

A slight tremble ran through his hands and his chest expanded as he drew in a deep breath. All while he watched her, and since he did, she decided to give him a show. Licked her tongue over him before taking him deep inside. She sucked and kissed and worked her mouth up and down his length while her hands caressed and squeezed his balls.

His hips shifted forward, drawing him in until she deep-throated him. She could taste him and feel the sweat gather on his skin. His fingers clenched against her skull as he whispered her name. *"Rebecca."*

Exactly what she wanted.

She traveled up again, spending time licking the tip of his cock and touching her finger against the dampness there. With a slight lift of her head she looked up and saw his gaze boring into her. Her lips smacked against his skin and a grumble escaped his lips.

"Stand up." His order sounded breathy and the tension etched across his mouth spoke to waning control.

She treated him to one last sweep of her tongue across his balls before getting her feet under her. Her fingernails raked against his skin as she stood, trailing her hands up and over him. She'd almost straightened when he grabbed her around the waist and her body took flight. She landed on the counter with his body between her legs.

He pushed the hair back off her face then held it in his hands. "I'm going to fuck you."

Instead of kissing her on the mouth, his teeth skimmed over her breasts. One nipple then the other, touching just enough to entice but not enough to relieve the ache building inside her.

"Jarrett, please."

He continued to suck on her nipples while his fingers dipped between her legs. With an arm around her butt, he pulled her to the edge of the counter and slipped his middle finger inside her.

From the kissing and touching, she was ready. Her body grew wetter with each pass of his finger, and her heels rested against the back of his thighs, pulling him in tighter against her.

He put her hand on his cock and pumped it up and down. Using her palm as a guide, he slid his tip over her slit. Back and forth until she lifted off the counter in an attempt to drag him inside.

His shoulders stiffened. "Wait."

"What?" Lost in a sensual haze she almost shouted the question. "Now?"

"Condom." He rested his forehead against hers. "Give me a second."

He blew out long breaths. With his teeth clenched, he shoved away from her and bent down. She heard the rustle of clothing and the ding of his belt buckle. Then he was back. His face swam in front of hers.

"This time will be quick." His fingers fumbled with the condom packet.

"Here." She grabbed it out of his hand and rolled it over his cock, watching him grind his teeth as she touched him. "I vote for rough and fast."

His nod turned to a groan as he pushed inside her. He withdrew then slowly plunged again.

"Faster." She grabbed on to his bare shoulders and flattened her chest against his.

"I want it to last." He whispered the words, right before he licked a line from the bottom of her ear to her neck.

"Harder." She dug her fingernails into his skin for emphasis.

"Fuck, yes."

The words ground against her as his tempo increased. His finger found her clit and he rubbed as he pushed. The joint pressure had her gasping. She'd been so primed, so ready for him, that her body responded to the friction as if they'd been rolling around naked for hours.

"Jarrett." She put her mouth against his ear. "Make me come."

"Yes." Whatever he said next got lost in a grunt.

But her patience expired. "Now."

She shivered and the tiny muscles inside her pulsed and tightened. When he thrust into her the fourth time, her orgasm exploded. That's all it took and she felt it in every cell and every fiber. Her toes pointed and her back strained. Her heels dug into his legs as a harsh breath ripped out of her.

"Jarrett . . ." She whispered his name right before her head fell back.

Her body left the counter as he pulled her up and into his arms. One hand balanced under her ass and the other traveled over her back. His hips never stopped moving. He pumped into her. His breath blew over her neck as he kissed her there.

With a final shudder, he buried his face in her hair. His hips punched forward as the orgasm roared through him.

A good minute passed before she roused herself again. Her body had turned to jelly. When he lifted her off and let her body slide down his, she worried her feet wouldn't support her. Good thing he continued to hold her tight.

When he finally pulled back and glanced down at her, her heart flipped. Actually shifted, stopping her breath. Somehow she forced out a word. "Impressive."

"Uh-huh." His affect flattened and a sudden coolness spilled off him.

Panic rose in her stomach and clogged her throat. "Jarrett?"

"Next time when I tell you to take the shirt off, do it." Then he stepped away from her. Pulling up his pants, he walked to his bedroom and shut the door behind him.

A few hours later she rolled over in her guest bed. She caught the sliver of light in the hallway and heard the soft thud of footsteps. When a shadow fell across her doorway, she closed her eyes and held her breath. If she could will him inside, to her, he'd be climbing into bed right now.

Instead, he stood there. She could feel his presence even though he didn't make a sound. Didn't shift. Didn't rustle his clothes.

It seemed like hours, but was likely closer to a few minutes when she heard the footsteps recede again. Her eyes popped open and she stared into the darkness. Looked like he wasn't ready to lower the wall between them at all. She knew that would set back her attempts to collect the information she needed. But the sensation tearing into her had nothing to do with work.

NINE

He hadn't slept a fucking minute and there was only one person to blame—Becca. Jarrett shook his head as he straightened his tie and reached for his suit jacket. Now that he had her again and knew she would react to his touch as if the months never passed, he spent every minute wanting to get back upstairs to be inside her. The weakness shook him and last night's kitchen sex proved how far his control had slipped in such a short time.

He wanted distant but hot. He only succeeded in finding half of that.

The five miles running on the treadmill that morning didn't help clear his mind. Probably had something to do with how much he hated running inside. He didn't need a lot of time outside, but he did crave the fresh air pumping through his lungs as he ran through the early morning D.C. streets.

That was just one more thing he lost when Becca tried to destroy him eight months ago. No way was he willingly putting a target on his back and giving the CIA or any other government agency a free shot at him by following his usual running trails. If that meant staying close to home and work and limiting his outings to places he could sneak to by car, so be it. At some point enough time would pass or he'd have enough leverage and he could venture out without worry, but having Becca land on his doorstep ensured the time wasn't now.

He walked out of the bedroom and closed the door behind him. The reason for his common sense's destruction stood right there at the breakfast bar, ass out, bare legged and sexy as hell as she sipped coffee and made notes on a legal pad. Clearly she'd taken another spin in his office.

But that wasn't his main complaint. "Shirt."

She shot him a smile over her shoulder. "Good morning to you."

Gone was the initial wariness she wore when she arrived. Twenty-four hours and she'd fallen back into old patterns. Flirting while pushing him and looking too delicious for him to fight her.

But they no longer had a real relationship, if they ever did, so he held the line. "I want it off."

She stood up and turned around, taking away his perfect visual shot of that ass. "I was cold."

Only took him a second to see she hadn't bothered to button his shirt. This was the one he wore yesterday. She had him so messed up that he didn't even remember taking it off. "That's convincing."

"Why are you even up? You had a late night and it's only nine."

The quick change in conversation didn't throw him off. He debated dragging her back to the clothing topic. Might have if she hadn't run her hand over her flat belly and pulled his stare even lower.

"I have a meeting." Though now he was thinking about moving it. He could visit the second floor and deal with an irate Elijah anytime.

"Okay." Her fingers tightened on her coffee mug.

The move was so slight he almost missed it. Might have if he wasn't studying every inch of her so he could torture himself with the memory all day.

"No need to panic. If I intended to turn you over to the CIA, I would have done it yesterday," he said.

"I'm thinking maybe you wanted another round of sex first and now my time is up. Maybe today is the day you get your revenge."

As if a few rounds were enough to satisfy him with this woman and let him move on again. "Using you for sex is enough vengeance for now."

"Interesting, since sex with you is not a hardship for me."

She just had to go there, had to keep pushing. He wanted her at his mercy and she wouldn't even give him that. Oh, she'd act like he was in the lead and she feared him turning her in, but he sensed that underneath she kept plotting and maneuvering. No question he was at least ten steps behind. Last time that happened, he ended up in a jail cell.

He needed her to know the screwing didn't trump his dignity. He still thought with his brain, not his dick. "You came to me. You set the parameters of this game when you walked up to my door and let me catch you."

"You figured that part out, did you?"

"From the bits and pieces I've picked up on, like how you once slipped into an embassy without being spotted." He skipped over the more unbelievable parts of her file, the ones about her kills, and stuck to the ones involving break-ins. "Another time you snuck into a high-tech security company and made it out with a rogue computer program without being caught."

Her eyes narrowed. "You've been busy reading my résumé, I see. I'm wondering how that's possible."

"The point is, I'm pretty sure you could figure out a way around my security if you wanted to."

"Not without some planning."

"Which means you're playing me, and I'm wondering why you would think that's a good thing. I have a reputation and it's not as a nice man, Rebecca."

"I know." She didn't even blink. "I read your file. The parts my bosses gave me."

He'd bet that was enough to spell out his years running the streets, then owning them with Wade by his side, enforcing the rules and collecting the cash. "Then you know how dangerous it is to yank me around."

"I'm here for protection and a bit of breathing room. I've been spinning for years and want to sit still for a few . . ."

"Few what?" It was the closest she'd come to putting an end on her visit. The idea of an expiration date should satisfy him, but it left him uneasy.

"Days, weeks. I don't know what it will take, which is why you should help me."

He'd had about enough of this. He had no idea what to do with her or how to deal with her access request, but he was not playing ball with the CIA and handing her over. Disloyalty in any measure was the one sin no one could ever lay at his door.

"Listen to me." He put his hands on her shoulders and regretted the touching the minute he went down that road. "I'm not turning you in."

"Good."

The smirk did him in, as if she were just waiting for him to give her the green light. He went with yellow. "Yet."

She pushed his hands away. "You always have to do that. Have the upper hand, keep me guessing."

"Just testing. Consider that last part a joke. The one thing I promise I will not do is give you over to those fuckers at the CIA."

"You don't joke and you don't promise, so you'll forgive my skepticism."

Now she was pissing him off. If she wanted a battle, he'd give her one. Hell, he could fight all day. At least then he'd have some control and a slice of that much-needed emotional distance. "Again, I didn't volunteer for this gig. You picked your savior."

"Interesting word."

Between the eyes flashing with fire and the way her crossed arms pushed her breasts up and open for his view, he knew it was time to go.

He put his jacket on, taking time to button it and run a hand down the lapel. By the time he was done with the show, his spark of anger died down to a livable level again. "I'll be back. You know the rules."

"No clothes. No moving. No rooms on the left side of the condo." She sat down on the barstool.

"See, not so hard."

She closed her eyes. When they opened again, some of that fire had disappeared. "This is never going to work if I just sit up here doing nothing."

"You have the legal pad and pen."

She rolled her eyes. "The goal is to move me out of here eventually. That means I need to track everything that happened with

Spectrum over the last year. Figure out who was really in charge of the day-to-day and who called the final shots."

"You know that information."

"I know the normal office division of labor and what I was taught about protocol, but this job went sideways."

Making him collateral damage, which seemed just fucking fine with everyone, including her. "And crashed into me."

Her words stammered and she hesitated before taking off again. "Someone pulled the plug on the operation after changing its parameters. Someone picked burning field agents over moving us or simply disbanding the group."

That part pointed to something deeper, and Jarrett guessed the information he turned over to the CIA was at the heart of it. "Sounds like an expensive intelligence decision."

"Once I know all of that, I'll know who took out my team and put my name on the list to be next." She finally wound down, but energy still vibrated off of her. "And then, Jarrett, you can be rid of me forever and celebrate however you see fit."

The words shot into him with the force of a bullet. He fought hard not to flinch. "Okay."

"Because that's what you want, isn't it? Me gone as fast as possible?"

"Stop acting like I'm the problem." She was determined to make him feel guilty and he refused to wear that tag. "Again, you're the one who came to me."

She clenched her jaw hard enough for it to click. "Stop saying that."

"I didn't go searching for you."

"I get that. Believe me."

"The way I see it, the last time you lived here you were fucking me over. Now you'll just be fucking me. That can go on for as long as I enjoy your body." Saying the raw words helped him regain just enough control to keep from touching her. From saying something stupid he would regret and she would use to emotionally bludgeon him. "Then there's the part where it's only been one day, so try being patient."

"I stripped on command for you."

"And why was that again?"

"You insisted."

She acted as if that explained anything. He knew better. "You're not exactly the type to be ordered around. Except in the bedroom, where you prefer it."

She started to say something then sputtered to a halt. It took her another few seconds before she blew out a haggard breath and started again. "I need your help right now."

From the mood to the tone of her voice, one thing was clear. The balance of control shifted back to him. "So, you're willing to do anything."

"I guess we'll see when you get back." With that, she spun her chair around and picked up the pen.

He decided that's as much of a win as he was going to get, so he walked out.

Wade balanced his palms on the kitchen counter and stared at the flecks in the granite top. The last month brought him a stream of steady, unbelievable sex and someone to share his condo. But it was all so unstable and tenuous.

Then Eli dropped that "because of you" comment a day ago

and made it sound as if being in the apartment made a difference to him. Wade had no idea what the hell to think about that.

He knew Elijah's history. He slept with men and women, together or apart, whatever the assignment demanded. Even now he insisted he preferred women. Never mind that he spent every night all over Wade, entering him, sucking him off. There wasn't an inch of Elijah that Wade hadn't kissed and touched, and vice versa.

Getting in this deep was so fucking stupid. Something about the man had Wade ignoring his own rules about holding back and being careful before trusting the man he was with. Biggest problem was the lapse came from something more than the impressive broad shoulders and what Elijah could do with that cock.

The idea the punch of desire probably went only one way, that he was convenient to Elijah and not much more, sucked the life right out of Wade. For years the blur of time before Jarrett dragged him out of the streets and into an office, Wade had killed men on command. Yet now he couldn't stop from falling for the disinterested guy in bed beside him every night.

"You okay?" Elijah ran a hand over Wade's back. Up and under his T-shirt. Over his bare skin, kicking his nerve endings to life.

Wade exhaled more to calm the grinding in his gut than shut off the slap of lust that always hit him when Elijah stood so close. "No."

His mouth touched Wade's hair. "Admittedly, I didn't let you sleep much last night."

As if Wade needed that reminder. The closeness, the confusion backed up on him. "What are we doing?"

"Getting a straight answer from Jarrett and a timetable for Becca's exit."

Not what he meant at all, but Wade knew there was a time for relationship conversations and this wasn't it. With Elijah, there might never be a time for more than hot sex with a guy whose body begged to be explored.

"Right." Wade stood up. Tried to throw Elijah a smile he'd buy as genuine. "Wonder what he'll say."

"Hey, hold up." Elijah grabbed Wade's arm when he headed for the family room.

The sudden concern and spontaneous touching where it couldn't lead to sex were both new. Wade welcomed it all, but instead of making things clearer, the change just muddied everything.

Wade pushed down the confusion and tried to play the moment like it was any other, even though in his head it blew bigger. "What's up?"

Eli frowned and this time the look didn't appear to come from anger. "Did something happen last night down on the floor?"

"Like?"

Elijah's frown deepened. "I don't know, but something's got you half here and half somewhere else."

"I just—" The sharp knock at the door cut off what was likely to be the wrong answer anyway. "There's Jarrett."

He could walk in since he owned the building and included the condo as part of Wade's compensation. But Jarrett never did. He honored privacy and kept confidences. For a guy who wrestled with darkness and insisted on handling most things on his own, he understood friendship and loyalty.

And Wade sure tested that bond. Elijah arrested Jarrett all those months ago and did it with fanfare. In the most visible and reputation-punishing way possible. Eli now insisted he acted on Todd's orders, and Jarrett for whatever reason decided to overlook the embarrassment and let Elijah stay.

Wade took it one step further and had sex with the guy. All the damn time. Guilt walloped him at the beginning. He made the decision not to compound the betrayal by covering up Eli's move into the apartment. It was pretty clear the guy hadn't slept in the small crash pad across the hall once he healed enough to move around.

Other than issue a warning for Wade to watch his back, Jarrett didn't comment on the new second-floor sleeping arrangements. Wade once tried to apologize, but Jarrett told him to shut the fuck up and live his private life however he wanted.

And that summed up how their friendship ran from the beginning. Jarrett had been the first business associate to know Wade was gay. Didn't even blink, certainly didn't care. When he heard a second knock, Wade tried to break Elijah's hold, but he tightened his grip.

"We're not done with this conversation," Eli said.

"Okay." But Wade feared the finish line hovered right in front of them.

He pushed his worries and fears to the back of his mind and went to the door. He opened it to find Jarrett standing there in a suit. Not that the guy wore much of anything else. This or exercise clothes. Wade tried to remember if he'd seen Jarrett in anything else since Becca left. He wore casual clothes back then, but his wardrobe was one of the many things that changed after being in jail.

He glanced up from his phone. Then his gaze skipped over Wade's shoulder. "Am I interrupting something?"

Wade decided he needed to work on his poker face. "Come in." He stepped back so his boss and friend could enter.

Elijah didn't mess with small talk. He stood in the kitchen, muttering under his breath.

Then he went for full vocal. "What the fuck is going on?"

So much for the calm of the last few minutes. The furious line-bending popped up again.

Wade tried to rein Eli back in. "Let's settle down."

"Good advice." Jarrett dropped the cell in his pocket as he walked across the open space to stand in front of Elijah. "Maybe you should listen to Wade and get ahold of yourself before you say something you regret."

"You plan to shoot me again?"

"It's tempting."

Wade stepped up, forming a semicircle with the other men. Not that he could stop either of them if they decided to launch into full-scale violence. Even with his strength and the gun at his side, Wade was at a disadvantage. He'd support Jarrett, but Elijah wasn't wrong about being ticked off at Becca's presence.

And the shooting did happen. Elijah had shown up at the wrong time, injured and going down hard, when Jarrett wasn't in the mood to listen or forgive. Talking fast, Elijah had pointed his finger at the rest of his team and refused to leave when Jarrett made a threat about what he liked to do to trespassers.

Elijah admitted one night much later that he never thought Jarrett had the balls to shoot a guy who was bleeding and lying at the threshold to his club. Elijah now sported a shoulder wound to prove Jarrett did. The thing that concerned Wade was that Jarrett wouldn't hesitate to shoot again.

Jarrett exhaled. "Why am I here?"

"Becca Ford." Elijah smacked his fist against the counter as he talked.

Jarrett's gaze went to Elijah's knuckles, then to his face. "What about her?"

"She's here. You're fucking her."

"Eli, Jesus." Wade knew he had to step in or these two really would rip each other apart. "That's enough."

Jarrett's cold reserve didn't change. "Watch your language."

"What, she's your girlfriend again?" Elijah threw his hands in the air and paced away from them to the sink. Also didn't do anything to cover his swearing and head shaking. He finally turned around again. "She set you up last time."

Jarrett nodded. "So did you and I took you in when you knocked at the door."

Wade cleared his throat. "After shooting you, of course."

He hoped the reminder would sink in and Elijah would calm the hell down. Wade knew the signs. The stiff shoulders, the nerve ticking in his neck—rage gripped Elijah.

Seemingly oblivious to the frustration that pounded down every wall of the room, Jarrett shrugged as if he barely cared. "There is that."

Elijah stepped forward, got right in Jarrett's face. He pointed and spit out his words through clenched teeth. "You brought me in and let me stay because I offered you something. I gave you the information you needed to build a case and show how you were being unfairly hounded and subjected to extortion. To gain leverage, against the CIA."

"Eli, you should—"

Jarrett stopped Wade with a lift of his hand. Then he faced Elijah again, his mouth now flat and his features pinched tight. "You seem to forget I was already out of jail and working on a final deal when you came along. You sped up the process and made things easier for Bast to prevent a trial, and I am paying back that debt right now by providing a place for you to hide and investigate, but you did not *save* me."

Elijah snorted. "Right, because the CIA never fucks anyone over during negotiations."

The louder Eli got, the softer Jarrett's voice grew. Wade knew that was a really bad sign. His boss held his temper through staff whining, childish member complaints and whispers that his business fronted an escort service. But when Jarrett blew, he fucking blew.

Wade tried to diffuse the tension with some common-sense talk, even though he didn't quite believe it. "I'm guessing the same people who think they killed you, Eli, also tried to kill Becca."

"Listen to Wade."

Elijah looked from Wade to Jarrett and back again. An angry red colored his face. "You're both wrong."

"How exactly?" Jarrett asked.

Elijah wiped a hand over his face. Some of the fury left him as he exhaled. "You ever think maybe Becca is at the bottom of this?"

"You've been telling me Todd is the problem. Your boss. The man in charge of the operation against me."

"I'm still digging but the timing is suspect, don't you think?" With the burst of anger behind them, Eli leaned back against the counter. "I finally make headway on figuring out who is at the bottom of this double cross, and she shows up at your back door."

Jarrett's chest visibly rose and fell as if he were weighing the words and not liking what he heard. "I'm aware of the timing."

"Yet you get her naked and take her—"

"Enough." Jarrett's shout bounced off the walls and stainless steel appliances.

Wade didn't blame him. There was arguing and there was stepping way over the line. Elijah struggled with a hot temper, but this was suicidal.

"Eli, what the hell are you doing?" It was as if he wanted Jarrett to throw him out.

"You agree with me that she's trouble." Elijah looked at Wade but pointed at Jarrett. "Tell him."

Before Wade could find the right words, Jarrett saved him. "I know Wade is concerned about Becca being here and being near me. He hasn't lied about that."

"Concerned?" Elijah scoffed. "This is a nightmare."

"No, Elijah. Getting set up for something you didn't do, then sitting in a jail cell while you wait for a CIA team to take you out by faking your suicide, that's a nightmare." Jarrett opened the button to his suit jacket.

The subtle move had Wade shifting his focus. "Jarrett?"

But he was on a roll and not stopping. "This is controllable. Becca will not see you unless I want her to see you."

"Jarrett, come on. Send her away," Elijah said with a mix of anger and pleading in his voice. "Hell, if you can't do it, let me take care of her."

"Excuse me?" Jarrett's voice was deadly soft.

With their backgrounds, all of them ready to fire a shot or land a punch if needed, Eli's meaning wasn't a mystery. But that didn't mean Wade couldn't deflect the message. "That's not what he meant."

Elijah never broke eye contact with Jarrett. "Your boss understands me just fine."

"Son of a bitch." Wade wanted Eli to stop before the explosion blew everything apart. Wade wasn't ready for Elijah to leave and he feared Jarrett was on the border of making that happen.

"Listen up." Jarrett moved so fast he registered as a blur. The businessman gave way to the old crime boss. With his hands on

Elijah's shirt, Jarrett shoved him hard against the counter. "If you touch her, if you think about touching her, I will fucking end you."

Elijah winced as his back rammed into the granite edge. "So, she matters."

"That's not your business."

"Actually, it is."

Wade couldn't disagree. "He's not wrong on that score, boss."

Jarrett stood there, his body stiff and his hands clenched at his sides. A full minute passed before he spoke again. "She has my protection."

Elijah closed his eyes on a look of pain. "That's just great."

"She is my business and if you want to continue enjoying my protection, using my resources and sharing a bed with Wade in this building, you will get in line."

A stark silence settled on the room after Jarrett's threats. When some of the color left Elijah's face, Wade wondered if the other man were really so clueless to think Jarrett didn't know about the sleeping arrangements. The crash pad consisted of a cot and kitchenette and little more, but it was still fine for an unwanted visitor, which was how Jarrett viewed Elijah.

The bigger kick in Wade's gut came from realizing that face likely meant Elijah wanted the sex to be a secret. Like he viewed what they did as dirty and wrong.

Elijah finally broke the quiet as he turned to face Wade. "You're not saying anything to that?"

Because whatever he said would be wrong, Wade went with the party line. "I think Jarrett was pretty clear."

TEN

Four nights into her stay Jarrett opened the door to the condo and stared into the quiet shadows. Becca had left a light on above the stove, but darkness fell over the rest of the floor. It was after two and the club officially closed an hour ago. The obligatory hour of winding down had begun.

Wade volunteered to take over the task of ordering car services and escorting into cabs the few stray club members still around, most of them impaired by too much alcohol and too little self-control. One of the many services Jarrett provided. At a substantial cost, of course. Because avoiding scandal and trouble always qualified as a costly affair. His success depended on that and discretion.

He should have been exhausted, but his nerves rode a fine edge. They had all day and he knew the reason. He'd managed to go without seeing Becca. And that took a force of willpower he didn't know he possessed. Since breakfast he'd stayed in his office, didn't venture upstairs, and only now walked across his family room, hoping to catch a few hours of sleep, shower and grab a clean suit since he wore the office spare.

Conversation he could avoid. Call it self-preservation, but the more he saw Becca in the house, the more right it felt. She fit there. Despite the lies and betrayals, and his vows to stay strong, his defenses weakened with every hour. He long ago promised when he saw her again he would bring her to her knees, inflict a tsunami of destruction on her life to repay her for ripping him apart. He'd held out about an hour before he broke again.

"Damn it." He massaged the back of his neck, trying to ease the growing ache there.

When he lifted his head he spied the papers spread out on his breakfast bar. Since he hated clutter and hadn't been home, there was only one excuse for the mess. He stripped as he walked over into the kitchen. The suit jacket hit the back of the sectional and he abandoned his tie next to the sink. By the time he loomed over the documents he had the top of his shirt unbuttoned and his sleeves rolled up.

He scanned the information in front of him, not sure what he was looking at. Flipping through, he saw the notes filled the entire notepad. Many pages had been ripped out and taped together to form a timeline of some type. He recognized some names and most places, but couldn't figure out how they fit together or what they had to do with the loss of her team.

Before turning away, he traced a finger over the black ink of her familiar handwriting. Bold and unique, just like her. "What a mess."

"I can explain it all to you, if you want."

At the sound of her voice, he closed his eyes. He had them open again before he turned around to face her. Good thing he did because she stood at the edge of the kitchen without a stitch on.

Of course she picked now to follow his orders and remain naked. Damn stubborn woman.

"I thought you'd be asleep." Hoped she would.

She stood there, not even trying to cover up. Her body glowed in the soft light. With every curve highlighted, every part of her on display, his already shaky control took a nosedive.

"You've avoided me all day." She stepped closer with her bare feet tapping against the floor.

"Not that long."

"Jarrett."

He beat back the instinct to shift away from her. "I had work."

"Then it had nothing to do with my promise when we last saw each other?"

I guess we'll see when you get back.

The words tumbled in his mind like a song on repeat. "I don't know what you're talking about."

She talked about being willing to do anything for him. The comment sent him running like some sort of pathetic kid. Somehow he'd lost control over his life and his brain when she broke through his personal space.

"You left me alone, unattended." Her head tilted to the side. "What's a woman to do?"

His gaze shifted to his bedroom door.

"I didn't go in there, but I couldn't do much else either. No clothes. No way to even use that workout room of yours." She ran her hand over her breasts. Cupped the weight as she flicked a finger over her nipple. "I can't exactly run without a bra."

The self-touching was the last straw. She knew he loved that.

Reality was he hovered too close to the edge to take her on tonight. "You should go to bed."

"No."

Not what he expected. "Excuse me?"

With a sigh, she stepped directly in front of him and wrapped her arms around his neck. The temptation continued when she pressed her lean body tight against his.

"Kiss me." She whispered the order a breath away from his lips.

Sweet hell. "No."

"Let me have this."

They'd drawn battle lines when he let her into the building. She would be his sex toy. He would give her sanctuary. The deal guaranteed a sexual release and little else. The plan, already tenuous, shook and faltered as she launched this offensive sensual strike.

"This isn't going to happen." But as he said the words, his hands slipped to her waist and one continued down to caress her bare ass.

"I miss the taste of you on my lips."

Christ, how was he supposed to fight that? "Kissing is over."

She skimmed her lips across his chin. "Is it?"

It had to be. "This is about sex only. Nothing more."

Yet, since she'd been there he explored her with his hands and his tongue. Didn't let one inch go untasted. The intimacy of how and where he touched her didn't escape him. But kissing her always sent a rush of blood to his head. He couldn't afford whatever the feel of his lips against hers might cost him.

"You can make this about anything you want." She licked his neck then trailed kisses through the dampness. "You can hold yourself back."

Hardly. "I will."

She blew a heated stream of air over his skin. "Not want me."

He did not have one ounce of self-preservation when it came to her. No shield at all.

"Don't do this." He made it sound like an order but inside his head he recognized it as a plea for feminine mercy.

Instead of backing away, she kissed his throat and under his chin. When he moved his head, she took his face in her hands. "Let me do this."

"Becca, I don't—"

But her lips found his. He fought for distance and disinterest. Struggled to keep his mind clear and his body from reacting. He counted and held still.

None of it worked.

With his surrender inevitable, he hoped it would be a quick kiss, one that meant nothing and didn't linger. But she didn't let him pull back or stay detached. She kissed him deep and long. Need and desire whipped around them as her hands roamed.

The last bit of blankness in his brain snapped when heat surged through him, spilling out through every pore. The grumble deep in her throat only spurred him on. As his control shattered he didn't so much as fall into the kiss as run headlong into it. Straight for her with no turning back. Blood roared in his ears and his muscles relaxed. His hands traveled over her back, into her hair— everywhere he could touch—as his footing stumbled. He leaned against her and she leaned back.

He couldn't get enough. His tongue danced across hers as need pulled at him. He wanted to be over her, around her, with her. Forget acting aloof. Electricity crackled between them, and the urge to burrow in closer flooded him.

The room spun around them as he pushed her up against the wall. Gone was any pretense of holding back. The memory of every kiss they'd shared rushed up on him. Now that he kissed her again he didn't want to stop. Didn't think he could.

Her fingers slipped into his hair as she held him held close. When they came up for air, both of them panting on stuttered breaths, her head fell back against the wall. He didn't waste time waiting for his heart to slow down. He kissed her neck and her cheek before returning to her mouth with a need that possessed every cell.

The second round of kisses tasted as good as the first. The sparks, the rumble of unspent sexual tension. He felt it all. If anything, they burned hotter the longer the kissing stretched. His cock almost exploded with the need to be inside her.

She broke away from him, leaving a sudden cool breeze lingering between them and his head spinning. She could say anything, ask for anything, and he'd likely give it to her in that moment.

Instead of leveling the killing blow, she threaded her fingers through his. "Sleep with me."

The established pattern of sex-and-run kept him sane. Leaving her bed zapped all his strength, but he knew staying would double him over. But when she looked up at him with those soft eyes and lips bruised from his kissing, he couldn't deny her. Not when he wanted it, too.

Letting her lead, he followed her to the guest bedroom. They'd christened the bed. The promise of hot, sweaty sex lingered. But this time struck him as different from the others. Deeper, more reverent somehow.

She swept him inside and went to work on his pants. With a tug, his belt gave. The scratch of the zipper came next. He stood, watching her slim fingers strip off his clothes. Determination showed in the lines of her body and graceful curve of her neck.

Rather than take over, he let her run this. His hands brushed up and down her bare arms as she dragged off his shirt. When she dropped to the edge of the bed, he waited for the touch of her mouth over him.

She didn't disappoint. With his clothes piled on the floor and shoes kicked off, he stood before her naked. Need pounded on him, inching him closer to the time when he pushed her back on the bed and entered her. Nothing else mattered but getting inside her. This time he'd kiss her, catching every delicious sound she whispered as her orgasm crashed over her.

She wrapped her fingers around his cock and glanced up. "Condom?"

Damn, he'd almost forgotten. Near the end of their relationship they'd skipped the condoms, relying on her birth control and their monogamy coupled with regular physical exams to ensure safety. He'd never acted that way before, but with her the freedom felt right. But continuing now required a level of trust that was long gone.

Still, with her hand traveling up and down his cock he could barely speak. "Pants."

With her he'd been transported back to his teen years. Always carrying protection. Always ready to go.

In a few quick moves she had the condom out and rolled over him. Then she grabbed his arm, bringing him down on top of her on the mattress. His breath caught at the friction of their bodies, but he didn't have time to inhale. She was kissing him, touring her hands over him, grabbing his ass in her palms and fitting his cock to the heated space between her legs.

His fingers skimmed over her breasts, stopping to cup and caress them. But the need inside him had his fingers traveling lower. After wetting the tips with a lick, he pressed against her opening. He rounded her labia, circling and touching until she grabbed his hand and pressed it hard against her.

The noises at the back of his throat matched hers. Sweat gathered over his shoulders. Still, he held back. He wanted her hips lifting and her mouth begging. Lightly thumping his finger against her clit did the trick.

She tore her mouth away from his and stared up at him. "Jarrett."

That was it. Just a hazy look and a tremble in her hands.

He kissed her again. His tongue flicked across hers as his fingers plunged in deeper. The steady rhythm had his body shifting and pressing over hers. Between her soft skin and wet clit, his brain shut off. He couldn't think or regret.

Pushing her legs open, he fit his body between her thighs. He swiped the head of his cock over her slickness. By the third pass her hips rose. He didn't wait another second. Knowing he'd never last, he slipped inside her, holding back as every one of her internal muscles adjusted to his size.

Then he lost control. His body pushed and retreated, loving every inch of the clenching warmth inside her. He dropped his head into her neck and inhaled the scent of shampoo in her hair.

When her legs clamped against him and her nails dug into his back, he let go. All the winding and tension inside of him exploded. His hips moved without a signal from his brain and a moan rumbled up his throat.

She chanted his name and he spilled. His cock jerked and his balls pulled tight. Sheets rustled as he held her and thrusted. When her arms fell to her sides on a harsh exhale, he knew this time wiped them both out.

It took a few minutes for Becca's breathing to slip back to normal. She opened her eyes and saw the outline of the closet on the far wall. The light from the hallway cast shadows by the door, but she could make out the important things. Like the male arm thrown across her breasts and the hot breath blowing across her neck.

Before she could say anything, Jarrett's hand clenched in her hair as he turned her face toward his on the pillow. She expected him to walk out or say some smart-ass thing to break the satisfied mood falling over them.

He kissed her.

Not quick. Not searching for another round. This was long and lingering, testing her in small nibbles before deepening the touch to a blinding kiss she felt to her toes. He reeled her in and pulled her close. For a second it was as if the long lonely months had never happened.

After a few dragging seconds, he pulled back and his gaze wandered over her face. "Tell me exactly what you need."

"Oh, I think you handled it."

He smiled. "I mean with the computer."

She sat up so fast she almost smashed him in the nose. Only a duck and shift move on his part averted disaster.

"Maybe try not to knock me out."

As fast as she got up, she sprawled out again. She leaned on her elbow so she could see every expression and wait for any sign of deception on his face. "Are you serious?"

"You think we're just going to do this forever? You live here, we have endless sex and neither of us leave the building?"

Something punched hard inside her when she realized she didn't hate the idea. "The list does have some pros."

After all those years of running, she wanted to find a place. A half-crazed, all-furious father dragged her all over the world in an attempt to punish her mother for having the nerve to divorce his hard-drinking ass. Becca repeated the pattern by cutting off her father for good and picking a career that ensured her endless shifting.

Jarrett had been the one man to make her rethink the life plan. Even undercover, she shared bits and pieces of her real backstory. Let him know she'd once been a pawn and never wanted to play the role again.

For him, she'd debated leaving the job. Just walking away from the only adult life she'd ever known. Then she found the drugs, and the allegations proved true and her world crumbled.

"It's not working." He delivered the blow without moving or even raising his voice.

Everything inside her froze. "Meaning?"

"I can't keep doing this."

"I still don't get what you're saying."

He sat up, not bothering to cover his bare body as he propped his back up on the pillows and threw an arm behind his head. "It's too much."

"Jarrett, really, what are you talking about?"

"Forget it." He reached out and covered her hand with his. "Tell me what you need."

Maybe it was the coaxing in his voice or the feel of his skin, but the list she meant to dribble out in pieces came pouring out. "Computer access, any files you've collected on me, Spectrum and my team, and don't bother saying you don't have them. You know things about my work and the very fact Spectrum exists, or did. You shouldn't know any of it."

"Yet, I do."

"I also need any background, documents and articles about the deaths of my team members so I can look for a pattern in how they were eliminated."

He cleared his throat, but he looked like he really wanted to laugh. "Gee, is that all?"

Having gone this far, Becca didn't see a reason to go back now. "No."

"Did you miss my sarcasm?"

She rubbed her thumb over the back of his hand. "I want access to Sebastian Jameson."

Jarrett's muscles tightened to the point of snapping. She could see each one freeze in place and half expected to hear cracking as the tension running through him and mirrored on the grim line of his mouth caused something important to break.

His eyes narrowed but he did not drop her hand. "Excuse me?"

"He got you out of the CIA charges. He might know something helpful."

"He knows how to negotiate."

"I don't believe for one second he managed to clear the charges and your name and hand your life back to you because he was top of his class at law school. He had information. From you or from somewhere else, and I need it."

This time Jarrett did let go of her hand. With his palms at his sides, he pressed against the mattress and sat up even higher. "You understand what you're asking, right?"

"We're talking about my life."

"You could be talking about mine."

There it was again. A one-liner that didn't fit and begged for more. "Explain that."

He threw his legs over the side of the bed and stood up. His gaze went to the floor and around the room. "I'll consider the request. Some of it, not all."

"Wait a second." She lunged forward and grabbed his wrist before he could pull away. The clothing search could wait. "You just said you would give me what I need."

"No, I asked you what you wanted." He just stood there. Not pulling away but not holding on either.

"Verbal gymnastics."

"You heard what you wanted to hear."

She dropped his hand as she scrambled to her knees. Something about half lying across the bed right now seemed wrong. "Jarrett, we're not playing a game here."

"We're not playing house either."

She threw up her hands. "Care to expand on that? I mean, you're a bit more cryptic than necessary this morning."

"You can't ply me with sex." He walked to the end of the bed and scooped his pants off the floor.

"You think I'm trying?" The direction of the conversation had her head spinning. Just a few minutes ago they were all over each other. Entwined and open. His kisses had touched off a firestorm inside her and now he rebuilt that cold wall between them.

He was making her crazy.

He didn't fight back. Didn't even rise to the challenge. He just shrugged. "Sure feels like it."

"Did you ever think I am in your bed because I want to be?" The question sat out there in the ringing quiet. She stared at him, refusing to break eye contact while mentally making him deal with her instead of running away.

"I bought that line from you once before and it landed me in jail."

She jumped out of bed and stood in front of him. When he started to fold his pants, she tore them out of his hand and threw them on the bed. "That's what you get for dealing drugs."

"Last time, Becca. So, listen the fuck up." He pointed at her as an icy darkness moved into his eyes. "I have never used drugs and certainly never sold drugs. You can lay a lot of shit at my feet, but never that."

"I saw—"

He yelled right over her. "You got played."

"By whom?"

He picked up his pants and threw them over his shoulder. "For the last eight months I assumed you were the mastermind, but since we both got played, who knows."

The fight whooshed out of her as his arguments bombarded her brain. "I didn't set you up."

"So, you keep saying."

"Do you really think I wanted you to go to jail?" Once out, the words left an ache behind.

"I thought you wanted me." He put his hand behind her neck and brought her head in close.

A rough kiss singed her hair.

"Jarrett, we need—"

Then he walked to the door, sparing her one last look. "Shows how stupid I was back then."

ELEVEN

The next night Wade finally closed his eyes after a long shift downstairs on the floor. Grown men went to battle over a parking space. Another guy tried to hide a cocaine problem while running to the bathroom every few minutes. Thanks to Jarrett's no-drugs policy, Wade had an excuse to escort that fucker out for good. Wade came back to find another idiot who had bounced two monthly payments at the bar still expecting service.

It had been a hell of a night.

The way Wade saw it, a percentage of the membership needed a priority check. He rolled onto his side and tucked an arm under his pillow to prop up his head. Tomorrow would be soon enough to work out all the club problems. Now he needed sleep.

"I screwed up."

At the sound of Elijah's voice, Wade's eyes popped back open and his muscles tensed. "What?"

"When I lost my temper yesterday and put you in the middle."

Wade didn't need a road map for this conversation. After the showdown, Wade had unloaded on Eli and gotten hit with the silent treatment in response.

Turning onto his back, Wade opened both eyes and stared at the exposed pipes on the ceiling above the bed. In the next second, Eli moved and his face swam in front of Wade. "Jarrett is not a man you fuck with."

"I have the bullet wound to prove that." Eli balanced on his elbow, hovering close as his hand flattened against Wade's chest.

"I'm serious."

Elijah's fingers tightened into a fist. "Her nosing around, him losing control . . ."

Hoping to calm whatever storm was brewing and keeping Eli talking, Wade rubbed his palm up and down Eli's arm. "What?"

At first Eli shirked off the comment, but then his eyes focused again, as if he'd wrestled with sharing and decided to take the risk. "I could end up dead."

There it was. The nightmare scenario. And it wasn't exactly an argument Wade could ignore. They were all on edge and double-checking locks and security feeds since she showed up in the building . . . again.

Still, he'd been trained, had spent his youth fighting and his twenties crossing the line. After a lifetime of working dirty jobs he was out of the business, but he'd step back in. For Eli. For Jarrett. If he had to lay it on the line, even if it meant hurting Jarrett by going after the one woman who mattered to him, Wade would.

He didn't issue the vow out loud. Didn't need to. He knew it to his bones and that was enough, but he did want Elijah to figure out a way to silence the battle waging inside him. "That's not going to happen. I won't let it."

"Others are dead. Strong agents, smart agents." Eli dropped

his arm and his fingers speared through Wade's hair. "People I worked with and trusted."

"Did you ever trust Becca?" Wade had at first. He wasn't sure what to think about her story now.

"I'm not convinced she's on the run, or needs help, or whatever line she sold Jarrett."

Wade noticed Eli hadn't exactly answered the question but let it drop. "Me either."

"Then work with me," Elijah whispered into the dip at the base of Wade's throat.

The conversation blinked out on him. The combination of Eli's mouth and hand wandering lower had Wade's concentration fading in and out. "I'm trying, but you losing your shit makes that tough."

"Because you have to support Jarrett no matter what."

Wade's hand slipped to the back of Eli's head and pulled him even closer. "Because Jarrett responds to logic and respect. When you go off, the only thing he's thinking about is how fast he can get rid of you.

Eli lifted his head. "You lived with danger."

"A long time ago." Wade wanted more than anything to put those days behind him.

"Did you stay calm and rational under fire back then?"

Leave it to Eli to drag out the logic now. "Not always, no."

The corner of Eli's mouth kicked up in a smile. "Well, do you blame me for having the same problem now?"

Despite the sparkle in Eli's eyes and the way his fingers explored, Wade refused to be reeled in. "When it comes to Becca you won't listen."

"Tell me you think she's not setting him up."

"If she is, Jarrett will stop her." Or a bullet would. Wade wanted the decision to belong to Jarrett, but when the end came that might not be possible.

"He couldn't before."

"He's smarter now." Wade ignored the part where Jarrett was pretty fucking smart before but still got wrapped all around when Becca stepped into his life.

"Is he?"

"He has a weakness for her." And that qualified as the understatement of the century.

"I get that."

This time Wade laughed. "No, you don't."

Wade tried to imagine Eli growing weak over anything or anyone. Even when he stumbled into the club those months ago, beaten and broken, he held his body with an assurance that dared them to try anything. Shot and bleeding, he continued to stare Jarrett down until Jarrett blinked.

"What the hell does that mean?" There was no anger in Eli's voice, but surprise swept around him.

Wade weighed each word to keep from sending the conversation to a dark place where Eli got worked up all over again. Wade preferred him right where he was. "I doubt anything ever threw you off the job."

"You did."

Elijah brushed his lips over Wade's collarbone as he angled his body closer. They lay interconnected now from their chests to the tangle of legs just below the thin white sheet. Eli's warm breath blew across Wade's skin.

"I don't know—"

Eli bit into Wade's shoulder. "Get on your stomach and I'll show you."

Becca propped her head on her hand. In this position, leaning over Jarrett's chest, she could watch his chest rise and fall on deep breaths. Study him.

His long fingers lay on his chest, and his other hand stayed tucked under her. Black eyelashes and a relaxed mouth. In sleep the churning darkness inside him faded.

She'd wondered if he would hide from her today. After last night and her delivery of the long list of what she needed from him, he bolted from the bed. Something she said freaked him out. She had no idea exactly which point did it. She only knew that when he slid in beside her an hour ago, leaving the club floor well before closing, his arm came around her and his finger slipped inside her.

Day five of being back in his condo and he hadn't wasted much time unleashing his revenge. He went to work, came in and out of the condo, and kept her on her back and any bit of clothing off. The fear of him hurting her faded away to nothing. Being freed from the worry this fast was a surprise. She assumed he'd toy with her, keep her dangling and on the defensive. Emotionally, he did, but not physically.

She'd searched his place and spent hours trying to crack his computer password. She even took a few hours and worked on the door alarm. Not that she planned to leave. She just wanted to know she could break out if needed. If the world imploded on her, she'd already devised an escape out the window. To quell the anxiety, she needed that alternative. But explaining any of that to him would only start an argument and make building any trust impossible.

"You're making me nervous," he mumbled without opening his eyes.

The grumble of his voice had her jumping. She forced her body to still, but tension ramped up in her at the unexpected noise. "You're awake?"

"Staring makes me twitchy."

She spread her fingers and touched as much of that hard chest as possible. "I couldn't sleep."

"Any reason?" His eyes blinked open. "Other than being tracked by the CIA and targeted for elimination, I mean."

"Funny how that seems to be enough."

"Imagine that."

They lay there in the silence for more than a minute. She could feel him staring and see his face with the help of the hallway light cutting through the darkness.

Reaching over, he flicked on the small lamp next to the bed. "Okay, I give up. What's going on in your head?"

She squinted until her eyes adjusted to the light. "Nothing."

"Uh-huh. Not believable at all, by the way." He pushed up until his back rested against the pillows. "If it's the list of things you want—"

"No."

"Then it must be that you want me to exhaust you." His smile promised he could do it, too.

"You already did."

"I seem to remember a few favorite positions we haven't revisited." His fingers skimmed down her bare back to the top of her ass as she cuddled in closer.

"Are you asking to try something specific?"

Something dark fell over his face. "I don't have to."

She sighed inside but kept it hidden there. At least he was consistent. He gave an inch and showed her some softness then quickly slammed the gate shut again. "Because you own me?"

"Your body. Temporarily, yes." The way he slid his hand over her and kissed along her jaw contrasted with his verbal shots.

Words kicked around in her head and she fought the urge to say them. Any sense that she didn't feel his revenge and he would balk. But still, a part of her wanted to know . . . "What if I told you I wanted something else?"

His shoulders stiffened. "I'd remind you of our deal."

"Right."

His eyes narrowed. "What?"

"Forget it." She shimmied up his body, pressing tight against his and ending with her mouth kissing his chest. "The answer is yes."

With his hands on her face, he pulled her head up and kissed her until her body shook. Her hands teased his shoulders and hair. Cutting through his words, she sunk into the trembling excitement of having him take charge.

He lifted his head without moving his palms from her cheeks. "Get on your back."

"What?"

"You can lie down or I can put you how I want you."

She didn't know what came next and didn't care so long as he took her. With her insides bouncing, she scrambled off her knees and dropped back against the mattress. The move put her body next to his with her feet flat on the mattress near his head.

He didn't let the position go to waste. With a quick grab of the knob to the nightstand drawer, he opened it and pulled out a condom. Then he was back, his body touching hers with his hand wrapped around her ankle, keeping the connection.

Before she could steel her body for the pleasure, his fingers danced up the inside of her thigh. He pushed her legs wide open as he kicked off the sheet and crawled between her knees. A kiss trailed up the inside of one leg until he reached the fleshy part of her thigh.

"I want to go in deep." The rough words rumbled against her bare skin and skidded across her senses.

She had to grab the sheets underneath her, ball them in her fists, to fight off the tension already spiraling through her. "Yes."

"You won't be able to control the fucking and I won't hold back," he said in between kisses. "You'll take every last inch."

"Jarrett, please." She wasn't sure if she said the plea out loud or only in her head, but she felt it in every cell.

He licked a long line over her skin, down farther until it swept over her. "What do you want me to do to you, Rebecca?"

She jerked at the slick contact against her sensitive flesh. "Fuck me now."

Two fingers disappeared inside her. They thumped against her as he plunged and withdrew in a steady rhythm.

Barely able to move but so desperate to feel his cock inside her, she raised her head and saw her wetness glistening on his fingers. Still he thrust his fingers inside her. In and out with his thumb flicking over her clit every time her hips lifted. Her insides quivered and her thighs shook. Fire burned through her as her skin heated and she feared she'd implode.

"You're soaking wet."

Gulping in air, she tried to answer him. "For you."

She hovered on the edge. If she could press her legs together tight enough, she'd come, but his shoulders blocked her and the rubbing of his thumb over her clit stopped every time she got close.

He bent down and sucked on her clit. Her gasp filled the room as her vision went dark.

His finger replaced his mouth when he sat back on his heels again. "I decide how I fuck you."

She would let him do anything, touch anything, try anything. "Yes. God, yes."

Both hands were on her now. Fingers rubbed her thigh as his other hand kept up the pulsing beat inside her. Need swamped her and she lifted her head again, thinking to bring him in for a blinding kiss, but his concentration centered on her clit and the pump of her hips in time with his presses.

"Your body belongs to me."

"Jarrett . . ." The rest of the words caught in her throat. She did and he knew it, but she had to hold something back.

"Say it."

Before she could give in, he pulled his fingers out of her. Those small inner muscles clenched in frustration and her lower half lifted off the mattress. She tried to inch closer, but he clamped his hands on her legs and held her still.

Rational thought fled. If he wanted begging, she'd beg. "Please fuck me."

A warm breath blew over her wetness, making her twitch and squirm. "You know what I want to hear. Give it to me and I'll let you come."

"Yes." She chanted the word and didn't stop until his fingers plunged inside her again.

"All of it."

She forced her eyes to stay open as she stared up at him. "My body is yours."

"Good girl." He bent over her once more and that talented tongue swirled over her. "Are you sure you're ready for me?"

"Yes." She fought the need to shift and moan. Her body rocked as the tension ramped up inside her.

He pulled away again and she almost screamed. She might have if she had any breath left in her body. Sweat dampened her hair and broke out on her chest.

Just when she found the voice to demand he enter her, he shifted. He lifted one of her legs and pushed her thigh back against her chest. He somehow got the condom on without her noticing and now he pushed into her with one long demanding stroke.

Her sensitive tissues felt raw. The pleasure was so intense her mouth dropped open. And he kept moving. He plunged inside her, pushing until he filled her and every nerve burst to life.

The position meant she couldn't hold back or control his thrusts. He was in control. Total control. Going as deep as promised as he wedged her foot against his shoulder. Satisfaction filled his expression as he focused on the push and pull of his cock inside her.

She was so primed, so ready for his entrance, that it didn't take much for her body to tighten. When he stopped to grind his lower body against hers, the world exploded. The orgasm rocked through her. Her body bucked and her mind went blank as her body kept lifting off the bed to get closer to his. She tried to breathe as every part of her tingled.

His pace picked up and his breathing grew heavy and she knew his orgasm was about to hit him. When it finally did, all she could do was drop her hands next to her head on the pillow and watch his shoulders stiffen.

Then a thought floated through her mind: he was right, she was his.

Becca gave up on sleep somewhere around five and headed for the shower. Jarrett had already slipped off around four. Later than usual, but he cut out just as he had night after night. Screw-and-run seemed to be his MO these days. They had sex, he picked a fight, they had sex again, but this time with an intensity that knocked her near unconscious, then he walked away to sleep alone. This time he'd stopped to turn off the light on his way out.

Early this morning she snuck out to see what he did once he left the bed. The answer wasn't all that original or difficult to figure out. He beelined for his bedroom where the door remained closed for the rest of the night.

She'd debated busting in on him. Even walked across the great room several times with that very intention in mind. But she refused to beg. Forcing him to kiss her, going to him on his terms while obeying his no-clothing rule, all cost her enough. So, she'd stayed in bed. Pulled the covers over her and settled in their softness. She expected to drift off to sleep, but it never came. The water revived her but not by much.

When she came out of the bathroom wrapped in a towel, because she would be damned if she'd walk around naked for him at all from now on, she spied the stacks on the bed. Flicking the bedroom light on, she froze. For a second she didn't know what she was seeing but then she did.

The pile on the left consisted of her sneakers, along with underwear, running shorts and a bra. The one on the right was nothing more than two of his dress shirts, her preferred outfit these days.

She didn't know what it meant, but it meant something.

With a shaky hand, she picked up the blue shirt on top and brought it to her nose. Inhaling deeply, she searched for the scent of his soap. The combination she couldn't identify by ingredient but associated only with him. It lingered in the morning long after he was gone. It wrapped around her when she slipped on the shirts he'd worn and abandoned.

These were clean and fresh. His but not intimately him.

She still wasn't sure what he wanted from her, but she now knew she needed more than his help. And this move on his part was a start.

TWELVE

Jarrett sat in the second-floor conference room and stared at the information spread out in front of him and highlighted on the three large monitors lining the wall. This room once served as a place for him to conduct business meetings, leaving his downstairs office private. But then Elijah moved in and it became a command center.

Jarrett looked at all the photos and notes and still didn't know what the point of it was. Elijah had showed up two months ago, begging to be heard. Crawled right up to the same door Becca used. For his trouble, Elijah got a bullet in the shoulder. Jarrett would have done more damage if Wade hadn't stepped in with worries about new criminal charges.

When Becca pretended to get caught, even though she all but knocked on the door, Jarrett ushered her inside. The reason for the different treatment wasn't a mystery. He used all sorts of excuses, trying to trick his brain into believing inviting her in was about revenge and cold fucking. But he knew the truth.

Despite the lies, despite handing him over to the feds and tearing his life apart. Despite everything and regardless of the passage of time and the festering anger, he loved her. Right down to the dark lonely place in his soul. And it fucking sucked.

He leaned back and stared up at the ceiling, trying to call up what little common sense he had left. What he felt for her made him vulnerable and stupid. He could lose everything and he doubted he'd fully recover a second time.

He'd just closed his eyes when the alarm dinged and the door opened. He sat up in time to see Elijah walk in looking six-feet-two-inches of furious. But that wasn't new. He'd been sporting a frown for days and Jarrett knew Becca was the reason.

"What are you doing?" Elijah nodded at the table top as he asked.

The snapping, the questioning—Jarrett was damn sick of all of it. "Sitting in a chair I paid for, in a building I own."

"It was a simple question."

Jarrett didn't get lured in by that one. Nothing had ever been easy or straightforward with this man. He'd worked as an assassin on the government payroll. Trained and paid for by the CIA and used for its purposes. He retrieved data, did whatever he had to do to collect information and killed on demand. The only reason he lived at the club now was because he turned over information that helped Bast negotiate Jarrett's safety.

After all, the public would not take kindly to a tape of a CIA operative talking about how he got an order from above to frame an American citizen in order to bribe him for information. The CIA could deny it and claim Elijah's tape was a fake, but the people in charge wouldn't want even a whiff of the allegations out there. Combined with the certain defense weapon intel from a former member now relocated to Spain, it helped buy Jarrett's freedom and hold back a second round of blackmail. So far.

That meant, as much as Jarrett hated to admit it, he owed Elijah something. Jarrett had repaid that debt in the form of room and board and a level of security while Elijah investigated who lied to him about the real reason behind the arrest at the club months ago. The way Elijah saw it he'd been used and double-crossed. That seemed to piss him off more than the attempts to kill him and wipe his existence from every database. In reality, Elijah looked for many of the same pieces Becca did. Jarrett decided just that morning to give them to her. Maybe if Elijah knew Becca worked on the same puzzle, he'd have more incentive to get the job done and get them all out from under this weight.

Jarrett jumped right in, expecting blowback. "We need to reconfigure the system to add a user but limit internal access to protect your identity and work."

"Who?"

"Just do it."

Elijah crossed his arms over his chest. "Going to tell me why?"

The man hadn't led his team, but he was born to the task. That made dealing with him a total pain in the ass for Jarrett. "I'm not sure why you think you're in charge here or entitled to explanations."

"Are you telling me I don't have a legitimate reason to know?" Elijah pulled out the chair across from Jarrett.

Jarrett couldn't argue with that. "To give Becca access."

Elijah froze in the act of sitting. "What the fuck are you thinking?"

Here we go. "That this is my building, my computer, my resources, and you're living here on my good graces."

"I handed you the information you needed to get out from under the criminal charges." Elijah dropped down. "Have you forgotten that already?"

"You gave me leverage. In return, I've given you cover, helped you fake your death and have not once unleashed the unholy hell you deserve for dragging me into your bullshit."

With his elbows on the table, Elijah leaned in. His voice didn't rise above a hoarse whisper. "I don't trust her."

"I don't trust either of you." And that was the truth. Becca and Elijah—hell, the whole CIA crowd—lied for a living. They got paid to engage in subterfuge. Becca only crossed his path because she showed up claiming to work for a satellite company, and he ignored her words and any potential alarm signals in favor of luring her into bed.

Looked like that joke was on him.

"After everything you still think I'm the problem?" Elijah asked with a voice filled with shock.

"Possibly."

"Well, I'm not."

"You'll understand why I'm skeptical of most everything you say." Which was why Wade was supposed to be watching Elijah and why Jarrett double-checked every move Elijah made.

The locks and security codes that kept intruders out also let Jarrett track everyone's movements. He didn't care what Wade did with his private life, except to worry he'd made a bad choice throwing in with Elijah, but Elijah was on Jarrett's personal watch list.

Elijah flattened his hands against the tabletop. "I'm not the one you need to worry about here, and you know it."

"Find a new topic."

"You're the one upstairs fucking her." Elijah threw out his hand. "Letting her work her way into your head."

Jarrett slowly rose to his feet. His legs hit the chair with enough force to send it spinning behind him. "This is your last warning. One more word about Becca, and you're on the street. You can explain to Natalie and her crowd why you're still alive and take your chances on staying that way."

"You care about Becca that much?"

"Just follow the advice."

Elijah slumped back in his seat. "You are playing games with my life."

The words mirrored the ones Becca had said. The same tremor of worry carried in Elijah's voice as had in hers. With anyone else, Jarrett would write the comments off as overly dramatic. But Becca and Elijah knew nasty people. Both enemies and friends could be after them.

Which brought Jarrett back to the point. "The two of you are looking for the same thing. Underneath it all, you both want to know who set up Spectrum for termination and why, and find a way off the hit list."

"Unless she is the one at the bottom of it all. She could be the one who wrote the hit list."

Jarrett wanted to believe that possibility because then he could hold on to his anger, but the theory fell apart every time he mentally walked through it. While this whole "I need to be in the club" thing could be one more assignment for Becca, he doubted that was the case. There was no reason for her to delay or win him over this time around. The longer she lingered, the harder it would be for her to get the jump on him, if that was the plan.

She'd had ample opportunity to remove him and search for his files. If she was on an information hunt or looking for Elijah, she could have gone on a rampage or at least be working on a way to get around his security system. As an expert, she could find a way or turn a weapon on him. He knew that much. More important to him, every time he climbed on top of her, she could have plunged a knife in his back. She didn't, which was why he decided to open the information to her now.

As far as he could tell, except for a case of restlessness and balking at his nudity requirement, she wasn't fighting being confined. Part of him wondered how long that would last and, trust or not, dreaded the day she'd walk out of his life again.

The constant battle between being so angry and wanting her so much robbed him of sleep and good sense. Maybe Bast and Wade were right. Maybe he should let her be someone else's problem, if for no other reason than to spare him from the inevitable gut shot to come.

At the very least, he could step out of the battle. "I should put you two in a room, let you hash out whatever pissing match you have and then put you both to work finding a solution."

Elijah dropped his head in his hands. His fingers massaged his skull as he sat there. A minute passed before he looked up again. "Tell me why her."

Jarrett wished he fucking knew. There had been other women and plenty of great sex over the years. None of that compared to being with her. "We're not discussing my private life."

"The last time . . ." Elijah shook his head as his arms dropped against the table.

No way was Jarrett letting that just sit there. "What?"

"She disagreed with how I was handling the operation back when she lived here."

Jarrett bit the inside of his mouth to keep from yelling that he was not an operation. "Why?"

"Ask her."

"I'm asking the man who trespassed on my property and lived to talk about it. Which, I would remind you, was by my choice."

"My shoulder still aches." Elijah rubbed it as if talking about it reminded him of the pain.

"I don't care."

Elijah hit Jarrett head-on with a full push of eye contact. Elijah didn't even blink. "Here's the part you're not going to like."

"I haven't enjoyed much of this conversation so far."

Elijah rubbed his hand up and down his thighs. "Before I could tell Todd my concerns about her cover, he moved up the timetable."

"Meaning?"

"He fast-forwarded having you dragged off to jail."

A stark silence followed Elijah's statement. Jarrett knew the other man was telling him something important, something that incriminated Becca. Rather than jump in and pepper Elijah with questions, Jarrett sat there. Elijah wanted to spill this story and only needed the room to do so.

He waited a full minute before launching into another comment. This time he seethed with anger. It poured out of him and showed in every inch of his tense body. "When you and Becca get together things get fucked up, and that time you messed up my timing."

"How?"

"I thought you knew everything."

Jarrett made a hard grasp for his temper. Calling up his control, he kept his expression blank and his voice even. "Elijah, spill."

"We were off plan and I didn't know why, or how far up the chain the orders were, but I knew the entire operation could end up with me being sacrificed."

The plan all fell together in Jarrett's head. Elijah played hard at not caring and insisting his life was about killing on command, but he'd known something was off back then and tried to derail the operation before it went to hell.

Jarrett felt a punch of admiration. It almost overcame his usual urge to shove Elijah out the window. Almost. "You were planning to take Todd out yourself and end the operation."

"If necessary, yes."

"Instead, it blew up on you. My arrest. Your team members dying. Hell, Todd getting attacked. It all meant whatever had you worried should have had your worried."

"Exactly."

Jarrett had never gotten this far, never broken through Elijah's reserves and the layer of silence covering the intricacies of the operation, so Jarrett treaded very carefully. "For some reason you blame Becca for the destruction?"

"For everything. We fought about what was happening with the operation back then, and she snuck out, broke protocol and went to Todd. Next thing I knew, the order came down to take you in."

Jarrett's insides shook from the force he exerted to keep his anger from bubbling up and over. "You're saying she made sure I got arrested."

"I'm saying I don't trust her." Elijah slapped a hand against the table. "And a little advice? You shouldn't either."

Wade walked out of his condo bathroom and slipped a T-shirt over his head. His hair was still damp from a shower as he searched out his coffee mug in the kitchen. When the alarm chirped, he did a quick check over his shoulder.

Elijah came in and slammed the door behind him. He wandered

around wearing a furious scowl. He seemed too busy swearing under his breath to notice what was happening around him.

Never a good sign.

"Where have you been?" Wade asked.

Elijah barely spared him a glance as he looked around the family room area with his focus not stopping on any one thing. "Conference room."

"You okay?"

His head snapped up. "Do I look okay?"

Sounded like they were back to pissing and moaning. Wade grabbed the mug and walked over to stand behind the couch and wait for the storm to hit. "More like half-possessed."

"That's about right."

"I'm guessing that means you found something." Wade didn't know whether to be happy or not. Finalizing the investigation meant moving on. Elijah wasn't one to stay in place.

Wade recognized the type because he'd once been the same way. Then Jarrett yanked him off the street and out of his loan enforcer job. Jarrett went legit and insisted Wade do the same. Being raised in a family of petty thieves, finally finding stability suited him. Wade never looked back and never regretted.

But he would regret Eli.

"Jarrett's lost his goddamn mind." Elijah rested his hands on the back of the chair. His fingernails dug into the dark leather.

Wade didn't need an explanation. Only one thing set Elijah's anger firing at this level these days. "So, we're dealing with a Becca issue. Again."

He pushed off and stood up straight again. Pacing started right after. "What is it about her?"

"Hard truth is that Jarrett wants her. He probably even loves her." *Had from the beginning and always would.* Wade was convinced of that now. Really, there was no other explanation for his usually steady boss's loss of control.

Jarrett ran his business with an iron fist and historically relegated women to the roles of dates and temporary sexual partners, never permanent and always living separately from him. Becca broke that mold, and no amount of crushing his will or wrecking his life seemed to change that.

"That's fucking ridiculous." Elijah shook his head. "Jarrett is a grown man, and a smart one."

Wade didn't disagree, but Elijah was missing the bigger point "He's still human."

"Wait a second." Elijah stopped walking and grumbling long enough to focus on Wade. "You're saying Jarrett told you how he feels about her?"

"Didn't have to. I've known him a long time." Wade had seen Jarrett attracted and intrigued. This thing with Becca was a totally different ballgame.

"The two of you are close."

It was the way Elijah said it that had Wade leaning against the back of the couch. "As friends."

"So you've said."

"Not sexual partners." Though in the midst of an alcohol-induced state after losing Becca, Jarrett wondered aloud, circled the idea. Wade knew the bright light of sobriety would prove that a huge mistake, so he dumped Jarrett in bed and stood watch until morning. He doubted Jarrett even remembered.

"You've been together since back when you lived on the streets." Elijah said the words as he moved across the room. By the time he hit the last syllable, he leaned on the arm of the couch, facing Wade.

He didn't know where this was going, but he'd shared these pieces of his past in week two or three of having Elijah here, so there was no harm in agreeing now. "Yeah."

"Back when you did everything to survive."

"Eli, what are you—"

"Talking about you." The heated look on his face suggested Eli was done talking about Jarrett.

"Why?"

"You're more interesting than your boss."

"I think most people would disagree."

"You're the one I want to fuck." Elijah maneuvered around the edge of the couch so fast he was practically on top of Wade.

That's all it took to send Wade's pulse racing. "I thought we were arguing about Jarrett."

"I have other things on my mind." Elijah slipped his hands under Wade's tee and trailed the tips over his stomach.

Not that Wade fought the move. "Like?"

Elijah walked around, skimming his hands up and taking Wade's tee off with them. They shifted until Wade stood next to the armrest with Elijah behind him. Then came the brush of Eli's lips over Wade's ear and the fit of his body against Wade's back.

"Feeling that beard against my cock." Eli kissed Wade's neck, scraping the skin with his teeth. "Sliding into you."

The mix of the words and touching hit Wade like an electric jolt. "I'm not saying no."

"That's one of the things I like about you."

"What?" A hand slid over Wade's chest while the other traveled lower.

"The way you say yes." Elijah rubbed the material over Wade's cock. Back and forth, slow and steady, clenching and unclenching his fingers. "So damn good."

The friction of Wade's jeans against skin built into a blinding heat there. He didn't realize he was holding a breath until it hissed out of him. "Let's go—"

The words cut off when Elijah pushed. Wade put his hands out to stop the fall and ended up bent over, balanced on the armrest, with Elijah's cock pressed against his ass. The layers of clothing didn't matter. Certainly didn't provide a barrier that couldn't be shredded in a frenzy to get at each other.

"I'm thinking to take you over the couch. Maybe throw you on the bed and watch your face as I fuck you." Elijah kissed his way down the side of Wade's throat and around to the sensitive spot at the base of the back of his neck. "Or do you want to be on your knees with me in your mouth?"

The words rumbled against Wade's skin. This side of Elijah, a little rough and full of need, broke Wade's will every time. He didn't have a shield for this. Couldn't figure out how to say no and mean it.

"Couch," he whispered, surprised by the low grumble of his voice.

"Don't move." Elijah put his hand on the center of Wade's back and pressed down. "Not an inch."

"What are you—"

"You better be in this position when I get back."

"Or?" Wade forced the words out over the want churning in his gut.

"Be patient and you'll be rewarded." The last of Elijah's words faded as he slipped out of sight and into the bedroom.

Wade shifted, keeping his hands on the arm of the couch. He

twisted and turned until he saw Elijah come right back out, having shed his shirt and in the middle of opening his pants.

Wade could barely see, barely hear over the thrashing of excitement inside him. "You going to tell me what we're doing?"

A tube of lube landed with a thump on the cushion in front of Wade.

Eli laughed. "Guess."

"Here on the couch?"

"That's right." Elijah lifted Wade just enough to undo the button on his jeans and plunge a hand deep inside his fly. "Are you ready for me?"

"Damn." Wade threw back his head, loving the weight of Eli's body over his shoulders and the brush of hair against his cheek. "Yes."

Wade's jeans dipped on his hips. With a tug and a shove, they fell past his knees. Since he hadn't bothered to wear underwear, the striptease left him bare and ready. His cock twitched when Elijah ran his palm up and down his length. Then his fingers curled around him and Wade's vision blurred.

"Are you sure?" Elijah glanced over Wade's shoulder as his hand pumped up and down. "Well, you do look like you're getting there."

His breathing hiccupped as he slipped his palms over the outside of Elijah's thighs. Anything to touch him and be close. "Damn right."

"If you're a very good boy, I'll let you come." Eli kissed Wade's hair. "Then we'll move to the bed and try it again."

"Elijah, please."

"I love how you say my whole name, all drawn out and hot, when you want me inside you. Very sexy." With a hand pressed on the groove between Wade's shoulder blades, Elijah pressed down again and didn't let up until Wade was bent over with his ass in the air. Then Elijah kissed a line down Wade's bare spine. "In a few minutes you'll scream it."

Wade gave up all control in this position. Eli would dominate the tempo and the thrusts. Wade knew from experience he could plead but he'd remain powerless. When he saw Elijah reach for the tube and felt the cool gel rub all over his ass, Wade stopped thinking.

He dropped his head and let the sensations tumble over him. The heat of Elijah's body. The push of fingers inside him, readying the way for a firm and eager cock. The kick of longing so strong it had Wade's knees buckling.

When he felt Elijah's tip move against him everything else washed away, slipping inside.

"Fuck," Wade said as he forced his muscles to relax.

Elijah bit down on the tight muscle at the back of Wade's shoulder. "Oh, I'm definitely going to fuck you."

Pain mixed with pleasure. "Then move."

Elijah licked the spot he'd bitten. "Ask nicely."

"Damn it, Eli—"

Firm hands settled on Wade's hips. The full and intense penetration started a second later.

"Consider this Round One." Then Elijah finally started to move.

THIRTEEN

The next morning Becca hugged Jarrett's shirt close to her body. The crisp cloth hung on her, reaching down her thighs.

She'd never been the fanciful type. When other little girls dreamed of big weddings, she worried about having enough food. Instead of poufy white dresses, she practiced how to pack up her few possessions and get back on the road in less than two minutes, per her father's insistence. The question of whether she'd have to hide from police or nosy neighbors trumped fairy-tale endings.

Becoming a fighting machine followed from her messed-up childhood. She used to beat up anyone who made fun of her and played grand mental games where she created new identities and spun wild tales of what her life would be. Sliding into the role of professional identity-changer as a grown-up actually seemed right. Predestined, even.

When her job had required sex with men to get information, she separated her mind from her body. When she killed, she'd hang on to the knowledge she was doing good. Never mind that she had trouble sleeping or couldn't trust anyone ever. Well, except one.

Her fingers slipped down the row of tiny white buttons as she stared at Jarrett's closed bedroom door. This was the last level of privacy she hadn't breached. He ordered her to keep out and she had. But the door pulled her like some sort of magnetic connection that kept sucking her in.

Even though she knew there could be something important behind that door, she'd waited. Because the idea of going into the room she once shared with Jarrett turned out to be the step too far.

Living in the guest room, she could trick her brain into thinking she'd maintained detachment. Enjoyed the sex and handed over her body but kept her mind her own. But it was all bullshit. They'd mentally raced around each other, shouting their respective positions, each thinking the other committed the greater past wrong. At this point she no longer knew what was right or real.

All those years of killing on command ended with a death squad on her tail. That shifted life back into perspective. The one man she could trust just might be the one she handed over to the CIA. That made her the betrayer, an idea that doubled her over in side-splitting pain.

Which is why her hand hesitated on the doorknob now. She didn't want to search the room. She wanted a specific shirt. The one he last wore. The trade would only take a second and she'd be out again.

Before she could think twice, she turned the knob and pushed the door open. Standing on the threshold, she peeked inside. The king-sized bed with the light gray comforter dominated the large room. The furniture fit the rest of the house—clean lines, no clutter, taking up minimal space.

The doorway on the wall to her left led to a massive walk-in closet. The type with drawers and a chair in the center. She knew because she helped him design it. Changed it from a large room with a single bar on each wall to something usable.

Beyond that sat the bathroom with the marble floors and jetted tub. Memories bombarded her brain. The two of them relaxing in there, making love under the water spray.

She shook her head, trying to push out the stray pieces of the life she left behind eight months ago. This was a mission for the comfort of his scent and nothing more.

Tiptoeing across the plush rug, because for some reason that felt right, she looked around for any sign of the clothes he wore the night before. As expected, they'd been put away in whatever place he assigned them. He traditionally used a cleaning service, but she hadn't seen evidence of it since she got here. Not that the man needed help. He kept the place pristine and likely deserved a kick-back from the service he paid.

Anxiety kept welling inside her, spurring her to move quickly. She glanced around when a tingling sensation crept over her. She'd felt the prickling at the base of her neck often enough to heed the warning and not linger.

Unless he changed his habits, and he was not a man prone to change, the laundry and dry-cleaning baskets sat just inside the closet against the wall. She pushed the door open and clicked on the light.

And stopped cold.

"What the hell?" It couldn't be.

Ignoring her stated task and the possibility of detection, she walked to the right side of the closet as if in a trance. Her feet carried her, but her brain kept misfiring. Starting at one end, she ran her fingers over the item on each hanger. Black pants. A few shirts. That dress Jarrett bought for her to satisfy his fantasy of running his hands up underneath it.

Nothing expensive or fancy.

All of it hers.

He hadn't changed a thing. Each piece of clothing waited in the same place she'd assigned it. The discovery was right there. She could see the evidence and say the words, but the reality of what it all meant refused to settle in.

Her stuff. None of it moved. She just assumed he sold it or threw it away. Hell, with the way they ended it was conceivable he'd set it all on fire. That's probably what she would have done had the roles been reversed.

Her mind flashed to the exercise clothes he set at the end of the bed in a stack. They didn't just *look* like hers. They *were* hers.

She turned, thinking to check the drawers in the bedroom for T-shirts and bras and anything else she may have left behind. Pivoting on her heel, she ran right into Jarrett's broad chest. He caught her arms before she fell over and held her there.

"Jarrett?"

"You set off the alarm," he said in a flat voice.

Seeing him there, so sudden and out of context to what she found made it even harder to understand what he was saying. "What?"

"If anyone enters my bedroom or office without typing in the proper code, an alarm goes off on my phone."

The calm demeanor scared her. He should be yelling and talking about his rules and her failure to listen. Anything but the painful emotion-free affect.

She said the only thought she could hold in her head through the waves of confusion. "I've been in and out of your office since the first day. You didn't come running then."

"I disengaged that one. Left this one on."

"Because you assumed I'd come in here."

"Didn't you?" There was no heat in his voice. No disappointment or excitement. Nothing.

"For a shirt."

He rubbed the material over her shoulder between two fingers. "You're wearing one."

"I wanted a different one." The excuse sounded ridiculous in her head and even sillier out loud. She tried to shake the haze out of her brain and search for the right words, but she couldn't get there.

No matter what argument she tried to frame, her mind zoomed back to the fact her clothes were on hangers a few feet away. It was as if she never left. All by the man who hated her, vowed to destroy her and tried to break her will when he forced her to strip off her clothes in his office.

Liking her for sex or even the company was one thing. Keeping reminders of her near him was another. It struck her as some sort of strange self-punishment. The only thing that made sense was he kept it all as a reminder of how she lied to him so he'd never travel down that risky road again, but even that didn't make much sense. Not to a man like Jarrett who demanded loyalty and thrived on control.

"Why do you need another shirt?" he asked.

She couldn't exactly say she wanted to smell him while he was gone. At this point she wasn't sure what she could and should tell him. "I liked the blue one you had on yesterday."

"As far as subterfuge goes, you can do better than this."

He thought she was on another operation. Plotting against him.

God, they talked past each other and around each other and so rarely to each other.

"I wasn't searching for anything in your bedroom."

"Okay."

From the drawl, she knew he didn't believe her. Rather than debate, she focused on her question. "Why is all my stuff here?"

He never broke eye contact. "I never got around to throwing it out."

"And you can do better with lies than that, Jarrett," she said, parroting his words back to him.

His hands dropped to his sides. "I don't actually owe you an explanation."

She missed the warmth of his hands the second he broke contact. "Okay, I know this looks like—"

"What?" For the first time emotion seeped into his voice. He almost barked the word.

Forget her mistake. She wanted to focus on his choices. "It looks like you were waiting for me to come back to the condo."

"No." He turned and walked out of the closet.

"Then what is it? It looks like a weird shrine." When he stopped, she hurried to stand in front of him again. With both arms on his forearms, she squeezed until he looked at her. "I mean, what did the other women you brought up here say about all of this? One of them had to notice."

"No."

"Did you use the guest bedroom?" Her stomach rolled at the thought. Bile rushed right up her throat and fought to get out. She concentrated all her energy on not throwing up on his shoes.

"I mean you are the only woman who's been up here."

Yeah, right. "You expect me to believe you haven't had sex for eight months."

"I didn't say that."

The words, so unexpected, hit her like a slap. Her head actually snapped back. The news shouldn't matter or surprise her, but it did. "So then what?"

"You want a number?"

"God, no." She really wanted him to stop looking at her with those dead eyes. Stop answering in short, clipped sentences. Never mention sex or other women again.

"None of them came up here."

"None?" That made it sound like he had a damn list and ran through it one by one. "That sounds like there was a waiting line once I was gone."

A spark of fire lit in his eyes as he pointed at her. "You don't get to judge me or who I fuck. You gave that up when you had your team arrest me before I pulled up my zipper."

Damn but he was right. His personal life, his sexual exploits, did not fall within her right to know. But the idea of it being so easy for him to move on sliced at her until she expected to see a thin line of blood welling across her stomach.

"I was making a statement about the other women in your life," she said.

But he was already talking. "You left me."

The words robbed her of breath for a second. "I don't want to fight about this."

"Then you should have obeyed my rule and stayed out of this one room."

There it was. Finally he circled back around to his requirements for giving her shelter. For some reason, the consistency gave her comfort. She could handle this debate. It wasn't as if she had an excuse for being in there anyway. Not one he'd believe.

With her chin up, she looked him straight in the eye. "You're right."

She expected a grunt of satisfaction. A smile. Something positive. He didn't give her any of that.

He frowned as his hands went to his hips. "Now what game are we playing?"

"You lost me."

"You're not exactly one to abandon a fight. We once argued about Chinese food restaurants for ten minutes until you admitted you hadn't tried either of the ones we were considering for takeout."

Guilty. The character flaw rose up at the oddest times. But the bigger point was she could not win this battle. Laying out the specifics of her side meant opening herself up and telling him how broken she had been back then. How, after a lifetime of jumping to her feet and moving forward, losing him drove her to her knees. Days of blankness and those stupid bouts of crying. She'd never considered medication until her life tilted and nothing made sense.

She'd cried three times in her life—when her father took her, when she returned to Pennsylvania after all those years away and found out her mother had already died. And when she realized she'd fallen in love with the type of man she'd always despised and hunted down—a sick liar who endangered everyone he met.

Nothing in that definition matched the man in front of her or the one she lived with without seeing even a hint of drugs. Back then she couldn't get out of the emotional tailspin enough to question all she'd been told and seen. If Jarrett hadn't meant so much, she could have separated all the pieces out. When it came to him, she lost perspective and slipped back to the green newbie she was on the first day of training.

But she could question the extent of his real role in everything now. Can and did. The drugs, the way Spectrum imploded, how he got out of trouble so fast . . . and why he let her in the club and his bed without launching an attack of revenge.

When she investigated Spectrum's demise, she planned to reopen the file on Jarrett and dig around like she should have when Todd ordered the takedown. If Jarrett's name should be cleared, she would figure out a way to get the job done.

Until she could fix everything else, she needed his help, which meant owning up to her mistake today and blocking out the rest. "I messed up."

"Fine."

He walked out of the bedroom, leaving her standing in the middle of the room. Whatever she thought would happen, this wasn't it. She also never thought she'd be the type to go running after a man, but she was doing that as well.

Before she could say anything he tapped his finger on the stack of files sitting on the kitchen counter. "These are for you."

She skidded to a halt on the floor. "What are you talking about?"

"Here is your password." He held up a piece of paper that had been folded in half. "You can use the setup in the office. It will also give you access to watch the club's security monitors, except for those on the second floor."

The world kept spinning and she didn't know how to catch up. "What's happening?"

"I'm giving you access. Limited, but still more than I planned."
He flipped the edge of the files. "Wade's place, storage, the conference room. Those are off the table. You stay on this floor and I'll
provide what you need."

She'd been on the second floor a few times, mostly to watch
movies on the big screen mounted to the conference room wall.
But all but one time Jarrett accompanied her. On that occasion
she'd poked around and seen the crash pad Jarrett said he kept up
just in the rare case of a special member being unable to return
home.

The storage room with the tapes and locked cabinets proved
more interesting. She spied it for a second when Jarrett relocked
the door. The thing had redundant security and she hadn't figured out how to break it before the world came crashing down.

"You have a computer, articles on the fake deaths of the rest of
your team and the attempts on you and Todd. All events were
termed accidents or natural complications, so who knows how
much of that info is real." Jarrett shuffled the files as he talked. "I
also have some information I collected."

He moved a few files and picked up one from the center of the
pack. When he held it up, she lunged for it and smacked it against
the stack again. "Why are you doing this?"

"You asked for help."

"We both know that's not the full answer."

He treated her to an uncharacteristic beat of hesitation. "You
need to move on."

At the words, her heart clunked. Actually made a screeching
noise that reverberated through her. "You mean you *want* me to
leave."

"Isn't that the end goal here? You get the evidence, you strike a bargain and you leave."

She couldn't tell from his tone if he liked that plan or not. "So, this is all about rushing me out the door as fast as possible."

Her hands flexed as he clamped down hard, grinding his teeth together. "I'm doing everything I can not to lose my temper right now."

She was pretty sure they had raced past that point minutes ago. "Can we go back for a second and talk about what happened in your bedroom?"

"Not necessary."

"I know I overstepped when I went in there."

"Damn right you did."

"I won't go in there again."

"It's a little late for that, unless the plan is to search for drugs." Those sexy eyes narrowed into menacing slits. "Or plant them again."

No matter where the conversation went, it always roamed back to this. A mutual distrust and sense of anxiety. A joint feeling that the other wasn't telling the whole truth. The scary sense that she might have been used as someone else's pawn and included Jarrett as her collateral damage.

"Tell me why Todd green-lighted the operation on the day he did," Jarrett asked.

Another zig when she expected a zag. "What are you talking about now?"

"You'd been living with me. I gather you were collecting data and reporting back. So, why that Tuesday?" He sat on the barstool. "Why pick that exact day, that time?"

With everything raining down on them, she had no idea why

this mattered. But his sharp breathing and stern face suggested it did.

"Todd was in charge of the operation," she explained. "He made the decision."

"Don't fucking lie to me."

The burst of anger stopped her from moving. "I'm not."

"But you're not answering the question. What did you do?"

"Why does this matter?"

"You're evading, so I'm guessing it does." Jarrett wiped a hand across his mouth and when he was done the blank stare had returned. "Why that day?"

"Because I told Todd there was no reason for my cover to continue." Truth was she threatened to blow her cover and walk away from it all. But she didn't add that. Jarrett wouldn't be able to hear it right now as anything more than a ploy.

And admitting it would make her vulnerable in ways that made her bones shake. It was the only time in her life the temptation to walk away trumped the dedication to the job. Because of him.

If she told him that truth and he laughed, or worse, she didn't know if she'd ever be able to put the shattered pieces together again. As it was, her legs barely held her and her heart thudded loud enough to pound in her temples.

"Why not wait and see what you could get out of me? That had to be headquarter's preference," Jarrett said.

Because I loved you, and setting you up pricked at me until I thought my head would explode. "Because I never saw you with drugs and thought our intel was bad."

The frown came back. "Who gave you the intel?"

"I don't know."

"Come on, Becca."

"That sort of thing was above my pay grade." She forced energy into her legs and made her muscles move until she stood next to him at the breakfast bar. "We got the assignment because someone much higher up at the CIA had the tip. We were following up. Just a piece of the operation and we never knew how drug charges fit in with a CIA operation."

"But at some point you believed I was innocent."

"Not the word I'd use because I'd seen your file and knew your history." She knew what she realized was likely a sanitized version. The series of strip clubs. The escort service. The loans that had to be repaid or he'd find another way to collect. "But I didn't see the drugs."

He swore under his breath. "You told Todd you were out because you didn't find drugs and then the drugs appeared. How fucking convenient."

The red flag waved high and proud now but she'd been so messed up and flailing eight months ago that she couldn't see it. By the time she noticed the whole operation carried a stink, he was out of prison and she couldn't understand how. And then her life blew apart—literally. "I know how it sounds."

"Do you?"

She sighed as she struggled to bring together all the facts and the bits of everything that happened since she'd gotten here. At some point she should be able to turn the pieces and make it all fit. Had to. "Can we talk about—"

Before she could touch him, he stood up and shifted away. "I have a meeting."

"Now?"

"I do run a business."

And he spent most of his day downstairs doing just that. "This is important."

"Is it?" He put his hand on the stack of files. "Funny, but I thought this information was all that mattered to you."

For a smart man he sure as hell got that one wrong.

FOURTEEN

More out of habit than anything else, Jarrett stood up when he heard the knock at his downstairs office door less than an hour later. Bast stayed in the chair he'd been in since his arrival a few minutes before. But when Wade ushered Natalie inside, Bast jumped to his feet again. Looked like whatever manners prep school training instilled in him hadn't disappeared. Jarrett had learned most of his manners through Bast's shining example, though Jarrett would much prefer to sit this meeting out.

Before Jarrett could say anything, Wade took off without saying a word. The running part made Jarrett envious. He'd rather be anywhere but listening to whatever emergency Natalie wanted to unleash.

And his head was not in the game. Seeing Becca in his bedroom and opening up his choices to logical explanations had him floundering. He didn't get rid of her clothes because he fucking couldn't. Every time he tried to clear the possessions out he'd get tripped up in the idea of wiping her out of his life forever.

The woman had him by the balls and she just kept squeezing.

Natalie didn't wait for an invitation. She walked across the room in her usual businesslike navy suit and sat down. "You kept me waiting almost fifteen minutes. I don't appreciate the delay."

As far as Jarrett was concerned, it was a miracle the woman got through the door. That only happened once Bast was in the building and ready to go, which was Jarrett's requirement for the meeting. "I thought we had a rule about you stopping by."

She nodded in Bast's direction. "I went through your guard dog."

"Now that's not very nice." Bast pushed away from the wall and took up the standing position next to Jarrett's desk chair. "Of course, I wish I could say no one has ever called me that before."

"This isn't funny," she said as she took out a small notebook.

Bast raised her one by dragging his phone out of his pocket and turning it on. "What it is, Natalie, is a waste of time."

The bickering and verbal jabs, Jarrett wasn't in the mood for any part of this pissing contest. He had enough trouble with the woman upstairs. He didn't want to invite more from another woman in the building.

"What do you want?" he asked.

"Becca Ford."

Every damn thing came back to her. Jarrett had to fight to keep from showing any reaction.

Bast didn't miss a beat. "Then go find her."

"I think she's here."

A fissure of concern had Jarrett talking when he'd promised to let Bast handle this meeting. "She isn't—"

Bast talked over Jarrett. "You think he'd be so fucking dumb as to invite her back in here after what she did to him? To his life?"

Jarrett didn't have to look up and check Bast's expression.

They'd been friends long enough for Jarrett to know the underlying message in Bast's words was meant for him, not Natalie. Not that Bast had been all that subtle in questioning the decision to give Becca shelter in private either.

For a few drawn-out seconds, Natalie sat there with her gaze going back and forth between the men. She finally settled on Bast. "Rumor is Jarrett had it bad for her."

"I'm sitting right here." The ignoring-him thing ranked pretty high on the annoying scale in Jarrett's mind. "You don't need to refer to me as 'he' or any other pronoun."

"Answer me this." Natalie tucked the notebook under her elbow and leaned forward. "What's with the hard-on for Becca?"

"Those days are over."

"It looks as if she's been very busy, cleaning up loose ends. You could be one of those." Natalie looked back and forth between the men. "Both of you "

"We know the score. Her team is dead," Bast said. "Except for Todd."

Jarrett wished that guy had been taken out first. "Someone killed them. Probably your friends at the CIA."

"The order didn't come from us."

Jarrett wasn't falling for a line. "Because you would tell us, you being so honest and all."

He'd heard about every line of the negotiations from Bast. The CIA had demanded every word of information Jarrett ever collected on club members. Even then, they stuck with the drugs story and only offered a reduced sentence.

A few weeks later Elijah stepped up—more like showed up at the door—and filled in a few blanks. Clued Jarrett in on the pieces the CIA absolutely needed to know. Jarrett sold his soul for those.

Keeping his name out of the news as someone who turned on his clientele was one of Jarrett's main concerns. Last thing he needed was a mass exodus from the club, but Bast's impressive PR machine spun tales and made comments until the spotlight moved off Jarrett. The club members were never the wiser.

"According to the news, the Spectrum team members, all normal citizens, died in random accidents." Bast held up his phone as if to show off the evidence of his claims.

Natalie snorted. "Don't be a jackass."

Jarrett glanced up at Bast. "Bet you've heard that before, too."

He shrugged. "Once or twice."

"Enough of this. Where is she?" Natalie stood up. She eyed both men until her gaze settled on Bast.

"You're asking the wrong person" he said.

"You're an attorney."

"Your point is?"

Her fingers tightened on the edge of the notebook until the tips turned white. "You have a duty to act within the law."

"That is not quite the oath I took."

"I'm done playing games." Her false façade of calm dropped and her anger raged through the room like a killing beast. "I will take this place apart brick by brick if I have to."

Jarrett knew he should be immune to the threats by now. He'd heard so many, most directly from her mouth. He'd dodged almost all of them . . . eventually. But every time a government agency promised to tear him apart, doubt started thumping deep in his gut.

Not that he would ever let her see his rumble of panic. "That should be interesting."

"It will be when I station people at the club's doors and start asking questions of your members. We'll see how quickly business dries up when law enforcement starts nosing around, picking apart their private lives and yours." Her smile grew with every word. "What, you think we don't know what a naughty boy you've been?"

"My record is clean." And Jarrett knew he had Bast to thank for that.

"Is it?"

Bast looked at her with one eye closed and his head tilted to the side. "I continue to be confused by your vision of the CIA's reach."

"This goes beyond the CIA." She glared at Jarrett. "We could be talking criminal charges."

"Like what?" Bast asked.

But Natalie's gaze never left Jarrett's face. This wasn't about empty promises. No, this production was for him. To make a point and throw his continued freedom into question.

"Whatever we can think up," she said. "Won't be the first time we came up with a reason to bring you in, to throw you in prison."

"More threats, Natalie?" he asked when he couldn't think of anything else to say.

"Ask yourself if Becca Ford is worth the clusterfuck your life will become."

Jarrett refused to answer that. "You can go now."

Natalie's mouth dropped open. "You're dismissing me?"

The woman clearly didn't understand how close he hovered to the brink. "I'm trying hard not to tell you to go fuck yourself."

Bast put a hand on Jarrett's shoulder and held him in his seat. "That's enough."

"Listen to your lawyer." Natalie glanced at her watch. "I'll give you three days to realize what you need to do."

Then before either man could fire questions at her or throw in a "you've lost it" comment, she turned on her comfortable heels and stormed out of the room. Her butt swayed but it was hard to see anything through the pounding fury that followed in her wake.

Bast moved around the room and sat in the chair Natalie abandoned. "That woman does like to leave a room angry."

"She's just doing her job."

Bast laughed. "Since when do you defend Natalie Udall?"

Damn good question. But truth was Jarrett dissected her actions, looking for evidence of being played. Natalie liked to bend the rules, but she mostly had her orders and followed them. Jarrett could respect that. "Since I realized I'd handle this about the same way she is."

"She's tough." Bast tapped the end of his cell against his thigh. "And she wants your ass."

Jarrett feared she wouldn't stop until she had it. "Figure out what we can do to prevent what she's threatening."

"That's pretty easy."

He didn't even have to ask. "I'm not turning Becca over to the CIA or anyone else."

Bast shook his head, gave the exaggerated exhale. Threw out every sign of a friend on the edge. "You ready to admit you're treading water when it comes to her?"

Jarrett shook his head. "I wish I was doing that well."

Becca leaned against the stove, holding a bottle of water and thinking about the last seven days at the club. She didn't remember twisting the lid off or taking a sip. She stood there, tapping the tip against her top lip and thinking. The events of last night and the early morning ran together in her head into one big blob.

With a practiced concentration, she closed her eyes and mentally pulled it all apart. She'd learned the trick during training. When facts and fear and adrenaline spun together and backed up on her, she broke it open and fought off the freeze. For some reason the skill worked better with trained killers than with Jarrett.

As soon as she thought about him, he appeared. She blinked, looking from those broad shoulders under the charcoal suit to the clock on the microwave. He'd been gone about a half hour. Not enough time to burn that pissy look off his face, unfortunately.

She went with the obvious. "You're back."

"You didn't get online." He didn't stop walking until he rested next to the fridge and across from her.

"How do you know?"

He reached into his suit pocket and pulled out his cell. "I'll get a message when you sign on."

With all his tricks and the load of paranoia he carried around, the guy could give lessons to her former desk-riding bosses at the CIA. "Interesting tracking device you have there. You pick that up from a club member?"

"Wade took a class."

He didn't smile but the deadpan delivery had her brain scrambling. "I kind of hope you're kidding."

"Did you think I wouldn't put any restrictions on what you did up here?" He took the water bottle from her hand and frowned when he turned the lid and produced the distinctive crack of breaking the seal. "Maybe I should rephrase that since I put plenty of restrictions on you up until now and you ignored them all."

Something about the way he said it made her defenses rise. "Not all."

She'd kept her quiet defiance to a minimum as she stripped for him, opened her body to him . . . refrained from stabbing him. She could kill a guy with a good-sized spoon and shimmy down a heating vent to sneak into a room, so as far as she was concerned, he should be grateful she stayed put for a few days. God knew, sitting still battled with her personality and training.

"Name one," he said.

"I waited until today to go into your bedroom." And holding back had used up a good portion of her willpower.

He rolled his eyes as he took a sip. "I wonder if you know delaying is not the same thing as obedience."

"Not my favorite word."

"You're too busy trying to outmaneuver me to try exercising it for a change."

Through all the banter, she noticed the lines at the corner of his mouth and stress around his eyes. Some of the fighting spirit seeped out of her. "What happened downstairs?"

He screwed and unscrewed the lid to the bottle. "What are you talking about?"

"Your mood is on fire." Much more of the smart-ass comments and she might refresh her takedown skills right there in the middle of the family room.

"Did you miss our last conversation? We didn't exactly part on friendly terms."

"It's still ringing in my mind, trust me."

He threw her one of those the-man-is-done frowns. "Then you know I'm tired of the bullshit."

Oh, no. She'd own her garbage, but he left with anger spinning around him. He came back with his shoulders weighed down with what suspiciously looked like exhaustion. "This mood—whatever this is—isn't about me."

"You sure about that?"

Eight months ago he would have grabbed her hand and drawn her down on his lap on the couch. After some prodding, he would have shared something, at least a clue. Talked about problems with members or staff infighting. Even his disgust at having a business-man sit in his office and explain that he *had* to stay in the club even though his last few payments bounced.

The point was, she'd seen this look before. "I know you."

He studied her as he twirled that damn lid in his hand. "I wonder how it feels to be able to say that and believe it."

"So, we've taken a giant step backwards, I see." Not a surprise. Her insides still trembled at the thought of her clothes hanging right there next to his. "We're back to short angry sentences and barely making eye contact."

"I've given you almost everything you wanted. There is no way you can complain."

She snorted. "Of course I can."

"Becca—"

The tension swirled around the small space, bouncing off every counter and cabinet. She rushed to diffuse it before it built to an explosion. "And you didn't give me everything I want."

"What the hell does that mean?"

No way was she elaborating on that. "Tell me what happened downstairs."

He put the bottle on the edge of the sink. "Nothing you need to worry about."

"I'm here. Talk to me." She wanted to go to him. Skim her hands over his chest and dip her head in for a kiss.

She leaned in to do just that, but his words stopped her.

"You are a convenient sex partner. Nothing else."

The tightness ran out of every muscle. Her chest and shoulders

fell. Hell, she'd bet she lost three inches of height. He crushed her
and stared at her as if daring her to complain about the killing blow.

"You always have to do that," she said, forcing the hurt out of
her voice.

"What?"

"Put a wall between us."

"You mean like a prison wall?"

God, he just wouldn't stop. "It doesn't have to be this way."

"We're not dating."

The verbal thrust slipped right through her ribs, pinning her to
the cabinet. Her stomach ached. Without thinking, she held a hand
to her middle before her insides could spill out. "I'm aware of that,
Jarrett."

"And I don't trust you."

For some reason, that cut sliced even deeper. He launched his
shots so fast and so furious she couldn't take cover or find an inch
of armor. "Maybe, but you need to talk with someone."

"What I need is a good hard fuck."

Every word carried a zinger. With each syllable he tried to bat
her away. This was about flailing and thrashing. About throwing
verbal punches and landing them faster and faster as she fought
back but lost ground.

The obvious choice was to stomp off and say no to him for the
first time since she showed up at his door. She considered it as she
bit her bottom lip. Then her gaze slipped to his hands and the death
grip on the counter behind him, and she decided to hold on tighter.

"Okay." That's all she said. One word.

His eyes widened. "You're volunteering?"

"Do you have another woman waiting somewhere to service
you?" If he said yes, she might just find that killing spoon.

"Not right now."

She took that as a green light and moved. Her hands skimmed up and under the edges of his suit jacket. "Then I'm here."

"Just like that?"

"You need relief." She kissed his chin. His neck. "I'll provide it."

He grabbed her hands and held her out from him a few inches. "Why in the hell would you agree to those terms?"

"That was the agreement I made when I walked into the building."

"Tell me to go to hell." His grip eased, but he didn't let go. "Christ, Becca. I'm not one of your assignments."

The blows kept coming. His face flushed as he found new vicious ways to phrase things. Ways that would hurt the most.

"You think the sex is just for you? That I don't want it, too?"

At her words, his thumb traced a pattern against her palm. "I'm the one demanding it."

"And I've taken the lead." Little did he know there were times when she wanted to cross that huge room between their bedroom and bust down the door. "Do you want to know why?"

"No."

"You are raging and fighting me, but deep down you hear me. You understand the wanting runs both ways."

He shook his head. "This is about bodies."

"You're telling me *any* female body would do?"

He opened his mouth, but whatever he was going to say got lost when he shut it again. A few seconds ticked by before he finally came up with something. "It's just sex."

"Not for me." Her hand brushed over his cheek. When he didn't push her away, she caressed his lips and chin.

"What are you saying?" The words whispered between them.

She smiled when the puff of air blew across her lips. "Let me show you."

Before he could back away or come up with a new sentence to show her how little she meant to him, she closed in. Her hands went to his tie. With a tug, she pulled him into the family room. He turned to head for the guest room. She was having none of that.

"The floor." She kissed him then. A long and lingering touch of her lips against his. "You on your back." She licked her tongue around the outside of his ear. "Me straddling you."

"Fuck, yes." He said the words on a harsh breath.

Not giving him time to change his mind, she slid her fingers into his hair and held him close. He swept her up in a kiss that robbed her balance. Heat wrapped around them and his muscles tensed. No longer trying to duck out of her hold, he had his arms around her waist now.

"You remember my favorite position, don't you?" She nuzzled the sensitive space just under his ear and felt him shudder. "How you suck my nipples as I ride you?"

He ripped his jacket off his shoulders and let it drop to the floor. She stripped off his tie. Four hands and deep breathing. In the rush to get to his bare chest, she tore at his shirt. The expensive material ripped but he didn't even flinch.

"Now you. Take the shirt off." He ripped his hand down the front of the dress shirt she wore. The buttons pinged as they flew off and bounced against the floor.

The room tipped and her feet left the floor. When the blur of movement focused again she was on top of him on the area rug. "Impressive."

He swept a hand down her stomach then lower. A finger rubbed against her. "I want your pussy, your nipples. All of you."

She sat up and threw the shirt off. When she lay down again his finger inched into the crease of her ass. It traveled lower with the tip rimming her. "Right there, Jarrett."

His gaze searched her face. "You make me . . ."

He kissed her until the last of her breath left her body. She clung to him as she rubbed her lower half over his cock.

She smiled when he groaned. "Hot?"

"Weak."

The compliment sent a shot of light through her. "When I'm done with you, you won't be able to walk."

FIFTEEN

Jarrett had no idea how he got downstairs an hour later. He'd tried to ignore the text messages he'd been getting since yesterday. When he got up to number four, he threw up the white flag.

Leaving Becca proved harder. He'd never be able to sit in that family room again without seeing her looming over him as she pressed her breasts to his mouth.

Damn.

He got off the elevator and headed for the bar. With a quick wave of thanks to the chef who stood guard, Jarrett cleared the room. All except the woman at the bar.

He took in the black skirt and slim-fitting sweater and knew he was going to regret this. "Kyra?"

She spun the stool around and flashed him a welcoming smile. Her shoulder-length blond hair fell around her face but her long legs stayed crossed. "If it isn't D.C. powerhouse superstar Jarrett Holt."

"Have you been reading my email again?" He leaned in for a hug and short kiss on the cheek.

"As if you share your emails with anyone."

"Very true." He slid onto the stool next to her and leaned against the bar. "What are you drinking?"

"Club soda." She shook the glass and the ice cubes clinked. "Your award-winning chef was nice enough to scramble around behind the bar and find this for me."

"Probably had something to do with how cute you are. He has a weakness for twentysomethings." Jarrett hitched his chin in the general direction of the glass. "Still, nicely done."

"Thought you'd approve."

After diving into one whiskey bottle after another when he got out of jail, he refrained from alcohol. Losing control qualified as one of his greatest fears. Between the member issues and running his club, he didn't have time to waste recovering from a hard night.

"Now that we've exchanged greetings, what's with all the secret phone calls and requests for a private meeting?" He held up his phone and shook it.

"Can't a girl say stop by and say hi?"

He saw the trap right there in front of him ready to spring. "Sure."

"That's convincing."

Laughter filled her voice and he wondered how the boys at college resisted her. For their sake, he hoped they did. He'd hate to have to kill some kid for looking at her funny. "Since you never do, I'm wondering what you're doing here."

"I wanted to see you."

That sounded bad. "Really?"

"You underestimate your charm."

But he recognized hers and stayed on his game. She was about to try to wrangle something out of him. And she was one of the few people with that gift. The other was upstairs in the shower. "Not even a little."

Kyra shrugged. "Well, I tried."

Jarrett glanced at the hidden camera over the bar and started the countdown to Wade storming in. "You're going to get us both killed."

"That's awfully dramatic."

"There are security cameras in here, you know. Wade is probably on his way downstairs to beat the crap out of me right now." When it came to being a big brother, Wade took the role seriously. Since Jarrett thought of Kyra as a sister, he did, too.

"I'm not afraid of Wade. "

"Then you're one of the few."

"He's an overprotective big brother but pretty cuddly underneath."

Jarrett wondered how hard he'd get punched if he called Wade cuddly to his face. Hard to image the former enforcer tolerating that nickname. "Let me assure you that you are one of the only people on earth who thinks so."

She frowned at him. "Tell me why would he care if we were talking."

"Haven't you heard? I'm trouble." Not that Jarrett played with women this young or so close to home.

"Oh, Jarrett." She put her hand on his knee. "Any woman with half a brain would recognize that."

There was nothing sexual about the touch. She was one who hugged and reached out. It meant nothing, but that didn't promise it would translate that way for the camera. "Always knew you were a smart one."

"Got the whole 'hide the women and lock the doors' speech about you from Wade long ago." She waved her hands as she talked in an exaggerated drawl.

"I'm thinking I should be insulted."

"Nah, it was typical big brother stuff."

"Just so you know, Wade has threatened to beat me to death if I even look at you for more than two seconds."

"He's an idiot, but I love the big lug." She shook her head. "And I can't believe he threatened his boss."

"He likes to think he's tough."

She winked. "Your virtue is safe with me."

"Good to know." Now that they'd circled and stalled, he went in for the hunt. The club didn't open for hours, but he had mounds of paperwork and a call from Bast that needed a return. "So, if you're not here to drag me to bed, why are you here?"

She wrinkled her nose, something she'd been doing since her gawky teen-girl days. He'd known her for more than a decade and watched her grow and change. There was nothing awkward about her now. The braces were long gone, as was the stick figure.

Her ability to gain his full attention wasn't. "Kyra? Spill it."

"A job."

Not the request he expected. "Excuse me?"

"I want to work here."

He glanced at the kitchen door, then to the dark back hallway. There was no place for her in his world, which made his response quick and easy. "No way."

"I am finishing up my master's degree. I need some cash."

International business. He knew this part because he'd helped her decide between graduate programs. "I'll give you money."

She shoved against his arm. "Now who's being insulting?" She rolled her eyes, looking every bit the troublemaker she'd always been. "What I want is a chance to make some money."

"Pick one of the million other businesses in the D.C. metro area. Tell me what you want and I'll make some calls."

"I don't want you pushing people around to get me in somewhere. I want to be here."

"Wade will never let that happen."

"He insists the business is legitimate."

A kick of satisfaction hit Jarrett at that. Seeing where Wade was now, strong and sure of who he was, compared to before never got old. He was self-made with his criminal past well behind him. "It is."

"Then why can't I put on an apron and help out? Metaphorically, of course. I doubt the women here wear aprons." She wrinkled up her nose. "Not sexy."

His mind flashed to the overzealous, too-much-drinking dinner groups that set up in his club at least once per week. Gambling was a regular part of the club activities, and Jarrett could see some of the conscience-light losers make getting her naked a sick game.

No fucking way. "I'm thinking the objection has something to do with all the men who hang out here and how Wade wants you fitted for a chastity belt."

"For God's sake. I'm not a virgin."

The reveal skidded across Jarrett's brain. "That is not information I need to know."

"Give me a chance."

He stood up and held out a hand to her. "What you can do is come into the office and we'll figure out where else you can work, preferably in an office that won't lead to my death at the hands of my club manager."

Her shoulders fell. "You ruin all my fun."

Becca sat in his condo office and stared at the empty space at the bar downstairs through the security feed. Ten seconds ago Jarrett stood there with a hot blonde. Now Becca saw nothing but abandoned barstools. She clicked on random computer keys trying to track them but nothing happened.

Then she tried the up arrow.

Then the tab . . . ah, there he was.

With a swipe of his card, he guided the woman holding his arm into his office and shut the door behind them. After nine slaps of the tab key, Becca realized the camera coverage didn't extend to his private office.

How freaking convenient.

She stood up, forgetting the files and notepads and even the computer, and moved to the doorway. She was debating the trouble she'd cause if she smashed the monitor against the floor. Or she could rip off the front door and pound down the walls until she got downstairs.

Yeah, nothing irrational about any of that.

Jealousy. She wasn't a fan.

Sure, the fact he "tried" out the female staff shouldn't be a surprise. She shouldn't care. She'd had sex on the job. Hell, he started out as her sex on the job. But there had been no one since him. The idea of letting another man touch her, kiss her, enter her . . . no way. Not yet.

She rubbed her forehead as she paced her way into the family room. Nothing about her surroundings registered. She couldn't get around the fact she'd been all over the man less than an hour ago.

Glancing down, she stared at the spot on the floor where they rolled over and she straddled him, taking him deep and riding him until they both sprawled out exhausted. He'd showered and gone downstairs, claiming he was already late. Unable to hold off another second, she'd headed for his office for a quick look around the computer. Now she was sorry she hurried or ever even ventured into that room.

"What are you doing?" Jarrett's voice cut through her mental wanderings.

She'd been so lost in her pacing and internal whining that she missed the lock and the door and any other noise that could have signaled his arrival. She froze in the middle of the floor and stared at him, wondering how long she'd been lost in her internal raging. Then she looked at him, really looked, for any sign that some part of his suit had spent a few minutes on the floor or around his knees.

Nothing obvious.

She squinted as she scanned him for evidence. "You were just in your office."

"I see you checked out the security system already." He threw his keys on the couch cushion. "Didn't take long."

"Was there supposed to be a waiting period?"

"Fair enough." He loosened his tie and dropped onto the couch cushion in front of her. He reached for the water bottle he stole from her earlier and abandoned.

The damn man even whistled.

"How did the meeting go?" she asked, knowing the answer.

"Fine."

"She was pretty." Becca meant to hold that piece in and prove she didn't care. The misfire wrecked that plan pretty damn fast and had her swearing under her breath.

He took a swallow of water then slowly lowered the bottle again. His throat moved but he didn't say anything.

"What, no comment from Mr. Super Businessman?"

One of his eyebrows lifted. "What do you want me to say?"

"For a guy who . . ."

"What?"

"Never mind." She waved him off. No way could she go there. The peace between them was shaky, at best. Bringing up his past—the forbidden subject—would guarantee more snapping and fury. The constant smash of anger exhausted her.

"Finish the sentence," he demanded.

She pretended not to care. Even flicked her wrist and waved him off. "It's your life. You can do whatever you want."

"I am aware of that."

His nonchalance finally broke her. The words came spilling out before she could call them back. "You throw around the word 'whore' and—"

"When?"

"Talking about your mother."

The relaxed stance disappeared. Now he sat up straight, fully engaged. "What does she have to do with this conversation?"

"Nothing." Becca expected an abrupt end, possibly followed by him leaving the building. Wouldn't be the first time. She got a confused stare instead.

"I have no idea what we're talking about."

"The blonde." When his mouth fell open, Becca picked at the wound one more time. No matter how she tried to block the image, it kept floating through her head. "What, did you forget her name already? Typical male. The bra is back on and her name is gone from your head."

The jackass had the nerve to smile. "Do you honestly think I had sex with you, then went downstairs and had sex with another woman ten minutes later?"

The arguments flooding Becca's brain just a second ago vanished. "What?"

"You fucking drained me dry, woman."

A sudden heat moved over her cheeks. Not one to embarrass easily, the sensation freaked her out. "But I saw—"

"Damn, Becca. I'm not sixteen." He leaned forward with his elbows balanced on his knee . . . and a stupid grin plastered on his face. "A guy needs some recovery time."

Now there was new information. "You haven't that I've ever noticed."

"Admittedly, I tend to bounce back quickly with you, but I can assure you I did not run downstairs and have sex with someone else."

A smile tugged at the corner of her mouth and she swallowed it. Yeah, that news made her far too happy.

She waved him off, hoping he didn't see the slight shake in her hand. "It's not my business."

"It is to the extent a woman has the right to know who's been climbing all over her."

Her hand fell to her side as her mind went blank. "When you put it that way . . ."

"There were days, long ago, when I did have sex with the staff. It was part of the strip club benefits. The women wanted perks and, well, I didn't exactly say no to much back then." He stood up and joined her on the same side of the couch. "It's part of the reason I wanted out of that business. I ended up playing part-time bouncer and full-time rescuer to some of the women. Not my thing."

She once craved the information, needed it for the job. Now she wanted to plug her ears and wipe it from her brain. "Okay."

"Point is, I don't have sex with the staff now. I have a pretty firm rule against it, actually."

And like that, he blew apart every rumor winging around town. People said he had a knack with the ladies, which she could attest to. Many people saw the private club as a front for sex. He probably would have been investigated for that if the membership rolls didn't included judges, prosecutors and quite a few elected officials.

The party line insisted this was an old-fashioned supper club. Food, business talk and that was about it. For a long time Becca questioned what happened in the back rooms, but something in Jarrett's stunned tone and calm body language told her he was telling the truth on this.

But Becca still had one question. "The woman?"

"Wade's sister."

"He has a sister?" Becca barely thought of him as human.

"Half, but he doesn't make the distinction." Jarrett balanced an arm along the back of the couch. "Did you miss the fact she's something like twenty-two or twenty-three? A tad young for me, don't you think."

Oh, please. "Right, because no old dude in D.C. has a hot, much younger second or third wife."

"You're calling me old?"

"Older." At almost thirty-five he was mature and hot and the perfect age for anything.

"I can accept that description." He cleared his throat. "I guess."

"In my defense, I thought all guys liked the young-and-firm sort of thing."

"That part is worth something, yes. But my feelings in this case, for her, are purely brotherly."

The idea of him thinking in family terms had Becca reeling. "Is she okay?"

"Her name is Kyra and she wants a job." He sounded confused by the idea. "Apparently she doesn't care if I give her one and Wade then kills me."

After fueling her anger with each passing minute while he was gone, Becca found her first laugh. "I'm guessing he's overprotective."

"Understatement." Jarrett sighed. "He'd go batshit crazy if I hired her and put her in the path of some of the idiots who have a membership here."

Becca tried to imagine what the men downstairs would do to a nice young woman. They'd make promises and show off their wealth and power. A potentially pretty ugly scene actually. "But he could watch over her here."

"Kyra tried that argument. The answer is still no."

"That explains why the meeting with her was so quick. I didn't think you'd . . . well, you get the idea."

"I'll take that as a compliment on my advanced foreplay skills."

One more second on that topic and Becca would have him on the floor again. "Okay, I need to take that shower."

She had to leave before the two remaining buttons on her shirt gave up the battle. He'd been inside her at least twice per day since she arrived. He'd leave her bed right after sex each night—and she hated reaching out and feeling the cool sheets—but she couldn't argue about performance.

"For the record." His voice stopped her. "I don't have a problem with prostitution."

She took her time turning around to face him. She kept the edges of her shirt wadded in a ball in her fist. "I'm thinking most men feel that way."

"I'm saying I don't care if a woman wants to charge to have sex. That's her business. Her body, her decision." He stood up and moved to stand in front of her. "I'd want her to be safe, of course, but if she does it to survive or for fun—that's not my place to judge."

The comment, offered without any judgment, didn't fit with what she knew or anything he'd said before. "But your mother—"

The amusement left his face. "She had sex for money, for food and one time for a television."

"Which is why you call her a whore." The logic had Becca confused. For some women it was fine, for others not?

Jarrett wasn't perfect, but he usually thrived on consistency. It was the one thing she depended on, which was why finding the evidence that supported the dealing had slammed into her so hard.

"I call her that because she sold her body, not to feed her kids, but to raise money for drugs." He cleared his throat when his voice began to fade. "That's what I object to."

No . . . but that didn't make sense. How could she not know this? "Your mother took drugs?"

His gaze bore into her. "Meth addict."

"I don't get it." How could such a huge piece of intel slip by her. It was as if someone purposely deleted it.

He studied her through narrowed eyes. "Clearly this is new information for you."

"Of course it is." It explained so much about the type of guy he was, controlled and serious. About the dangerous life he led before the club. More than likely, he'd never known much in the way of security or stability.

"If you say so."

The energy rushed out of Becca, deflating her heart and everything else inside her like a balloon. "Is that what she died from?"

"She died when she got high and ran a car into oncoming traffic."

Becca reached out and put a hand on his arm, anything to reassure him that she was there. "Jarrett, I'm so sorry. I had no idea."

"Not even hinted at in my file, huh?"

"No." And she wanted to know why.

He covered her hand with his. "Don't weep for my mother. Weep for my baby brother who had the great misfortune to be in the backseat and die with her."

The fact walloped Becca. She leaned into him. "I had no idea. You never told me."

"I never talk about it."

"How old were you?"

His fingers tightened around hers. "Eight."

She doubted he knew about the signals his body sent out. The pain on his face, the tension in his arms. Her heart ached for the little boy who lost so much. The hollow rumbling sat there, digging deeper and sucking away the small bit of life she had left. "It's all so horrible."

"And, Becca." His arm dropped and he stepped back. "That is why I can promise you I have never touched drugs."

SIXTEEN

This was an epically bad idea. Jarrett knew it. Common sense sent up a warning flare. A headache pounded beneath his temples. Hell, Bast even put on his lawyer hat and counseled against it.

Natalie had issued a three-day warning and time was ticking down. Not that Jarrett planned to do anything other than let her deadline pass. Well, not quite. Her little test pissed him off, mostly because it had him weighing his options. He could initiate the emergency parachute Bast created and hand over the information he'd held back the first time he made a deal with the CIA. He viewed the material as his protection, but it could protect Becca instead. Unless Bast killed him for even suggesting the move.

But Jarrett ignored all of that and focused on the one issue that still shocked him. Yesterday he broke his cardinal rule and told Becca the truth about his mother. Not small pieces about how she'd have sex with men right across the room from where he sat reading the book he stole from the school library. Not about how she'd eat the last hot dog and throw a few chips on the table for him and Jacob. Nope, he'd jumped right to the biggie. Mother as killer.

The only thing that saved his pride was the way she handled it. She nodded, thanked him for telling her and skipped right to a conversation about what he should grab from the kitchen and his chef for her dinner. No wallowing in pity here.

Her reaction was a relief but shouldn't have been a surprise. Like far too many people, she possessed an intimate knowledge of family dysfunction. Still, if he'd seen one peek of sadness or pity in those eyes, he'd still be in his office downstairs. The exact opposite happened. By the time he came upstairs last night after breaking up a fight between two members and a long night on the club floor, he was so hot for her that he almost ran from the front door to her bed.

He settled for waking her up with a sprinkling of kisses down her spine and over her ass. Dragging her to her hands and knees. Then he took her the way he wanted to her first night back.

Round one started at four in the morning and he'd have that movie playing in his head for days. But now he had something a bit less fun to handle. Something that required clothes and a huge dose of idiocy on his part.

He walked into the guest bedroom and glanced around. Empty. Huh, hard to make a big gesture when no one was around to see it. "Becca?"

The bathroom door opened and steam poured out. The scent of vanilla filtered into the room as she stepped out in the middle of wrapping a giant white towel around her athletic frame. Didn't bother to hurry either. Nope. She shot him a sexy smile as she brought the towel edges to a close by slow inches, leaving him a nice long time to gawk.

And he did.

"You sure you need the towel?"

She had the damn thing knotted between her breasts already but her fingers still hovered there. "I can be talked out of it."

All he needed was one word from her, one stray look, and he had to fight the urge to claw his clothes off. "What would that take exactly?"

"Well." She drawled the word out as her head fell to the side and her hair streamed over her bare shoulder. "It's been a long time since you pinned me down."

His temperature spiked and his cock twitched, which he guessed was her goal. "On the bed . . . yeah, I remember."

The memories rushed back at him. She liked being tied up. Not hit or hurt, which was good because that wasn't his thing at all, but restrained while he sucked and licked and rubbed her to breathless orgasm. And when she came it overtook her hard and fast.

Holy fuck, she could set him off.

"When you stretch my arms above my head and trap them there." She fiddled with the towel's knot as she trailed one foot up the inside of her other calf.

Damn her timing. "Remember that—every last second of it—because it's happening pretty fucking soon."

She smiled. "But not now?"

"You have an appointment."

Her mouth flattened. "What?"

In two seconds he'd be on top of her, using his tie to bind her to the headboard. Then they wouldn't be going anywhere for hours. Tempting, but not going to happen.

He held out the stack in his hands. "You'll need these."

"And that is?"

"Your clothes." Cargo pants and a blank tank. He'd included underwear, not because he wanted her wearing it but because she should be comfortable during the half hour he'd let her stay dressed. Then he'd clear his afternoon schedule and devote every ounce of his strength to stretching her out on that mattress.

She didn't move. Didn't reach out. "I don't understand what's happening."

"You have a meeting with Bast."

Her face blanched as white as the towel. "Are you kidding?"

The reaction took him off guard. Shook his confidence, which was not easy to do.

He wasn't sure what spun around in that head, but something did. "Do you know me to have a sense of humor?"

"Yes, actually. Warped, but it's there."

He laughed because it was either that or choke on the thick flow of tension pouring through the room. "Thanks."

She wiped a hand over the damp ends of her long hair. "Jarrett, don't play about this. It's too important."

The pleading in her eyes sobered him. "I asked Bast to come over. He's waiting for you in the second-floor conference room."

"He knows I'm here? You promised—"

"Stop." Energy pounded off of her. Jarrett could tell she was winding up, and he wanted to tamp right down on that.

"You could get me killed." She still hadn't left the doorway.

"I trust Bast."

"Why should I?"

"Because he got my ass out of jail and has kept it that way." Jarrett didn't understand why they were still discussing this. "Look, you wanted to meet him. I'm making it happen. I don't see the problem here."

"On my terms." She shook her head. "I thought we'd discuss how and what we told him. Maybe meet elsewhere so he didn't know I was staying here."

The woman had to control everything. He assumed that stemmed from her training, but right now it was pissing him off. "He's known since day one. Just like Wade."

She sighed. "That's just fantastic."

"My point is, if he wanted to turn you in or kill you or whatever you're worried about, it would have happened." Jarrett dumped the stack of clothing on the edge of the bed. "So, this is your one shot. My terms. My ground rules. My building. Yes or no?"

She swiped a flimsy white bra off the top of the pile. "You know the answer is yes."

"Then stop fighting me and get dressed."

"We're in lockdown. He actually banned me from leaving this condo. What the fuck is that about?" Elijah repeated Jarrett's order as he paced back and forth. Another few minutes and there would be a groove behind the desk chair in Wade's office area.

Even though he tried, Wade couldn't ignore his temporary bedmate. Probably had something to do with the clomp of his sneakered feet against the floor. Or the constant mumbling under his breath.

The steady stream of bitching was getting pretty damn old. In the past if someone acted like this around him, Wade would have taken him out. A punch, maybe use a knife, or when things got bad and a situation hit kill-or-be-killed status, Wade didn't hesitate to make sure he was the last guy standing.

Life had calmed down and now most of his frustration came

from dealing with idiot club members. Having stupid shit seep into his home pissed him off.

But this was Eli and for some reason this man crept under Wade's defenses. To keep from blowing up or leading them square into a fight he didn't want, Wade blocked out the man behind him, broad shoulders, hot face and all.

"Are you ignoring me?" Elijah asked the question from right behind and above Wade. Put his hands on the back of the desk chair and leaned it back. "'Cause I hate that shit."

Never mind that made two of them. Wade concentrated on not landing on the floor. He flattened his feet against the hardwood and started a mental countdown to keep his fury from rising to Eli's level. "Jarrett doesn't want Becca to see you."

"The best way to do that is to kick her the hell out."

Wade gave up trying to review the staffing schedules on his computer. He couldn't concentrate or see anything but black line blurs anyway.

"We've been through this." He shoved the chair back, forcing Elijah to take a step. When Wade spun the chair around, their knees knocked together thanks to the sudden closeness. "It's not going to happen."

"Then there's the part where she gets access to Sebastian Jameson." Elijah rubbed a hand over his face as he resumed the annoying pacing. "Must be nice."

Wade understood the frustration. Being held hostage in the condo ticked him off, too. But he knew he was only confined to make sure Elijah stayed that way. The fact lessened the force of the blow, but only a little.

Reality was, fighting with Jarrett on this issue—on any issue relating to Becca—led nowhere. The man had more than a soft spot. He had a hole a mile wide and Becca kept slipping in there, making herself at home, and otherwise screwing up everything.

But she wasn't totally the cause of the current mess. "You made it clear no one could know you were here."

"You think she didn't lay down the same rules while she was sucking his cock?"

The angrier Eli got, the more he targeted Becca with his viciousness. Wade didn't blame him, but Eli being all fired up and yelling made for a long afternoon and evening.

"I get that you're pissed."

Elijah stopped walking and spun around. The anger in his voice hadn't made it to his face. The frown looked more like confusion and fury. "That's it? That's all you have to say."

"It's not exactly easy to talk with you. In case you haven't noticed, I'm not the tiptoe type." Wade shook his head. If the guys in the old neighborhood could see him now.

"It's hard to imagine you doing that, not that I want you to."

Wade looked at the man who had come to mean too much and tried to believe where life had taken him. More than once he'd wondered how a gay man would have fared with the group of bruisers he used to run with. If they'd found out, he'd probably be dead right now. If not at the hands of their misplaced disgust, then by a bullet marked for his brain. Prison and coroner—those were the two long-term life options where he grew up.

"You know what it's like to live with you?" he asked.

"I'm not sure I want to hear this."

"Tough shit because I'm saying it." The burning frustration that ate away at his gut sparked until all Wade could see was flames. "Most of the time you're either up here buried in your notes and files or you're pissing about Jarrett's love life. It's pretty fucking exhausting."

"That's not all I do." Elijah wasn't frowning now.

Oh, yeah. That smile meant trouble. The good kind, but also the end to any intelligent conversation. Wade tried to figure out if he cared about that right now. "You know what I mean."

"Am I not showing you enough attention?" Elijah crouched down until they met at eye level. "Because I can fix that."

"Fuck you."

"Happily."

"I'm not talking about sex." But, man, that was the one time they communicated just fine. The heat, the touch of Eli's hands over his skin . . .

"I kind of wish you would." Elijah slid to his knees as his palms traveled up Wade's thighs then down to his knees and back up again. "It would be nice if we were on the same wavelength here."

Hell, yeah, they were. "I was trying to make a point."

"Spell it out for me." Elijah dipped his head and kissed his way up the inside of Wade's jeans.

"You can be a total shit." But not now. He was doing fine right where he was.

"I know."

The heated friction of hands and mouth had Wade squirming in his chair. He had to blink a few times to restart his brain and keep up with the conversation. He'd been trying to make a point about something. "Most of the time you're a pain in the ass."

"That's not news. I warned you about that before I crawled into bed with you that first time." Elijah's hands slid under Wade's ass and pulled his hips forward. "Remember that?"

The entire night was imprinted on his brain. Wade could see the shadow at the door and replay the mental debate if he should gave in and take what he wanted, which he had two seconds later. "Of course."

"You sure? I'd be happy to give you a reminder." Elijah's fingers went to Wade's belt. He tugged, then slid it open, letting the ends fall as he turned to the zipper. "How I slid the sheet off you and crawled between your thighs."

As his muscles turned to jelly, Wade grabbed the armrests to keep from sliding to the floor. "I remember setting a record for waking up."

"You didn't think I'd make the first move." He tugged the zipper down and opened the fly.

"I knew you'd slept with women and men and figured I was convenient."

Elijah laughed. "You are *not* that."

Unable to hold back, Wade speared his fingers through Eli's hair. The strands tickled his palm. "Meaning?"

Elijah's hands slipped into Wade's jeans and worked them down, taking the boxer briefs with them. "I didn't expect you."

His bare ass hit the cool leather. Whatever comment he might have made next died on his lips when Elijah lowered his head.

Elijah didn't stop. His mouth covered Wade's cock, drawing it in as his hand slid to the base. He licked across the tip then sucked on his balls. By the time he took Wade deep to the back of his throat, Wade's hips were lifting off the chair.

"What did you . . ." Wade swore as his head fell back.

"I love sucking you off. Watching your face." Elijah lifted his head and smiled at Wade. "Should I do it now? Make you come and then lick it off of you?"

"God, yes."

"I'm not going to stop." Elijah tightened his hand and slipped it up and down. His mouth followed his fingers and the constant touching and caressing didn't let up.

Wade could only force out a breathy exhale. "Don't."

The churning inside him built and thrashed. He tipped Eli's head to the side to watch his checks puff in and out as he sucked his cock in deep. A hand slid around and under Wade, finding his ass and slipping the tip of his finger inside. He lifted, giving Eli room and silently letting him know he could do whatever he wanted.

The jeans on his lower thighs trapped Wade in the chair and Eli's body held him there. Between the flick of his tongue and pump of his hand, Wade's mind went blank. He wanted to tell Eli to stand up so he could get a turn, but the words wouldn't form.

"Let go, Wade." Eli mumbled the words as his hand moved faster. "Come for me."

Wade gripped the chair even tighter and obeyed.

Becca stared at the closed conference room door. She'd been in the room a few times and remembered the oval table and the heavy curtains hiding the tall windows underneath. One monitor had turned into three. She assumed that addition could be traced back to her. Jarrett used heavy-duty security before. Now he locked the place down like a jail, which struck her as an odd choice for a man who lived in one for a short time and never missed an opportunity to throw that in her face.

She glanced across the table at Sebastian Jameson. Undeniably attractive in a way that came off as more polished and gentle than Jarrett's harder façade. Bast was an interesting mix of sharp good looks and undeniable power. He also had an ex-wife who liked to screw and tell. She opened up the bedroom door to their marriage, and thanks to the tales she told, more than one metro-area social-ite crossed Bast off the list of eligible bachelors for her daughters.

Despite the privacy breach, the man was a bit of a D.C. legend. If you had a problem, you called him. He made things happen and troubles disappear. And as far as Becca knew, he was Jarrett's only true friend other than Wade.

Right now, Bast was also the only other person in the room. "How long do you think he'll leave us alone?" she asked.

"Knowing Jarrett, as short a time as possible." Bast pulled files out of the box he brought with him and separated them into piles. "He didn't look too happy to get that business call and have to step out."

She scanned the stacks, trying to figure out what sort of filing system Bast was using. "He mentioned something about two mem-bers being locked in a business battle to the death over a private party that's supposed to be held in one of the private rooms next week."

"Idiots." Bast put a hand on top of the pile closest to him. "So, the privileged stuff and confidential agreement are off-limits, but here are the background files—"

"Agreement?"

"I thought you knew."

She had no idea what she was supposed to have known. "Obvi-ously not."

Bast leaned back in the oversized black leather chair. "We needed leverage to keep Jarrett from losing everything."

Something she always suspected. You didn't walk away from a

CIA-engineered prison sentence without putting up something the CIA wanted as collateral. "And what was the leverage?"

"Maybe you're unclear on what the word 'confidential' means."

From any other guy the comment would have come off on the wrong side of the jackass meter, but Bast could deliver a takedown in a voice so smooth the victim would be smiling. When she realized she was, she stopped. "Whatever they wanted is likely at the center of why he was targeted in the first place."

"What were you told?" Bast turned his pen end-over-end as he talked. "I'm assuming not much."

"Only that he had contacts with foreign nationals who are or were club members and he had collected certain information that could be vital to the security of the United States." She repeated the operation objective almost verbatim. "The job involved sur-veillance, routine searches, total infiltration of Jarrett's operation."

"You know you just used a lot of words and said nothing."

Clearly Bast wasn't impressed with her memory, but he had to understand her limitations as well. It wouldn't do her much good to avoid being shot only to pick up an espionage charge. "You're not the only one with confidentiality restrictions."

"I notice you didn't mention the drugs."

Funny how a talk about Jarrett always came back to that topic. Thinking about the charges even a few days ago had the power to drop her to the ground. She closed her eyes and called up the image of the evidence against him, and something deep inside her cracked open.

But the pieces no longer fit together as cleanly as they once did. She just accepted before. With her heart shredded and her belief in her instincts destroyed, she bought into the tale she was told. Now, with the story about his mother and watching him day after day, where his worst sin was coffee overindulgence, she doubted everything she'd ever been told.

Rather than let her emotions unwind in front of Bast, she stuck with the facts. "As you know, domestic drug running is generally outside of the CIA's purview. The briefing on this operation referenced the drugs as a way Jarrett kept a hold over some of the members."

Careful and deliberate, Bast set the pen down on the table. The click sounded louder than it should have, as if he'd exercised his control to keep from slamming it down and didn't quite succeed. "He's never used drugs in his life."

Once the words were out there, she grabbed onto them. She turned them over in her mind and they made sense. Sounded right and true. "That's a pretty strong statement."

"I've know the man for a decade."

But still, she had to be sure. The drugs charge was the one block that, if removed, could bring everything else tumbling down. "People hide things. Functional alcoholics. Recreational drugs."

"No way." He tapped his fingers against the hard tabletop.

"I saw them here. In the club and his condo."

"Planted."

His unwavering confidence was hard to ignore. "That's what Jarrett says."

Bast's frown eased and now he sized her up, searching her face with his gaze. "Interesting."

The whole assessing thing made her jumpy. "What?"

"I think you're questioning the truth of the charges now, too."

She thought about denying it but couldn't think of a reason to. She spent her life analyzing high-intensity situations and reacting. She worked on gut and instinct. She relied on both now. "It never fit. As Jarrett has pointed out, the timing was convenient since the op wasn't uncovering anything and could have been shut down."

"Instead, drugs magically appeared."

"I'm assuming that was part of your argument to free Jarrett."

"Yes, but not the winning one."

This. She'd been waiting for this. "Are you gonna fill me in?"

"Your bosses wanted the information Jarrett had collected on some troublesome members and figured out the easiest way to get it was to destroy Jarrett and make him hand it over as he begged for mercy."

She couldn't imagine him doing any of that, but if she could match the member to a case, she'd know who at the top needed the information—Natalie, Todd or someone else. "And the specific information?"

Bast shook his head. "Ask Jarrett."

Right, because it was that easy.

She sat up and curled a leg under her butt. "He's not exactly an open book."

Bast closed one eye and shook his head from side to side as if he were thinking the comment over. "Also interesting."

"You're making me hate that word."

"Professional hazard."

She skipped through the dramatics right to the issue on her mind. "You don't like me very much."

Bast almost talked over her. "I worry about the hold you have over him."

"He can kick me out at any time." She held out her arms and scanned the room. She hadn't seen anything that could hurt him. Weird how that was the case since he had the absolute power to wreck her.

"I think we both know that's not going to happen."

She shifted her chair from side to side as she sized up her opponent. He was supposed to be the best and she didn't like to lose. It was a potentially lethal combination. She thought about backing down and holding her plans in, but Bast might be the one person who could help.

For days, ever since she walked into Jarrett's bedroom and saw parts of her old life still hanging there, her priorities had changed. She'd brought him to his knees, and maybe the charges were true and he deserved the devastation, but somewhere deep inside she sensed that wasn't the case. He might not be innocent of everything, but the drug charges—the very reason she turned on him—appeared to be nothing more than the CIA working an angle to get what it wanted. The idea she played a role in that made her stomach heave. Made her question every professional move she'd made.

But maybe she could make amends in some small way. "If I told you I don't want anything bad to happen to him—"

"You better not."

For some reason the quick defense satisfied her. Never mind it came wrapped in a threat. "While I'm busy trying to stay alive, I plan on clearing his name."

Bast's eyebrow lifted. "I could point out that's my job."

"In part."

"Jarrett already made concessions, did things he didn't want to do, to buy his freedom."

"There's a difference between being free and being absolved." Right now she was neither and craved both. "And we both know the CIA will come back around if it thinks it can squeeze more information out of Jarrett."

"We have protections in place."

"So did I, and then someone tried to burn down my home with me in it."

"I heard." The chair creaked as Bast rocked back. "Does Jarrett know your intention?"

He'd probably tell her he didn't need her or say some other dismissive thing that ripped her in two. She decided not to give him a choice. "No."

"Any particular reason you're not sharing?"

None that she planned to say. "We have trust issues."

"I figured that much. Can't say I'm sorry to hear he's on guard this time around."

Anxiety spun through her at the thought of someone knowing her private business. She dug around to see how much. "The two of you are close."

"I'd guess I'm the person who is closest to him." Bast reached into the box and pulled out one last file. The box thudded against the floor a second later. "But that could change."

"What does that mean?"

"Someone could take my place." Bast shrugged. "Maybe you."

The anxiety ran out of her as quickly as it had stormed in. For the first time, she gave words to the need crashing through her and admitted it to herself. "Maybe."

SEVENTEEN

The next afternoon Jarrett took a break from reviewing club membership applications and stepped on the elevator. He needed to head upstairs for a few minutes to warn Becca about some household maintenance issues. Listening to the thud as the doors closed, he realized if he got her a cell he could avoid the number of trips upstairs during the day. Today he held himself to two, but it was early yet, only one in the afternoon.

But this trip had a real purpose. He repeated that as he pushed the number three button and rode in silence. He wanted to let Becca know he'd taken the cleaning crew off standby. The condo was about to run out of towels and he'd changed the sheets twice, which was two times more than he ever did. She'd handled the general pickup, but he was a guy used to pristine surroundings and the crew was on the payroll, so they'd juggle their lives for a few hours tomorrow to let the crew in.

She could work in the second-floor conference room. That meant keeping Elijah in his cage. Or it would if Jarrett had been smart enough to build the other man one. As it was, Elijah had to stay out of the hall and out of sight. Jarrett didn't relish that conversation. Between that and Natalie's deadline, Jarrett's life was filled with many unpleasant tasks lately.

When the elevator dinged, Jarrett stepped off and unlocked his door. He made it two steps inside before feeling left his legs. The door banged closed behind him, but he barely heard it over the rush of blood through his veins.

Becca leaned against the doorway to his bedroom and the den. She wore one of his white shirts with the sleeves rolled up and the buttons open. The position showed off a long sliver of sexy bare skin.

"Why are you standing there?" He hoped the answer had something to do with wrapping her legs around him, but he'd wait and see.

"I saw you on the security monitors and knew you were coming upstairs. I thought I'd wait for you."

"You do provide an interesting welcome."

Fuck the phone. He would rather get a look at this a few times a day than read one of her texts.

"You're not going to complain about me wearing your shirt again?"

"Not when you look like that in it and it's almost off." After all, he wasn't a complete dumbass. He'd learned a thing or two over the last nine days.

She smoothed her hand down the edge and over the buttons. "Well, I'm not sure why I'm still wearing it."

"Excuse me?"

"Yesterday you made me a special promise but never followed through."

He was too busy looking at her to follow the conversation. "About?"

She slid a hand up the doorframe, making her shirt drape open even more. "Tying me up."

Three little words and a heaviness settled in his lower half. In the space from one breath to another, his cock revved up for action. This woman took all his good intentions about separating his mind from his body, about concentrating on work, and flushed them away.

"We did have sex on the couch after your meeting with Bast." Jarrett remembered every damn second of it. "And then again last night."

"True but that's not the same thing, now is it?" She pushed away from the door and stood up straight. The shirt fell off one shoulder, exposing the most tempting bit of skin.

"The cleaning crew is coming."

Her eyebrow inched up. "Now?"

He'd be damned if she could even tell time at the moment. "Soon."

"Cancel."

He didn't even question her order. He dialed the number and moved the visit to another day. Then he looked up and saw her staring. He almost swallowed his damn tongue. "Now, what were you proposing?"

"We go in there," she tipped her head toward the area behind her, "and find your ties. About time those saw some action for something other than balancing out your pretty dark suits."

"My bedroom."

She didn't show any reaction as his voice got louder. "Yes."

"Why?" But he knew. The days-long power play had long since shifted to her favor. He let her in intending to use sex as a weapon. He was the one who got shot.

"There's the obvious reason about how you have posts on your headboard. Those come in handy when using the ties. The guest room doesn't have that feature."

He couldn't believe he was going to get beaten by his choice in furniture. "And that's all this is about?"

"I can see you're turning the idea of me in your bed over in your mind and not liking the suggestion." She made a tsk-tsking sound and stepped away, keeping one hand on the doorjamb. "So paranoid."

From experience, he had reason to be. "I wonder if I'm being outmaneuvered."

"What do you think my endgame is?" She let go of the trim and stood behind the couch.

The look, from those firm breasts to the sexy smile on her lips, reeled him in. He couldn't remember why he got on the elevator in the first place. And fucking did not care.

The game she played was a dangerous one. Made him think about the positions they'd tried and the ones left on his wish list. "You tell me."

"My safety."

"That's fair."

"Maybe some revenge."

Seemed to him she deserved to exercise a bit of that. "I'm a fan of that, so long as it's not aimed at me."

"Not even a little."

Unable to stand still for another second, he walked across the room to her. "That's good."

"And some truth."

His steps stumbled, but he tried to hide it. "You lost me on that one."

She leaned against the back of the couch and her fingers absently toyed with the soft fringe of a throw pillow. "What if I said I only told you half the story about why I almost broke cover months ago?"

He stopped in front of her. He would have reached out, but that question had him holding back. Also splashed a full bucket of cold water over his dick.

If this was the part where she admitted to making the call to bring him in, he would . . . actually, he had no idea what the hell he would do. In the back of his mind he assumed Elijah's comment about her going to Todd meant she pulled the trigger on the operation at the club. That she actually planned to have him grabbed while she was in the middle of giving him a blowjob, just to add to the shittiness of the moment.

With a flash of clarity Jarrett understood one thing—he didn't want to know every detail about her role in his arrest. He could let the truth sit there, unheard and never spoken from her mouth. That might be the only way to survive what happened long enough to put this piece aside and enjoy her now.

But the bigger question was why she wanted him to know. After all this time, why the seduction followed by the verbal bomb drop?

Before he could ask, she gave him the answer. "You deserve the truth."

Forgetting the type of man he was and how he valued information, he'd rather pretend not to know this part. "Look, Becca, I've had about enough of—"

"I wanted to break cover. Me. Not the office, not my bosses. Certainly not Todd." She put her hand on Jarrett's chest with a soft touch. "I walked into Todd's office and told him to pull the plug and leave you alone."

The words bounced around his head but refused to make sense. "Why?"

"I risked my job and talked to Todd because I wanted out of the lies, out of conning you, of pretending I was something I wasn't. I needed it all to end."

None of this was what Jarrett expected. Here he thought she'd come clean and lay her guilt on his shoulders. But this was something else.

He forced his arms to remain at his sides. "What are you trying to tell me?"

"I went to Todd and told him I couldn't do it. That you were innocent."

Jarrett had never heard her use that word in reference to anyone. "Because you didn't find the drugs after looking all over my building for them."

"No."

"That's what you said."

Her other hand slipped up his chest and over his shoulder to find a place at the back of his neck. The move brought her body in close to his. The scent of her shampoo, of her body, spun around him.

She pinned him with a look of fierce determination. "I thought the man I was falling for deserved to know who was in his bed. That's why I wanted out eight months ago. I wanted to come clean and tell you everything. Warn you."

He zoomed in on one word, the only one that mattered. Calling on all his will, he kept his hands fisted at his sides. "Falling?"

"Yes, Jarrett." She rubbed her cheek against his before pulling back again. "I know you don't believe me, but I'd lost perspective and all objectivity where you were concerned. I didn't want to double-down and head back for more training. I wanted to stay with you."

"Do you remember how that day ended, Becca?" He grabbed her arms, careful not to dig his fingers in, though the hammering of blood through his body made that difficult. He stared her down. "Do you really get what happened to me after you were gone?"

"I can tell you how it tore me apart."

This was wishful thinking or revisionist history, anything but the full truth. "But you didn't step up and help. You let me rot while your friends took turns ripping my life apart."

"I was a mess. It's no excuse, but I stopped functioning."

He wanted to shake her, make her stop lying, but he forced his muscles not to move. "You walked away."

"I did."

"And for some reason, now I'm no longer the bad guy in your mind."

"You never really were. Even when I thought you did something awful, I couldn't hate you. I mourned what I'd lost, but that's a different thing."

The rage seeped out of him and the strength left his body. "You can try to convince yourself, but we both know none of that is true."

"I know you're not ready to hear the truth about what I wanted with you." She cupped his face in her palm. "But I needed to say it. You needed to know."

"It doesn't change anything."

What a fucking lie. He knew the words were empty when he uttered them. Now he had to do something about Natalie's damn deadline. Something that would save Becca and end the stalking of her. Something more than just standing his ground.

This new cast of history already started shifting the facts around in his head. The fury he'd fueled and stoked since being in jail slipped further out of reach. Her being in his condo, so close, lying in bed with her and watching as she fought every rule he put in place to preserve his sanity, made revenge harder. Now she was saying things that mattered, and his last hold on making her pay slipped out of his grasp. And while he was surrendering, he went the final step and gave up the hold on his bedroom. He wanted her there, and there was no longer a need to pretend otherwise.

"I didn't expect anything I said to matter." Her sentence broke off as she shook her head. "Communication isn't our strong point, but there are some places we excel."

Funny, but he thought they were doing better this time around, under tense circumstances, than they did eight months ago. But he couldn't deal with it all now, so the time for talk was over.

They had better things to do. "You mean in bed."

"Yes."

"Let's get there." He pulled her into his arms and sighed in relief when she wrapped her legs around his hips and her arms around his neck.

"Are you sure you're ready for me?" she whispered the question against his mouth.

He hoped to hell he didn't drop her until they hit the bed because that tie thing was happening. Right fucking now.

"I'll show you just how ready in a second."

Somehow he got them into his bedroom. Between kissing her and sliding his hands over her bare ass, he was half done with foreplay. He'd slow it down for her but would probably explode in the process.

Satisfaction surged through him when he dropped her on the

bed. So many nights he'd made the long walk from her bed back to his, cursing his pride and her lying with every step. No more waiting. No more stopping his needs in order to feed his fury.

With his palms against the mattress, he leaned in and kissed her. Felt her unknot his tie and start on the buttons of his shirt. His mouth wandered and teased. When he deepened the kiss, his brain crashed. He didn't realize she'd stripped off his jacket until he stood back up again.

While she sat there and watched, he ripped off his shirt with jerky movements. Then he was on her again, his chest against hers as he pushed her against the bed. Her hands skimmed up his back while his went down her stomach. His middle finger found her wetness and slipped inside to rub over her clit. Back and forth, round and round until she moaned into his mouth.

Her legs shifted around him and her hips left the bed. But he didn't stop. He kissed her, letting his tongue mimic the in-and-out brush of his fingers inside of her. He waited until she thrashed. Until she pressed her thighs tight against him to let his body move to the next step.

"Jarrett, now."

He wanted her to beg but settled for the order. Forcing his body to pull back zapped most of his energy. When she threw her arms out and tugged him close again, he almost gave in. But she'd asked to be tied down and he was going to give it to her.

"Not yet," he said.

"I can't wait." When he sat up, she pressed her legs tight together.

He knew she was trying to clench tight enough to find relief. Not that he would let that happen.

"Oh, no." Sliding his palms up her legs, he parted her thighs again. "You have to wait until I give permission."

Knowing his control teetered right on the edge, he didn't waste time. He rolled his zipper down and pulled off the rest of his clothes. All while she watched. Her gaze never left him. It toured over his body as he revealed every part of him to her.

He reached into his closet only long enough to grab two ties off the rack just inside the door. Smoothing the silk through his fingers, he walked back to the bed. Before he could move her or give his next order, she raised both arms above her head. Long and sexy, stretching her body out to the full length of his bed. He had to grind his teeth together to keep from getting on top of her and ending this right now.

"Tie me up." She sent him a smile filled with sensual promise. "I want it."

Sitting on the edge of the bed, he reached for her wrist and brought her hand to his mouth. A lick against her palm. Then a kiss.

His gazed locked with hers as his mouth traveled up her arm to the soft inside of her elbow. When she started shifting on the mattress, he brought her arm back to the bed and slipped the tie around her wrist, looped it around the bedpost. She didn't say a word as he bound her second hand. Not tight. She could easily break free, but when she grabbed on to the silk, crushed it in her hands, he knew she planned to stay right where she was.

Taking a slow walk around the room, he ended back at her feet. With one knee on the bed and his hands on her ankle, he drew her legs up until he lay between her thighs and her feet balanced against the mattress. "Now, we play."

He dipped his head and swept his tongue over her lips. One pass, a second. When her leg fell to the side, he sped up, flicking over her until she thrashed against the sheets and tugged on the bindings holding her.

"Jarrett, please."

The begging.

He loved the begging. "You need to come first."

And she was right on the edge. Every muscle pulled tight and her body opened for him to do anything he wanted. His mouth continued and when he added his fingers, her hips went wild. Heavy breaths filled the dark room. Her feet flexed and her stomach dipped. With one final pass of his tongue, he felt her body shudder as she let out a stammered exhale.

The orgasm hit her then. Coursed through her as he watched. Still he used his tongue, feeling the sensitive muscles inside her contract and clench.

"Now, Jarrett." The punctuated words came out between pants.

This time he listened. Blood pounded in his cock and the room started to spin. Climbing up the bed, he fit his body against hers and kissed her again. He rubbed his tip against her, dipping inside.

She turned her head to the side on the pillow. "Condom."

The spinning stopped and everything inside him froze. "What?"

"Protection."

Guilt crashed over him. "Damn, I'm so sorry."

Her mouth covered his in an electric kiss. Not a quick one either. Long and firm, before facing him again. "Both our fault."

He lifted his hips away from her as a splash of cold washed over him. "Becca—"

"Get it."

His brain battled with his lower half. They were at two very different places. He might have pulled back, sat up, done something a decent guy running on his last ounce of common sense might do. Then she lifted her hips and rubbed her wetness against his cock and his mind went blank again.

"Are you sure?" He looked down in those eyes searching for anger or disappointment. He only saw heat.

"Find one now or I will rip these bindings off and you'll be the one tied down."

Her commanding tone snapped him out of his stupor. Moving now, he kneeled on the bed and grabbed for the knob on the nightstand. With the packet in his hand he looked back to her. Rolling it on, he shifted back to the bed.

Those sexy eyes watched him. Followed him as he moved.

Her legs fell open. "Do it."

"Oh, yeah." His body hadn't cooled after all. Blood pounded in his cock and his body begged for release.

With his hands under her calves, he lifted her legs and balanced her feet over his shoulders. She gasped as her hips rotated off the bed and he opened her wide to his penetration. He rubbed the tip back and forth, sliding over her, back and forth, until her body moved in time with his.

She pulled on the ties as her back arched. "Now, Jarrett."

Yes, now.

EIGHTEEN

A half hour later Becca lay sprawled across Jarrett. She moved her hand and felt a tickle. Looking down, she saw his aqua tie still wrapped around her wrist and flowing over the side of the bed. If she had an ounce of strength she'd take it off.

Not going to happen.

She tried to lift her head off his chest and gave up. She settled for looking around the room. This was her second trip behind the sacred door. The first was about getting in and out then getting the shock of her life. This time her initial focus centered on getting on the bed as fast as possible.

Now she scanned the room, taking in the clean lines and the small changes, like her photo no longer sitting on his nightstand. She never realized how much that mattered or what a huge gesture it had been for a man like Jarrett to include a piece of her in this space after such a short time together. Now it was gone. The loss of such a simple thing slammed into her like a punch to the chest.

To keep from focusing on the strange body blow, her gaze traveled back to the man under her. His arm wrapped around her for the first time in eight months and she welcomed the warming blanket of his touch.

When his breathing evened out and his hand brushed over hers where it lay on his chest, she knew he was awake. If he'd drifted off before, he was back now.

Her mind went to the look of disgust that crossed his face when she mentioned the condom. At first she thought the anger was aimed at her for slowing them down. Then she saw the expression for what it was—self-loathing. For a man used to exercising an extreme amount of self-control, she knew the lapse shocked him.

But the incident did bring up an issue. "That was close."

His eyes opened.

"I mean the condom," she said.

"Yeah, I know. Not my finest hour." Frustration still lingered in his voice.

She was all for chivalry, but she was just as strong an advocate for taking care of herself. "You know I was here, too, right?"

"I don't have a huge number of rules when it to comes to sex, but a decent guy—a smart one—protects the woman he's sleeping with." He rubbed a hand over his face.

She pulled it back down and leaned up on her elbow to get a better look at him. So much for all his protests about being a criminal and living on the dark side. A man who didn't care about anything would certainly put the full weight of responsibility for birth control on the woman.

"I'm a big girl. It's my responsibility, too. After all, I've been handling it for about a decade now. The slipup is on both of us, but it's my body."

He slipped his arm behind his head. "Tell me again why you're not on birth control right now."

"I haven't been since I left you. Being on the run, birth control pills were not my biggest priority. I reached for the Kevlar vest instead."

"Don't you need it for the job?"

She shouldn't have been insulted, but still the words squeezed tight around her heart. And not in a good way. "I haven't slept with anyone else."

He held her gaze for a full twenty seconds before nodding his head. "I guess that would have been tough, what with your team getting blown up and all."

Sure, she threw that out there, being flip. But she didn't want him hiding behind it. The full truth might scare the hell out of him, but it was still the truth. "That's not why."

"Okay. Then why?"

"The point is, if this is going to go on, we should think about getting me to a clinic for birth control. I can't imagine trying to take care of a little guy on the road." She sat up and tugged on the sheet beneath her. It didn't move. Nothing did. The lack of anything had her glancing up again into Jarrett's blank face. "What?"

In a move so slow it seemed to take forever, he sat up and leaned against the headboard. "You mean you'd have it."

"A baby?"

"Isn't that what we're talking about here?"

It wasn't until he asked the question that she realized what she'd said. Something so important and she'd tossed it out there without working it through or taking a second to figure out what it meant. "I . . . well, honestly, I hadn't given it a thought."

"Do it now." A certain intensity pulsed off of him and was mirrored in his unwavering stare.

"My inclination is yes. I know that's stupid because everything is in chaos right now, but . . ." The words felt right. Scary and stupid, yeah, most definitely stupid, but true. Growing up without a mother, she'd never felt the rush to become one herself. But the idea of having a part of him. Then she saw the paleness of his face. "Jarrett?"

"You would have the kid of a man you once hated."

"That is not true. I have never hated you. Never." She put a hand over his, trying to loosen his death grip. "Some days I wish I would have been able to, but no."

"A baby."

Then she realized this whole scene was as much about him turning over the idea as her. Clearly, he didn't like the idea. He didn't balk but his emotions had all but shut down. One more twist and he could actually hurt her arm, though she knew that wasn't on purpose. He was lost in his thoughts. Still, the idea of having a baby with her had him in its grips and he was fighting it hard.

And that pissed her off.

"For God's sake, Jarrett. I wouldn't make you see our hypothetical baby or give me one cent. You can stop worrying." She shrugged out of his hold and scooted back on the bed. Rubbing her wrist, she scowled at him, letting her anger flow through her as she wrestled with the idea of punching him in the stomach. "If you want me to sign some sort of agreement just in case, have Bast send it over."

Jarrett's hands dropped to each side of his hips. The open palms looked as if whatever had him stiff and tight had whooshed right out of him.

She had no idea what was going on.

Before she could ask, color rushed back through him and his face reddened. "You think I'd abandon you?"

She jerked back. Almost fell off the damn bed. "You'd want me to stay?"

"Yes."

What the hell was happening here? "Jarrett?"

He stood up next to the bed, naked and not showing any signs of caring. "Hell, I don't know."

That made two of them. But his reaction, the signs she could not piece together as shock and hurt, had her stammering. "We should—"

"Why are we talking about this when it's not even a real thing?"

"Because we're grown-ups and when grown-ups have sex, as often as we do, this topic needs to come up and get handled." Her voice stayed calm. She even managed to sound reasonable. Inside, her nerves jangled and twisted, but she maintained calm on the outside. Somehow.

His eyes narrowed. "Are you pregnant?"

"No." She didn't think so. They'd stumbled and came close to messing up here, but they'd otherwise been careful. She had no reason to believe the birth control failed and didn't fear that issue despite the conversation.

"You're sure?"

Not the more he talked about it. "We've come close to skipping the condom more than once. In light of that I'm trying to be realistic about where we go from here."

"But you'd keep my baby."

She blew out a long breath and stood up. They faced each other across the big bed. She didn't bother reaching for a sheet or covering up because he'd seen and touched everything. She wasn't ashamed of her body and he sure didn't have a problem showing his off.

"Yes, Jarrett. Standing here, right now, I say I would."

"Okay." He made the word last for three syllables.

Not exactly the response she wanted, but then she didn't know what either of them should say or believe right now.

"Now, before we start picking out names for our not-real baby, maybe we could—" When he turned and walked into the closet, she just stood there. Then the second wave of anger smashed into her. His house or not, walking away amounted to throwing down the gauntlet and asking for a fight. "Where do you think you're going?"

"Out for a second." He pulled on a pair of dress pants.

"Uh, now?"

Next came the shirt off the floor. He slipped it on and started buttoning. "Definitely."

It was as if the man didn't know she was a trained assassin. "We didn't settle this."

"I understand your position."

He was really begging for a kick. "Is this some weird male fear-of-commitment thing? If so, I gotta tell you it's kind of cliché. It also makes me want to punch you."

His head stayed down but he peeked up at her. "It's not."

"Then?"

He nodded to her. "I'll be back."

Before she could step in front of the door or shove him back on the bed, he was gone. Good thing the building had a camera system.

She planned to watch the weasel. Right now, he was safer anywhere but in the room with her.

Jarrett's head still spun from the conversation upstairs. One second he could laugh it off as ridiculous. The next it took hold and he had to fight off the need to run around doing stupid things, like letting her know how much the conversation meant to him.

Right now, all flustered and half out of breath from his race downstairs, he had all the confidence of a sixteen-year-old sneaking his first package of condoms out of the drugstore. Standing across the bar from Wade, seeing the stunned expression on his friend and manager's face after he asked a simple question, almost sent Jarrett running back to the angry woman upstairs.

He wasn't one to wallow in confusion. He acted and made practical decisions. Right now he wanted to jump in a car and forget all about the security measures he'd put in place. His mind had turned to mush and he'd be damned if he could figure out how to clean up the mess.

Then he remembered the coldness in Becca's eyes and the way she scanned the room looking for a weapon right before he left. She had that woman-scorned thing down, and when she thought he was throwing her and their nonexistent child out the door, she went all mama bear on him.

He'd take his chances with Wade.

The friend in question looked two seconds from shedding his own skin. Wade slowly lowered the glass he was cleaning. "What did you just say?"

"You heard me."

"You want me to get the car?"

"I need to go out." It was his damn car, after all.

Clearly unimpressed with a request from the boss, Wade's eyes narrowed. "Is that a great idea? I mean, have you even left the building since Becca got here?"

"The club doesn't open for hours." Jarrett sat down on the barstool. Yeah, sitting would be good.

He looked around. The female attendants hadn't started filing in yet. He could hear the low rumble of voices from the other room and assumed the kitchen staff had begun work on dinner.

"Natalie threatened you, giving you three days before . . . I don't know, something terrible. She basically insinuated that stepping outside would get you shot or arrested on a new set of trumped-up charges." Wade rested his palms against the bar's edge. "Or did I get confused about that part?"

"She won't see us."

Wade leaned in closer. "Us?"

"I'm taking Becca." And why did he sound like a little kid who got caught doing something bad. Jarrett hated that. He owned the place. He was in charge.

But, damn, this was uncomfortable. He wasn't the type to drag personal matters into the business and that's all he'd done since meeting Becca.

Wade's mouth dropped open before he talked again. "I don't get it."

That made two of them. The words and plans shot through his brain, and he said them before thinking. "You bring the car around through the garage, we get in. Maybe we have someone here drive a second car as a decoy."

"Do you hear yourself?"

He was trying not to think or hear or reason. "I want to leave for a few minutes."

Wade closed his eyes for a second. "So, this is a death wish of some sort."

"Just a car ride. I'm not looking for death."

"With the woman who once set you up—both of us—to be arrested." He smacked his hands against the bar as he said each word. "The same one you've kept trapped upstairs."

"She's not a prisoner." If anyone was stuck and unraveling, it was him.

She had him thinking things he shouldn't think and wanting things he couldn't have. He'd held back some leverage from the CIA, information people there wanted, to make sure he didn't become expendable. He purposely hadn't asked questions of what became of the Spectrum agents or who set him up. He thought he knew and that he'd been the sucker. Now nothing seemed clear except his need to keep Becca close.

"She hasn't left the condo in, what, ten days? Hasn't even seen sunlight, as far as I know," Wade said.

"For her own protection."

At least that's the excuse Jarrett ran through his mind. She came to him. He set the terms and she took them, and he would not feel anything but satisfaction about how the last few days rolled out. He was not a man accustomed to guilt and he pushed it away now.

Wade exhaled in the way that signaled an oncoming lecture. He reached under the bar and pulled up a water bottle. Sat it on the edge right next to Jarrett.

"Okay, I give up." Wade grabbed a second bottle and twisted off the lid. "What am I missing here?"

"She needs to run an errand."

He nodded before taking a drink. "I'll do it. Give me a list or whatever."

"That would be interesting."

"Meaning?"

That almost made Jarrett laugh. "You can't really handle this one."

"Jarrett, for God's sake. This is the most annoying game of twenty questions ever."

"She needs to see a doctor." He yelled the answer, then leaned in and lowered his voice. "Is that okay with you?"

"Did she get hurt?" Wade snapped his fingers. "Trying to climb out the window, right? That was Eli's prediction. I keep waiting to see her rappel down the side of the building."

Jarrett ignored that because if he spent two seconds thinking about Wade and Elijah discussing his sex life, they'd be the ones going out the window. "No."

"Give me a hint."

Fine, he wanted all the information, then Jarrett would give it to him. Maybe after that his friend would shut the hell up and find the fucking keys. "Birth control."

"I don't . . ." Wade shook his head as his eyes narrowed. "What?"

Enough. "This conversation is over. I'm the boss. We're leaving."

When Jarrett saw Wade's mouth drop open a second time he knew he should have led with that. Issue the order then demand it be upheld. This whole trying-to-spare-everyone's-feelings thing was not his style. At all.

"I have condoms upstairs," Wade said.

"So do I. That's not the issue."

Wade moved his bottle to the side and leaned down on the bar on his elbows. "You lost me again."

So much for thinking he was in charge. Jarrett made a last grab for patience. "As far as I know, Eli can't get pregnant."

Wade shot back up straight. "Becca's pregnant?"

"Maybe you could not yell that."

The man's eyes bugged. Looked ten seconds from popping out of his head. "Is she?"

Jarrett seriously considered messing with Wade until he realized this was a topic he did not find the least bit funny. "No."

"Then I don't—"

Jarrett held a hand. "It's a precaution."

"Let me get this straight. You can't take two seconds to put on a condom?"

They'd been talking like friends instead of boss/employee, but that comment was too much. "You are about to get your ass kicked."

"If it will knock some sense into you, fine. Let's go."

"I'm going stir crazy. She has to be, too."

"So, she's bored?"

Jarrett decided to ignore that. "I want her protected and I don't just mean from gunfire."

Wade dropped his head between his arms. He stood like that as he mumbled something.

Jarrett couldn't catch the comment. "I didn't get that."

Wade's head snapped up. "You know we're headed for disaster here, right?"

There was no reason to lie about this part. "Yeah."

"I don't see a way you can protect the business, yourself and her."

"And Elijah." The weight of all the people, all the lives, weighed down on Jarrett. It was getting to be a bit much, especially with Natalie sniffing around and giving deadlines.

Elijah meant something to Wade, which meant Wade was invested. They all were. This went beyond birth control and having a place to sleep. Elijah and Becca needed answers. Someone ordered their termination. They needed to know why and who. Without that, they were in the crosshairs and would stay there, especially since Natalie insisted this wasn't a CIA hit. Not that the woman had any trouble lying.

"Eli is just another layer of complication. Take him out of the equation and you still have a mess." Wade said in a low voice.

Jarrett focused on the sound of clanking pots not far away. "Remember the good old days when we ran a supper club and collected money and information and everyone was happy?"

"Were you?"

He could count so few times in his adult life where he was happy. Satisfied and determined he'd conquered. Happy, not so much. He wasn't even convinced that was a necessary component of anything. He'd survived without it when Becca left. He was a mess with her here. That had to mean something.

Instead of laying that all on Wade, Jarrett went with a shrug. "Don't ask that because I sure as hell don't know any more."

"Skipping the birth control conversation, because right now I'd like to get the visual image of you two humping like bunnies out of my head—"

"Thanks."

"Let's talk bigger picture." Wade spread his arms wide. "Like, what's the long-term goal here? We can't hide two adults in here forever, and I'm assuming you'd like to go outside at some point for something other than a birth control run."

Questions ran through Jarrett's head. Someone was using them all. For a long time he didn't care, as long as he wasn't in prison. But now he wanted to know. "I'm working on that."

"Want to clue me in on how you're doing it?"

This part Jarrett finally got. "I'm going to figure out a way to save everyone."

What?"

"It was a surprise to me, too." It had been building for days and now it was the only answer.

"Not really. It totally sounds like something you'd do."

The insight stopped Jarrett's mental planning. "That's not what most people think."

"They don't know you like I do, being one of your early rescues and all."

As far as compliments went, that was a pretty big one. He let it sink in and wash away some of the darkness. He'd spent a lot of years ripping people apart. Walking away from that, disconnecting, took time and money and more muscle that he ever thought he could throw. But he was out, legitimate.

Jarrett owed part of that to Wade, so he had to engage some payback. "Warning here. Eli isn't going to like anything that happens from here on out."

"Nothing new there. He spends a lot of time being pissed."

Jarrett looked at Wade's calm demeanor and feared he didn't get it. "This could push Eli away, and I don't know how to make that better for you."

"It's just sex."

No way. Jarrett had seen them together. More than once he'd looked away when Wade's growing interest worried him. "You know that's the crap I've been saying about Becca, right?"

"Meaning?"

"We're both screwed."

Wade laughed. "Guess you might really need that birth control then."

Common sense came rushing back and Jarrett didn't fight it. "I'll table that for now."

"Because?"

"I have bigger issues to handle."

NINETEEN

Becca spent most of the morning in the conference room, avoiding the cleaning crew that had now left the condo and looking through the information Jarrett gave her. Stacks and stacks of files. All the background on the deaths of her team members. Well, the published fake stories. She knew who they really were and what they did for a living, and no one was an accountant.

The idea made her smile until she spied the newspaper article talking about Felix Hernandez dying in a home invasion robbery. The murder didn't even make the front page of the metro section. It was buried pages back and pure bullshit. The man was a poisons expert with serious gun skills. He'd slept only a few hours at a time, and even then sitting up and ready to fight if needed.

Yet, someone got him. From the medical report Jarrett somehow possessed, Felix went down in a hail of gunfire. She wanted to know why.

The answer was in all of this paper somewhere. She smoothed her hand over her ponytail. Being back in her cargo pants and tank top gave her confidence. Probably had something to do with feeling less vulnerable. So did the pocketknife she took out of Jarrett's kitchen drawer.

Just as he used to demand she stay naked in the condo, he insisted she wear clothes when she came downstairs this time. She assumed he didn't want her parading around in front of Wade, but all the intel on him suggested he wouldn't really care if she did.

She'd welcome Wade or anyone right now. Maybe another set of eyes would help her see whatever lurked just out of reach. She'd spread everything out on the second-floor conference table from one end to the other. She stared, walked around it, rearranged it. Nothing made the pieces fall together in her head.

The lock clicked and the door swung open. The old fight-or-flight instincts kicked in and she pivoted, ready to fend off any attack. A sidekick, a punch, the knife—whatever it took.

Jarrett didn't even look up from his phone as he stepped inside. "I need the room."

He'd been gone all of an hour and morphed right back into the demanding, indifferent guy who wanted her naked every second. She fought this battle at least twice every day. He'd let his guard down, talk to her, then something would have the shield slamming back up again.

She had no idea what raised it this time. "Uh, hello."

He turned around as if to leave. Actually gave her his back as his fingers moved over the buttons. "Let's go."

"What are you talking about?"

"You can go upstairs—"

"No." And he could go to hell while he was at it. She'd reached the end of her patience on this dual personality bullshit. He gave her clipped orders and a boiling heat moved to her brain. No more.

He turned back around as his hand dropped. His focus switched from the phone to her. "Despite the great sex, I still own the building and I'm in charge."

Boiling. Rage. "Don't do that."

"What?"

"Be a giant douche."

She thought she saw the corner of his mouth twitch. Normally this was the point where he'd double down and his jerkiness would escalate off the charts. Instead, he sighed. He was not the sighing type.

"Remember how when you got here you didn't say anything but yes to whatever I asked you to do?"

"Only too well." She moved some files and made room for her thigh on the corner of the table. "A momentary lapse brought on by the fear of death, I assure you."

"The rules haven't changed."

"Jarrett, honestly, you're smarter than that. The rules changed almost immediately. I am not your sex doll or your slave."

It felt good to finally unload. For days she'd been accepting, waging a war of defiance without saying a word. Those days were over.

She no longer believed he'd kick her out or physically hurt her. Every day, in quiet moments, she saw the warmth in his eyes and felt the want in his touch. He might shout and throw around words like "betrayal," he might even still hate her a little, but underneath he needed something from her. She was willing to give it to him if he stopped being an ass.

She wrestled with what she felt for him and how to make it extend past the web of guilt and confusion weighing her down. She wanted him, had never stopped loving him, but repairing the shattered trust required more strength than she could muster. Trust had always been her downfall anyway. Add in everything that happened between them, and the task struck her as insurmountable.

Since he hadn't moved once she yelled, she tried again. This time in a normal tone. "If you need me to go upstairs, don't be a dick about it. Just ask."

"Go upstairs." He held his phone in a strangling grip.

She half thought he'd break the thing in two. "I can see you're unwilling to cede any ground on this issue."

"Yes."

"Fine, I'm patient. We can just sit here until you do." She swung her foot back and forth. Would have whistled if her mouth hadn't gone dry. Fighting with him fired her up, but a level of wariness remained.

"I'm trying to believe we're having a ten-minute conversation about this."

Since logic and stubbornness didn't win him over, she tried common sense. "Why would I leave? You said Bast was coming for a second meeting."

"I know. I set up the damn meeting."

Seemed none of the tricks in her arsenal were working today. That didn't mean she'd back down. He wasn't the only one who could dig in. She crossed her arms over her stomach and watched his gaze dip to her chest. Then she remembered, no bra.

Ah, yes. There was that trick. Not this time. She needed to prove they could work through something while keeping their clothes on.

She snapped her fingers to win back eye contact. "Then just ask."

He blinked a few times. "Becca—"

"Jarrett, you're an adult and I am done pretending you rule the world."

"I can put you on the street."

The ultimate threat. He hadn't pulled that one out for days. Amazing how the words still slashed through her, whipping and ripping everything they touched.

The jackass.

She lifted her chin and dared him to do it. "Go ahead."

Tension streaked through the room, cutting through the sudden silence.

They settled into a staring contest. When he didn't say anything, she lifted an eyebrow in a silent "bring it on" message.

"Fine." He gritted the word out through clenched teeth. "Would you go upstairs for a few minutes?" Every word sounded harsh as if covered in sandpaper.

"Please?"

He pointed at her. "Don't push your luck."

The man had no ability to lose with grace. She shook her head as she walked over to stand in front of him. She held out her palm. "Give it to me."

"What?"

Poor thing looked ready to smash a fist into the wall. She understood the feeling. It washed over her quite often when dealing with him.

She wiggled her fingers. "I need the keys and secret passwords and whatever the hell else a human has to use in this place to pass from one floor to another."

"The security card stays with me."

Apparently he wanted her to magically appear on another floor. "You are the very definition of stubborn."

"Right back atcha, sweetheart."

"It appears we're at another impasse."

He swore under his breath. "Come with me."

Turning around, he took off. Didn't even wait to see if she'd follow. She'd chalk it up to his confidence in his power over her, but she really thought he was tired of dealing with her. She was fine with either outcome. She'd made her point. The bullying and sexual game playing, other than the fun mutual kind, was over.

Using more strength than seemed necessary, he lowered the black door to the security keypad. The plastic cracked under the treatment. Rather than swiping his card he typed in a sequence. Seven-nine-zero-two-eight. She knew because she went up on silent tiptoes behind his back to watch him do it.

The elevator doors slid open. She stared inside. "Why not use the card?"

"It's synched to me. If I use it here, I have to use it upstairs. You can use the code one-one-four-nine-eight to get into the condo. It's a guest code."

Good thing she'd been trained to memorize numbers. "Let me guess, you're changing the number tomorrow."

"This afternoon."

"Your trust is lovely. Really." She stepped on. Thought about slamming the door shut in his face.

He must have sensed it because he put his foot in the threshold and hand over the door vent. He leaned in. "Trust has to be earned."

"Jackass."

Now he smiled. "As if you're the first person to point that out."

She made it upstairs and inside the condo. First thing she did was find a pen. With the guest codes for the elevator and condo now tucked in her bra, she headed for the office. Jarrett had something planned and she had every intention of watching it through the security cameras.

Sitting down, she pulled out the keyboard and started typing. The second-floor hall popped up. Her gaze went to the open conference room door but not inside. But someone would come. She could feel it. All she had to do was wait.

Jarrett stood at the far side of the conference room table, looking at the documents Becca put together. Not that he saw a damn word. The black lines blurred as he wrestled to get his anger back under control. Between Becca pushing him and Elijah declaring he'd be in the conference room, ready or not, for a meeting, Jarrett had just about had it with the former Spectrum agents.

Damn ungrateful. Both of them.

He looked up in time to see Elijah walk in. Scowl, stiff shoulders and all.

"For the record, demand my presence again and I will shoot you." Jarrett was sorry he didn't have a weapon on him. "This time I won't go for a shoulder wound."

Elijah stood in what could only be described as a fighting stance, with his hands behind his back and his feet slightly apart. "I need a status."

"On?"

"You're confining me to the condo and messing with my files in the conference room."

These days this guy threw blame in every sentence. Never mind he'd had Jarrett arrested or came asking for help when he didn't deserve it. No, this shithead thought everyone owed him something. Jarrett once again wondered what Wade saw in the guy. He insisted there was more to Eli than the anger festering now, but Jarrett didn't see it. From his experience, hot sex only went so far.

Reaching for his last bit of patience, Jarrett repeated the explanation he'd given Wade. "I'm trying to figure out a way out of this for all of us."

"You think you can get to the bottom of this mess faster than I can?" Elijah leaned in. "I'm fucking trained for this work."

"And that got you really far, didn't it?"

"Don't test me, Jarrett."

"And do not threaten me, Eli. This is a game you will lose."

Wade appeared over Elijah's shoulder. His gaze flicked from Elijah to Jarrett. "What's going on in here?"

Sonofabitch. Jarrett wanted to keep Wade out of this. Had sent him on a storage room run downstairs to get him away. Nothing was going right today.

"Our guest is dissatisfied," Jarrett said.

Wade's eyes narrowed as he stepped up even with Elijah. "Eli, why are—"

"Because someone had to." He held up a hand as he turned on Wade. "You make promises. You tell me to be patient. We've got that bitch in the building and—"

"Enough." Anger filled in all the space left behind by Jarrett's expired patience. He let the white-hot rage pouring through him wash over everything. "You're done here."

"You think you can kick me out?"

"I've officially reached the point where I don't care how long you survive outside these walls." The phone in Jarrett's pocket buzzed, but he ignored it.

Elijah shook his head. "Holy shit, you're going to do it."

The dropped mouth suggested the man finally understood he'd

gone too far. About fucking time, as far as Jarrett was concerned. "Yes, you're leaving. Consider this your half-hour countdown."

Elijah didn't move. "Not that. I mean, you're going to turn over whatever files you originally held back."

"What are you talking about?" Wade asked as he grabbed for his phone.

"He has leverage to keep the CIA out of here, to keep all law enforcement away, and he's going to give it up. For her."

Jarrett should have seen Elijah putting the pieces together. "This is not your concern."

"It's the only answer to why you're alive and not rotting in jail."

Wade's gaze kept roaming as he clenched his cell. "Let's calm down."

"Listen to me." Elijah grabbed the phone out of Wade's hand and chucked it across the room. It smashed against the wall next to Jarrett and broke into pieces as Elijah turned on him. "I'm not letting that happen. Whatever you have is protecting all of us. Without it, we're dead."

"Eli, what the fuck?" Wade's yelling now matched Elijah's. "There was a building alarm."

"Tough shit." Elijah whipped a gun out of nowhere and aimed it at Jarrett.

He should have seen that coming as well. The man was on the edge and trained. He'd been frisked, but Wade had firearms, and Jarrett guessed Elijah found them.

Jarrett refused to flinch or show any sign of fear. "You will never make it to the front door."

Elijah laughed. "You think Wade will kill me?"

"No, me." Becca stepped from behind Wade, taking his gun out of his belt as she went.

While everyone froze, the barrel pressed against the back of Elijah's head. A second later, she shielded her body with his much larger one.

That fast, Wade whipped out a second weapon from his ankle and aimed it at her. "Drop it."

The standoff snapped Jarrett out of his stunned silence. "Wade, no."

Anger pulsed off Wade. "Now, Becca."

"I will kill Elijah." She shoved the gun until he lifted his hands. "See, he's smart enough to know I'll do it. Follow his lead here, Wade."

Wade looked at Jarrett. He nodded for Wade to listen to her because he needed to defuse this . . . whatever it was.

When she shifted, Jarrett saw the gun in one hand where it aimed for Elijah's head and the knife she held to his throat with her other hand. Wade must have seen the double attack too because he slowly lowered the weapon to the conference room table, swearing and shaking his head as he went.

Putting the knife between her teeth, she reached over and took the gun right out of Elijah's hand and tucked it into the back of her pants. "I'll hold this."

Damn, that was sexier than it should have been. Jarrett shook his head to stay focused.

"Move one inch in any direction, Elijah, and I will blow your head off." When Wade stepped forward, she waved the knife in his direction. "Nuh-uh. That goes for you, too."

Wade's jaw tightened. "You have my attention."

"Then step back. And hands up."

Jarrett was about to call Wade back when she pressed the gun hard enough to push Elijah's head forward. Looked like this self-described sex toy was done playing games. The trained warrior was now fully in attendance.

Jarrett didn't hate the change. Even undercover, she'd been tough and athletic. Now that he knew she possessed skills to bring a man Elijah's size down, he knew she'd hidden her true strength from him all those months ago.

"Shoot her," Elijah said as he glanced at Wade.

"His extra one is on the table and I have the other, you idiot."

For some reason Jarrett found comfort with the idea of her being armed. But he'd bet Wade still had another weapon on him somewhere. Becca wasn't the only tough person in the room.

Wade watched her as his hands went up. "Let's all calm down."

She brought the tip of the knife right against Elijah's throat. "No one kills Jarrett."

Wade nodded. "We agree on that."

"Whatever else happens in this room, he stays safe." She glanced around as she said it.

Elijah closed his eyes. "For fuck's sake."

Jarrett didn't know what to think about her stand, but it sure didn't piss him off. Elijah, on the other hand, did.

"On your knees." She gave the order to Elijah and her hands stayed steady.

He shifted his weight. "That's not happening."

Wade's hand started to fall. "Eli, be careful."

"You should stop doing whatever you think you're doing unless you want a bullet in your kneecap." She glared at Wade until he obeyed. "And don't bother trying to use logic on Elijah here. He always did have to learn the hard way."

"Shit." Elijah jerked when she pricked his skin with the tip of her blade. He gave Jarrett a furious glare. "Maybe you can tell her what's going on before she actually does some damage."

Jarrett's gaze went back to Becca. Her eyes were wild with hate and her body practically vibrated with fury. He decided to call an end to this for her sake, not Elijah's. "Becca, I think—"

"I don't know how you got in here or upstairs with all the security, but Jarrett can fix that later." She pushed against the back of Elijah's head until he swore under his breath and his knees started to buckle. "In the meantime, everyone thinks you're dead, so let's go ahead and make that happen."

Hands still in the air, Wade took a step toward her. "Becca, no."

Her gaze snapped to Wade. "He pulled a gun on your boss. What the hell were you doing to stop it?"

Wade looked at Jarrett and waited until he got the okay nod before talking. "It's not what you think."

"I think it's time for Elijah to bleed."

"Damn it." Elijah switched to constant yelling. "Jarrett, tell her now."

"You can't kill him." Jarrett gave the order in a calm but firm voice. No yelling. No thrashing around or panic. A simple command.

At the sound of his voice, her gaze slipped to him. Only for a second but enough to break the red haze that seemed to blind her. "Why not?"

"He's been living here."

She eased up, bringing the blade a fraction of an inch away from Elijah's neck. "What?"

"Could you maybe lower the gun, or the knife? One trip and I'm out of here," Elijah said.

Jarrett didn't hate that idea. "Be quiet."

She tensed and her attention shifted to Wade. "You're moving again."

Likely going for another weapon if Jarrett knew Wade. Much more of this and Jarrett would have a bloodbath on his hand. "Wade, stop."

Too many gun-trained people stood in this room. All of them killed without regret. If Wade and Elijah figured out how to send the right signal and coordinate their efforts, they could go after Becca. Jarrett refused to let that happen.

Everyone finally looked at him, which was exactly what he wanted. All eyes on him and thoughts of stupid defensive moves gone. "Becca, Elijah didn't break in. He's been here, living here with Wade, trying to do the exact same thing you're doing."

"Minus the part about fucking Jarrett."

Elijah just begged for a bullet. Jarrett fought back the temptation to grab a gun and do it himself. "I can let her kill you, you know."

"I would advise against that," Bast said from the doorway.

Everyone looked at him but Becca. Her focus centered on Elijah.

Just what they needed. More testosterone in the room. Jarrett walked around the table to stand behind Becca. He put a hand on her shoulder and felt the fury bubbling underneath the surface. "Bast, you're early."

He shrugged. "Timing sucks. It's the story of my life."

Becca still hadn't moved. "You're perfect if you want to watch me kill Elijah."

Jarrett reached over her shoulder and put a hand over hers. With some effort, he pushed her hand down, taking the knife away from Elijah's throat. When Wade took a step, Jarrett sent him back with a shake of the head. "It's time to diffuse this situation."

Elijah swore under his breath. "You think?"

"I'd shut up if I were you," she said, her voice still raspy and low.

Bast cleared his throat. "Not to sound old-school about this, but how about we try talking for a second."

Becca's shoulders finally fell. She nodded at Jarrett. "Fine."

Before Elijah could swing, and it looked like he was tensing to do it, Jarrett grabbed the one gun on the table and shoved Elijah into the side. He pushed off and turned. He might have sent them all into a second, deadlier round of fighting, but Wade stopped him with a restraining arm across his chest.

"Much better," Bast said.

Becca held up both guns. "I'm keeping the weapons, except for the one Jarrett has."

Bast nodded. "I'm fine with that."

Everyone started moving, or they did until Becca spoke again. "But I want an explanation."

"*You* want?" Elijah acted like she didn't have a right to anything.

Not that Becca bought the argument or flinched from his rough tone. Her yell matched his. "This was supposed to be my meeting with Bast, so I'll set the agenda."

"Actually, I do." Jarrett used the tone that suggested everyone start listening. He still wasn't sure why she'd stormed in, if she even realized the stand she'd taken on his behalf, but she clearly remembered how much she disliked Elijah, so Jarrett cut right to the point. "The easy version of all of this? Someone tried to kill Elijah and he needed to disappear, so I made that happen. He's been here recovering and researching, trying to figure out why Spectrum imploded."

Becca frowned. "What did you get out of all of this?"

"Information," Bast said, jumping in.

"And then you showed up with a near identical story to Elijah's, so now you're both here, in my club and on my property, looking for the same answers."

Wade snorted. "Simple."

Becca snorted right back. "Hardly."

"On that we agree." Elijah pulled out a chair and dropped into it.

Bast gestured at the table. "Good, then let's all sit down and start the meeting."

TWENTY

Ten minutes later Becca's heart still raced. She'd seen Elijah walk into the room on the security monitor and knew Jarrett was in there. She reacted. No thinking. She used the codes, got on the elevator and vowed to kill Elijah with her bare hands if needed.

Jarrett in danger brought all her skills rushing back. She thought about pressure points and where to knife Elijah for greatest impact and quickest bleeding. She'd heard the threats and her eyes focused on the gun at Wade's hip. The rest blurred.

Except the part where Elijah lived in the building. She heard that bit of news just fine. Would have been nice to have that information sooner, though she had no idea how to process it or what it meant even now.

Leave it to Elijah to screw up getting killed. The man didn't even have the decency to be dead.

Jarrett said something but she only heard a rumble. When he called out her name, she turned on him. Watched him sit at the head of the conference table with Wade and Elijah on one side and

Bast on the other. The energy bouncing around inside her made it impossible for her to sit down. So, she stared down the length of the room at the man who shared her bed but refused to trust her with anything.

She said the first thing that came to her mind and didn't involve a lot of swearing. "I'm still trying to believe you took Elijah in after how he arrested you."

Jarrett had the nerve to shrug. "If it's any consolation, I shot him first."

"Allegedly." Bast didn't bother lifting his head from the file he was reading.

"Not allegedly," Jarrett said. "I did shoot him."

Wade raised a hand. "I was there."

Elijah rubbed what was likely the injury area. "It still fucking hurts."

They acted like this was some big joke. Becca wanted to find her gun and take aim at all of them until they sobered and started spilling every last piece of information on what had happened during the last eight months. Never mind that Elijah and Jarrett should be bitter enemies or that Elijah threatened Jarrett with a gun in this very room less than a half hour ago. Now they were joking buddies.

She would never understand men.

She glanced at Elijah and had no trouble calling up her anger for the man. Without thinking, her teeth crashed together in a grimace. "You're lucky it was Jarrett who shot you. I wouldn't have wasted a bullet on your shoulder."

"Now that we're all here, I think we can modify the agenda a bit. Let's get back to what we know and make sure we're on the same page." Bast made check marks on the list in front of him as he talked. "Someone gave the order to move on Spectrum. Natalie is claiming ignorance and is on the hunt for Becca to pin it on her."

Elijah shook his head. "Typical agency bullshit."

"I agree." Becca might hate most everything Elijah stood for, but he got this one right.

If Jarrett noticed the fiery glares she was sending his way or the rising stress evident on everyone's faces, he didn't let on. He sat there, calm, as if he were handling a boring board of directors meeting. "What about Todd?"

Papers shuffled and a pen rolled across the desk as Bast closed one file and opened another. "My sources are saying he's playing the wounded victim well."

"He got hit by a car." Elijah rolled his eyes. "Big fucking deal."

Bast flipped through a few pages. "The guy had a collapsed lung and was in a medically induced coma."

Becca bit back a smile. Bast night be a super negotiator and accustomed to working through people's problems, but he clearly didn't understand the undercover world or how easy it was to fake an accident. She decided to educate him. "It is hard to believe a paid assassin would knock Todd down but not finish the job."

"Absolutely." Wade nodded. "It's faked. I've said that from the beginning, even over Jarrett's objections."

"It's enough of an injury to lure suspicion away but not enough to permanently sideline him." Elijah backed them both up, emphasizing his argument by pointing to something on the crime incident photos.

"I would have circled back around and run over him." Not that she ever ran someone over, but she didn't need those months of training in Berlin to envision how she'd get the deed done if it had to be done. If it was a matter of survival or the only way to protect Jarrett.

"Me, too." Elijah said as he thumped his finger against the photo. "Wouldn't have given him the love tap in the first place. Gone right for the kill and sped away before my face or vehicle registered in anyone's mind."

Bast's eyebrow lifted. "Bloodthirsty crowd."

"What I'm wondering about is message management." Jarrett talked on as if the rest of the room hadn't been discussing the top ten ways to squish a guy with a car.

"Meaning?" she asked.

Jarrett made a face. "I'm not sure everyone at the CIA is buying Todd's tale."

"True, but Todd led an operation that brought in helpful intel, which buys him some time," Bast said.

"You mean me." Jarrett leaned back in his chair and grabbed for the armrests. "I gave up the intel."

She could see the tension pump through him. Those dark eyes didn't focus, and he slid into a world only he seemed to occupy. She wanted to snap her fingers to bring him back, but went with talking louder. "What exactly did you hand over?"

Jarrett being Jarrett, she expected him to dodge the question. Pull the "I'm in charge" crap and tell them all to move on. When it came to the unraveling of his life, starting eight months ago, he shut down. Whatever came before, this topic cut him off.

He looked at his fingers as he tapped them against the armrest. "Information having to do with the tenuous nature of the Chinese housing market."

The words fell into the silence. Elijah stared. Becca did, too, but for her own reasons. In that moment she didn't even care what he said. She was too busy being stunned by the fact that he shared anything. She tried to say something, but she stammered and nothing coherent came out.

Elijah didn't suffer from the problem of surprised silence. "You've got to be kidding. How is that top secret? Wade and I saw it on the news the other night."

"They're building huge cities and no one is moving in," Jarrett said, ignoring the outburst. "Everyone in charge knows that much, but no one is talking about it. Still, that's not the secret. The amount of the U.S. financial market tied up in the mess is the problem, especially for a few businesses and congressmen who are keeping it quiet after trying to capitalize in secret."

"Then there are the rumors about the military equipment being moved into some of those empty cities. As you can imagine, those same businessmen and congressmen are not happy to be connected with that part of the business." Bast flipped a photo around and showed it to the rest of them.

Becca made out buildings and equipment in the aerial views. Her gaze went to Jarrett. "You have satellite photos."

He didn't blink. "More importantly and more damaging, I have evidence from on the ground in China. Photos of powerful people being where they shouldn't be, having personal knowledge of the military buildup they now act shocked to hear about."

Only Jarrett would find it normal to have information that should be locked in safes deep inside the CIA and reserved for a few eyes only. "Why do you even know any of this?"

Did he really not understand what this meant for his safety? This wasn't just about government operations. They were talking about big money and bad PR for a lot of powerful people. If those people traced the leaks back to Jarrett, the CIA would be the least of his worries. There were plenty of mercenaries out there happy to collect a paycheck for taking Jarrett out.

The security system and designing the perfect takedown would be a game to those sick folks. She knew because she lived right on the edge of being one of those types.

He shrugged. "I hear things."

Again with the shoulder thing. The flippant attitude made her want to strangle him. Just reach right down that long table and wrap her fingers around his neck. Maybe shake some sense into him as well. She settled for a final question. "What does this have to do with international drug running?"

Jarrett dug his fingernails into the leather chair. "Not a damn thing."

"Because that never happened." Wade glared at her as he said it, as if daring her to debate him.

"Apparently not." She didn't doubt the protests anymore.

Somewhere between Jarrett's vehemence and the story about his mother, Becca became a believer. And that made her all the angrier because it meant she'd been used and lied to, and in the process lost Jarrett.

"So, basically, the operation here was fake." Elijah stood up and walked to the window. "Despite what the briefing material said, the only goal was to grab Jarrett and shake him down for info."

"Looks like it." Which meant Todd either got conned, too, or he led the subterfuge. Either way, she blamed him for this mess. He was in charge. It was his job not to just rubber-stamp whatever he got handed from above.

They were a CIA splinter group. They didn't have to worry about checking in and playing by the rules. They didn't have to talk with Langley every two seconds. They ran free. That was the point of their operation.

None of this should have happened.

Bast smiled. "Maybe they could have asked nicely and Jarrett would have helped out?"

"That's not really how the CIA operates." Elijah put a hand against the bulletproof glass. "The people there tend to shoot first, ask later."

Wade blew out a breath as he slumped back in his chair. "Bast was kidding."

Jarrett joined Elijah in standing. He gathered the photos relating to China and put them back in the file. "At least we're all on the same page."

Elijah spun around. "Are we?"

"All information is shared from here on in. You two use this room to investigate whatever you need." Jarrett turned all of his attention to Elijah. "And you stop being an asshole."

She thought about rolling her eyes but decided she wasn't the type. "Impossible."

Elijah talked right over her. "You're still assuming the person who made the hits isn't in this room."

"You managed to prove her 'asshole' comment true right after she said it," Bast pointed out.

With everything that happened today and the emotional upheaval, Elijah's words set off something inside her. She went from standing there, trying to stay on her feet while exhaustion ripped through her body, to wanting to tear Elijah apart. Hit him and keep hitting him. "I didn't kill anyone. If I had, and if that's what I wanted, you'd have a bullet in the back of your head right now."

"And if he wanted you dead, he would have made a move that

first night you got here," Wade said, matching his angry tone to hers. "He's known you were here the whole time. So, I guess you're even."

And she intended to have a long conversation with Jarrett on that topic. She wanted to know what Elijah could see and why . . . at least she thought she wanted to know. "How comforting."

Elijah groaned as he rubbed the back of his neck. "We're back to Natalie, Todd or one of the higher-ups, and the question of why they killed the team that brought in Jarrett and his information. Why they wasted assets."

"We'll figure it out." Jarrett's low voice sounded confident.

The firm tone was enough to ease the crazy spinning inside her stomach. At least for now.

Without doing anything more than shifting in his chair, all attention went to Bast. He looked at Jarrett. "Can I talk with you?"

Jarrett nodded.

Elijah snorted. "I thought we were all sharing everything now."

"He's the client. You pay my exorbitant bill and I'll have a private meeting with you, too." Bast ended the talk by pointing his thumb toward the door. "Go."

She wanted to balk, at least argue. But when Wade and Elijah moved to the door, she followed. Bast wanted privacy, fine. She'd give Jarrett two minutes to come clean once they were alone upstairs. He accused her of using sex to get her way. This time she just might do it.

Jarrett dreaded the conversation before Bast even opened his mouth. Watching the three others drag their butts out of the conference room, as if going slow would mean they'd overhear something, showed they didn't know Bast very well. The guy had enough patience for an entire town.

The door clicked shut and Bast started shaking his head. "No."

Jarrett tried to remember what he said last. When nothing came to him, he gave up. "What are you talking about?"

"I know what you're thinking and the answer is no."

"Care to clue me in because I don't know the topic we're discussing." Oh, but he did. Jarrett recognized the knowing look and scolding tone. Bast was a very smart man and he likely knew exactly where Jarrett's mind had jumped.

That's what happened when you shared a friendship and business relationship with someone who'd known you for a decade. One of the negatives people cited about him was his refusal to let anyone get close. He had with Bast and now this happened. No hiding.

"Stop pretending to be a dumb street kid." Bast turned his pen end-over-end against the yellow legal pad in front of him.

"Excuse me?"

"You're thinking to take some of that information we held back as leverage to save you and use it to flush out the person who put a hit on Spectrum."

Jarrett didn't bother to deny the plan. It had barely taken root but it was there and growing in his mind. It made sense and it might be the only way. "I've got to end this before Elijah does something that gets us all in trouble."

"Then cut him loose." Bast drew a line through something on his written list.

That sounded good, smart even, but there were other considerations. Elijah knew too much. Then there was the part where Jarrett had promised to help. He wasn't the type to abandon that. And he couldn't even think about what it would do to Wade if something happened to Elijah. Any way you looked at it, the guy was a pain in the ass, but he'd been useful and Jarrett owed him.

"How do I do that exactly?" Jarrett asked.

"I don't want to know how you handle these things, or once did, but you know people. Make it happen."

"Thanks for the vote of confidence in my legitimacy."

"I believe you're the one who referred to the concept as plausible deniability." Bast dropped the pen. "More to the point, you can't save everyone."

Jarrett stood up and walked to the side of the table opposite Bast. He didn't need to stall or analyze his priorities. He knew the answer. "Then I save Becca and Wade."

"I thought that might be your answer."

Jarrett recognized the tone. It carried a hint of "you're fucking up here," and Jarrett had been catching it from Wade and Bast ever since he let Becca back inside the building. "But you disagree with it. With Becca being one of my choices."

"I did."

"And now?"

Bast smiled. "Seeing her pull a gun on Elijah made me like her a lot more."

Not the answer Jarrett expected, but he'd take it. "No kidding."

"So, we agree. We're a no-go on turning over more files." Bast slipped two off Jarrett's pile. "We're done with the idea of playing your last card. We'll come up with something else and figure out a way to diffuse Elijah and make him play nice with Becca."

Jarrett slapped a hand against the folders before Bast could tuck them under his notebook. "Not exactly."

"Jarrett, come on."

"Put the pitch together using my plan with the information. We'll see how it would work and what it would cost me."

Bast sat back in his chair. "Clearly, we're having a communication problem."

"Becca walks away from this. That's my bottom line." Until he said the words, Jarrett didn't know they were true. He could take anything but losing her. She didn't have to stay with him or live in his condo, but he needed to know she was out there somewhere and safe.

"I'm so glad we had this talk." Bast shuffled the rest of his files and grabbed his briefcase from under the table. "I just love when I earn my fee."

"It's going to work out."

Bast froze as his head lifted. "Really, because I notice you forgot an important name on your list of people to protect. The one person who should be at the very top."

"You're fine. No one is coming after you." Jarrett didn't even entertain the possibility that it couldn't be true. "You have the protection of privilege, which I won't waive, and—"

"I meant you, dumbass."

"I'll be fine." Jarrett had no idea if that was true or if he even cared any more, but the fact his safety mattered to Bast meant something.

"You put it all on the table. Offer up names of businessmen and congressmen who know about the China military deal, the ones you held back, along with information on other brewing international political disasters and whatever other pieces you've discovered since we last talked about this. And what keeps any of those you name from making you a target?"

Probably nothing but Jarrett knew it was the chance he had to take. Maybe he always knew it would end this way. Otherwise, he would have locked the door and refused to let Becca in. But once he opened the door, he made a commitment. He'd honor it. Because that's what idiot men did when they fell in love. They got stupid and careless.

"I've collected other intel on other subjects," he said, because asking about updating his will would only piss Bast off.

"And how exactly do you plan to live long enough to use it? You've got me and Wade, but I don't know how to stop a bullet."

"Stay out of the firing line."

"Then who is going to step up for you?"

Jarrett's mind went back to the conference room scene. He had spent his entire life wondering about the answer to that question. Not his useless mother or the grandmother who gave up on him after a month and one broken window. Not the series of foster homes or the supposedly well-meaning judge who threatened to send him to juvie to "teach him some manners" after he ran away the second time.

Bast and Wade, yes. Jarrett appreciated their loyalty and didn't take it for granted, but he'd never let it come to that. And now he knew the one other person who would save him without hesitating— Becca. "I have to get lucky, I guess."

"You have a lot of that?" Bast shook his head. "Because I haven't seen it."

"I have to get lucky sometime." And Jarrett really wanted that time to be now.

"That's the kind of answer that makes me put the legal team on standby."

Leave it to Bast to inject a heavy dose of reality. "That's not very comforting."

"I didn't mean for it to be."

TWENTY-ONE

Wade stood in the shower. He didn't turn the water on. He stood there naked, letting the air conditioner blow over him and feeling the cool push of air prickle his skin. He should move, do something, but his muscles locked up and his brain refused to reboot.

When Elijah had pulled the gun, Wade went blank. He should have tackled Eli or threw the knife by his ankle. Even taken out his own gun and used it. But Becca beat him to it. She grabbed his gun and didn't hesitate to defend Jarrett.

Wade knew he'd have to somehow explain to the man who changed his life and had been a friend for years why he froze instead of stepping in to save him. Why, when the moment of truth arrived and every second mattered, he sided with his lover of a month rather than the man he'd always depended on.

Wade slapped a hand against the tile wall. When he heard Elijah call out, Wade turned on the water, letting the lukewarm spray wash over him.

He fucking felt nothing.

Balancing his hands against the wall, he leaned in with his forehead against the cold blocks as the water rushed over his back and into his hair. He closed his eyes to avoid the sting of water as it ran off him and down his face.

He blew out an exhale of relief when Elijah's voice faded away. For a second the only sound was the ping of water against the stone shower floor.

Metal rings screeched along the rod as the curtain pulled open. The few seconds of peace shattered.

Elijah stood there with a painful bleakness in his expression. "Did you hear me call for you?"

"I just need a minute." Wade didn't bother to yell over the pounding water.

Elijah didn't move except to frown. "What's wrong with you?"

He could not be that fucking clueless. Wade turned his head and stared at the man who played with his brain and emotionally punched him in the nuts at every turn. "Are you kidding?"

"Come out and we'll talk."

Since that usually consisted of Elijah yelling and stomping around, Wade took a pass. "I said I need a minute."

"And I need you."

Wade finally focused on Elijah. The water ran over his cheek and into his mouth, and Wade had to spit it out before standing up. "Since when?"

"How can you ask me that?"

Yeah, fucking clueless. "Experience."

"Since the day I met you."

The right words but piss-poor timing. "Don't do this now, Eli."

Instead of listening, he stripped his shirt off and stepped into the shower. His arms wrapped around Wade's bare body from behind. Jeans scraped against Wade's ass as a hand traveled down to his cock.

"Talk to me." Eli said as he kissed Wade's shoulder and ran his hand up and down Wade's length.

He closed his eyes, trying to block out the sensations bombarding him. Eli's smell and touch. The friction of body against body.

Space. He had to have space. "I need—"

"Me." Eli bit down on Wade's neck then licked the spot he nipped. "Let me touch you."

"Why?"

"I want you."

Three little words and they tripped right to Wade's chest. Hammered into him and burrowed deep. "Today sucked."

"I lost it."

It was the closest Eli had ever come to taking responsibility for anything. Wade tried to view the rough comment as progress. "You tried to shoot Jarrett."

One step closer and Wade would have reacted. In his head he knew that.

"I wouldn't have done it."

Wade wanted to believe that. "Seemed like it."

For his own self-protection he should walk away from this man—hell, run—and not give a shit. But he knew that wasn't going to happen. Even after only a short time, losing Eli was going to rip him up. Wade understood it. Felt the reality vibrate to his soul when Becca pulled the gun and had every intention of killing Eli on the spot.

Eli's mouth traveled over Wade's ear. "Let me fuck you. Please." His whisper carried over the sound of rushing water.

God, he was pleading now.

But Wade wanted it, too. He could deny it, but why bother. And why hold back? If he had Eli for a day or a week, it didn't matter. Somehow it would be enough.

Not trusting his throat to form the words, Wade nodded. He turned around, thinking to shut off the cooling water and head for the bed. "Let's go—"

"Here." Eli took Wade's face in his hands and kissed him. Their mouths met under the spray in a rough smash of lips and teeth.

There was nothing sweet or lingering. This kiss burned with a white-hot need. Their mouths moved. Their tongues battled. Water hit them straight on, blinding Wade and throwing off his balance. But he kept kissing Elijah.

In the blur, Elijah took Wade's hand and carried it to the zipper of his fly. "You do this to me."

Wade looked down. Without thinking, his hands worked on Elijah's belt and his fingers found the zipper tab. "You're killing me."

Elijah moved to Wade's neck, kissing and sucking until he shivered. He didn't know if the tremors came from the cold or the weight of Elijah's cock in his hand.

Elijah whispered against Wade's lips. "Then I'll heal you."

He closed his eyes, willing to believe, but only one phrase moved through his mind—*unless Eli broke him first.*

Becca fell against Jarrett's chest limp and exhausted. Her breathing stammered as she buried her face in his neck. The rapid thump of his pulse against her lips made her smile. He was so virile and alive. But, damn, she wanted to strangle him.

She'd demanded an explanation the second they stepped inside the condo. He picked her up and didn't stop until he was lodged inside her on the couch. With the frantic sex over, she could concentrate on weaseling some information out of him. After all, she pretty much had him trapped under her, inside of her.

She put her palms against the couch cushion on either side of his head and pushed up to stare at him. "You should feel free to explain."

"Well, we got here when you straddled my legs and rode—"

"Not that." Her fingers crossed his lips. "I am well aware how I landed in this position."

He had the nerve to smile around her hand. "It's one of my favorites."

The sexy playful side of Jarrett made her heart drop. He threw her a wicked smile and all she wanted was to jump on top of him all over again. It was his superpower. The commanding side of him made her hot. The adorable side of him made her swoon. And she was not the swooning type.

It took a lot of willpower not to get sucked in this time. "Jarrett, stop stalling."

"The sight of you over me is the only thing on my mind right now. Trust me." He put his hands on her hips and pulled her tighter against his body. "I'm thinking we could go another round. I'm in the right place."

Even now she could feel him swelling inside her. She had no idea how that was possible so soon. "I thought you needed time to recover."

"Never with you."

"Flattering." Like, toe-curling so. "But it's still not going to work to avoid this conversation."

She glared at him when he opened his mouth again. He clamped it shut, but not before giving her one of those "you're killing me here" sighs men did when they wanted sex right that second.

He brushed her hair over her shoulder and let his hand drift over her chest, palming the top of her breast. "He helped me get out from under the criminal charges."

There was no way they were talking about the same "he" here. "Elijah did that?"

"Shocked me, too."

Shock didn't even cover it. She thought back to all the arguments with Elijah while they worked together. The practical, no-nonsense way he handled tough situations turned out to be a benefit in the field, but he had a tendency to let his emotions take over. He pretended to be an automaton but actually struggled with his anger and many times failed. There were times when adjustments had to be made and getting him to pivot took a crowbar and hours of arguing. She admired how he'd turned his body and mind into powerful weapons, but the guy exhausted her.

"How?" she asked.

"Elijah handed over an internal memo detailing my surveillance and the call for my removal if I failed to comply. Me, a U.S. citizen who hadn't committed any crime except having the information the CIA wanted."

The news had her head whipping back. She grabbed for Jarrett's hands and pinned them against her chest.

"I never saw that." She willed him to believe her.

He smiled as his thumb flicked against the underside of her chin. "Your name wasn't on it. His wasn't either. There wasn't any way to identify the receiver and sender from the document."

"Where did he get it?"

"Swiped it from Todd, but who knows where he got it."

"Dangerous." But typical of Eli. He tended to fly off on emotion and take risks.

"Which was part of the reason I gave him a chance. Since I wasn't sure if I could trust you, and since I made a promise to him, I kept you two apart." That thumb found its way to her bottom lip. "And he can't see inside my condo or my office downstairs, so no worries there."

She remembered the perp walk Jarrett subjected her to and winced. But that is not where her mind focused. She realized he was sharing it all now, without coaxing or yelling. The comment about distrust almost sounded past-tense.

The dread that hovered just outside her vision ever since she lost her apartment floated away. But that took a momentary backseat to the Eli information. "Someone wanted you dead eight months ago."

"Seems like it, but it's not good practice for the CIA to be on U.S. soil bothering U.S. citizens and targeting them for death, so what Elijah did made a difference. He provided the final piece and gave me leverage."

"How?"

"Bast quoted the memo and made it clear it would be released to the public, along with the electronic footprints to trace it back to internal CIA communication, if anything happened to me."

She still couldn't wrap her head around the idea of the memo or Eli's quick reaction in grabbing it. Those things, the kind of orders that should never be documented, tended to get shredded as soon as they were issued. "Weird."

Jarrett laughed. "You don't think the CIA does shit like that?"

"Please, I'm not stupid. No, I mean Eli. He's not exactly the 'help others' type."

"Which has me worried." Jarrett dipped his head and placed a kiss in the space between her breasts.

She had trouble concentrating, especially when his mouth kept going and his tongue licked over her nipple. "You're afraid he'll double-cross you?"

"Not at all."

"Really?"

"Worse, I'm convinced he's going to mess up Wade."

"Isn't Wade an expert shot? I actually thought he was going to get the jump on me today." She tried to hold on to the words, but that hot mouth made her dizzy. "Honestly, the guy can be scary. I'm thinking Wade versus Elijah is a pretty fair fight."

"I mean emotionally."

With her hand under his chin she lifted Jarrett's head. "What are you talking about?"

Turning, he held her wrist with two fingers and kissed his way down her inner arm. "You couldn't tell? They're sleeping together. Have been almost from the very beginning."

"*What?*" She tore her hand out of Jarrett's palm and sat back. The move had them both groaning.

"Damn, woman. Much more of that and I'll go blind."

Temporarily distracted by the pulsing inside her, she chuckled at their ludicrous attempts to hold a conversation as his cock sparked back to life inside her. "I thought using your own hand did that."

"That's a nasty rumor started by people who don't appreciate the benefits of masturbation. I am not one of those people."

She fought for focus for just a few more seconds. This was too important to ignore. "Back to Eli."

Jarrett's head tipped to the side. "You didn't know he was gay?"

"I don't think he is." Her mind bounced from her sex life to Eli's. Not a place she really spent much time. "I mean, I kind of think of him as being very sexual, in general."

Jarrett pulled back a bit and gave her a look of confusion mixed with amusement. "I have no idea what that means."

"I never knew him to date. He slept with people on assignments, men and women. He didn't really show a preference."

Jarrett's smiled faded. "Like you?"

The words carried a slap. He kept them low and even, without the obvious touch of judgment. Still, they stung against her skin. At the beginning she looked at that aspect of her job as a necessary evil and tricked her mind into enjoying the control over men she didn't know. But with time the shine dulled and left her with a hollow emptiness.

Until Jarrett.

"I slept with men only and nowhere near as often as you seem to assume."

His fingertips traced the line of her neck to her collarbone. "I don't want to know."

"But you care."

He peeked up at her. "I actually don't. Not like you think. I understand sex as a weapon and part of a job. I don't judge those choices."

She searched his face for any sign of a verbal punch to come. "Doesn't matter because I'd never do it again."

"Do you get a choice in your job?"

She continued to try to read his emotions, but his face stayed blank. "Since my employer wiped out my bank accounts, put me on a hit list and is even now trying to frame me for murder, I'm not really inclined to follow protocol."

"Ah, yes. In that case, your position sounds reasonable."

She wanted him to yell and demand she never go back. Something other than sit there wallowing in calm and staring as his hands wandered over her.

"Besides, I hate that part of the game and I'm not going back to it," she said.

"Okay."

The same heart that thundered for him shriveled at his flat tone. "You don't believe me."

He kissed her neck right where her pulse kicked and thumped. "I do."

"I . . . Are you—"

A hand slipped to the back of her neck. "I said I believe you."

He treated her to a long, lazy kiss. Desire spiraled inside her.

After seconds ticked by he broke the kiss and leaned his forehead against hers. "Understood?"

She nodded. It took another minute for her to clear the shake out of her voice. "What if we never figure this out or we do and it doesn't matter because my name stays on the hit list?"

"We'll resolve this."

"I'm asking what if we don't."

"Becca, trust me." His hands smoothed over her back as he talked.

"I can't stay here forever." She regretted the words as soon as they were out. She winced waiting for him to agree.

"I'll keep you safe."

"I'm not sure we're saying the same thing." But relief flowed through her that he hadn't pulled away or set up a barrier between them. Like he used to do months ago, he caressed and calmed, making her feel safe. She kissed him in silent thank-you. When she lifted her head again, his body followed hers and he kept her close against him.

"We've had enough talking for one day."

His fingers skimmed down her stomach until he reached her entrance. His cock filled her, and he now rubbed her wetness where their bodies met.

"Avoiding a serious conversation. That's very guyish of you." A bunch of babble slipped through her brain after that. She stopped talking out of fear of saying the nonsense out loud.

"Maybe I'd rather touch you." That finger dipped deeper, stretching her. "Like this."

Air caught in her throat. "Thought you needed recovery time."

"I'm sure you can help me out."

She shifted to find a better position and her breast brushed his cheek. The second time it happened, he turned his head and pulled her into his mouth. His tongue flicked over her nipple as his hand picked up its tempo over her clit.

The joint caress had her hips rising and falling. Her knees dug into the couch cushion. The friction of his cock over her swollen sensitized flesh made her gasp. They careened right toward another orgasm and she didn't stop them or slow down. If anything, her pace increased as his fingers dug into her hips.

After letting her lead the tempo, he finally took over. His hips rose to meet her presses. He thrust and she took him in deep. The combination sent her head swimming.

She threw her head back and his mouth went wild against her skin. He kissed her breasts and her throat. With every touch of his lips she pushed down harder, wanting all of him to fill her.

When the orgasm hit her, it swamped her. Her body tensed and her toes pointed hard behind her. She locked her arms as her body bucked. Then her muscles weakened and she didn't think she could hold her own weight. It wasn't until he slid down on the cushions, angling in ever deeper, that she heard his ragged breathing.

She wanted to tighten against him, concentrate and make him lose his mind like he did to her, but her body's instincts and drive for completion took over. She closed her eyes and rode him hard. His cock twitched and his hips pumped even faster. She felt every inch of him. Loved the way he swelled until she didn't think her body could stretch anymore.

Their breathing and shifting, the creak of the couch, the grumble of a moan deep in his chest—every sound combined in her head until her body exploded. Through cloudy vision, she watched him. The muscles in his neck strained and his moan turned into a sharp shout.

Then, for the second time in an hour, she fell over him. Her body draped across his and his staccato breathing echoed in her ears. After the first round, the end came swift but his hips still pressed against her in the aftermath.

She didn't try to hide her shortness of breath. "Now *I* need time to recover."

One of his hands rested against her lower back. The other lay open, palm up on the couch beside him. "I think my heart stopped."

Seemed liked quite the compliment to her. "You're welcome."

TWENTY-TWO

Natalie walked into the club the next morning wearing a black pantsuit reminiscent of every movie version of an FBI character Jarrett had ever seen. Wade escorted her to the main room, a few feet from the bar, then stood behind her when she stopped at the doorway to the bar.

She surveyed the room before glancing over her shoulder. "I can walk the rest of the way by myself."

He didn't even look at her. "I don't take my orders from you."

The verbal slams and constant poking. Jarrett smiled at their fighting but hid it behind his drinking glass. He doubted either of them would appreciate his amusement, but some things never changed. These two taking shots at each other was one of them.

Jarrett put the glass down on the bar and rested his palms against the edge. "We're okay, Wade."

His second-in-command frowned but obeyed. Took his time leaving and Jarrett didn't say a word until he was gone.

Natalie wasn't quite so patient. "Your time is up. Three days, I even gave you a few extra hours."

And as expected, no one broke through the club's front door. Despite ratcheting up security and keeping Bast on speed dial, all was fine. For now. "Should I say thank you?"

"You should have given Becca to me before now."

"I'm continuing to ignore that nonsense."

"That's a poor decision. You should—"

"You might want to stop using the word 'should' since I stop listening when you do."

"You continue to think you're in charge."

No way was he listening to that again. "Now you're wasting my time."

Natalie sighed. "In that case I'm here as requested. What do you want?"

"As always, it's good to see you, Natalie." He waved her into the room. "What can I get you to drink?"

"Nothing."

Smart woman. Only an idiot lost control to liquor outside of the privacy of his house, and even then. But it happened to many people in this town. His business depended on that simple fact. Men ruled by liquor tended to spend too much and talked more.

She walked in and stood across from him, matching her pose to his. "You seem to forget I don't work for you."

"And I don't work for you." Best to make that clear from the start.

"Debatable."

He felt a kick of reluctant admiration for her. She was not one to flinch. "I'm not going to take up a lot of your time."

"Too late."

But there was a part of her that reminded him of Elijah. Something about the undercover agent type. They launched verbal volleys, took no shit and bitched about everything that didn't go their way. Then there was the part where they could kill you. Not a great combination.

Rather than waste time and tiptoe around, since that wasn't his style anyway, Jarrett dove right in. "Why is Todd still on the CIA payroll?"

"That's why I'm here? Do I look like the human resources department?"

He swished the water around in his glass and listened to the ice cubes jingle. "Skip the drama and answer the question."

For a second she looked as if she were going to turn around and leave, but she sat on the barstool. "Don't dig into internal CIA business. That can only end badly for you."

"That's not an answer."

This was usually the point where she started rattling off her credentials. The list of threats came right after. He stiffened, waiting for it.

Her gaze moved over his face before making eye contact again. "Why do you care?"

He couldn't tell what she was thinking. Couldn't read a single expression. He guessed she was sizing him up, but he had no idea what she decided.

He pulled a clean glass from under the bar and set it in front of her. "Because someone ordered the hit on the Spectrum agents."

"We've been through that. Becca."

"No."

"You sound pretty sure." Natalie pointed at the empty glass and nearby water bottle until he poured a drink. "I thought you didn't care about Becca or know anything about what's happening with her now."

No way was he getting dragged into that fight. "I care about being roped into someone else's mess, so I've been looking into the entire operation."

Natalie's glass stopped halfway to her mouth. "Don't."

Now that was more like the response he expected. Direct and to the point. "Something to hide?"

"You insist you have a right to know matters of national security. Being nosy here will get you arrested."

"You tried that already and failed."

She drained the glass in one swallow. "You are alive and free because we decided to allow that to happen. And we can revoke that decision at any time, without warning. You may want to remember that."

"More threats against innocent American citizens, Natalie? I wonder what the public would think."

She smiled. "Since when are you innocent?"

"You make it difficult to want to deal with you."

"Are we negotiating something?"

The word choice was careful. Natalie didn't just throw terms around. She analyzed and assessed. He'd called her here and she came without argument. That meant she knew this was big.

He gave her a peek at his cards. "A disappearance."

"Becca?"

Jarrett shook his head. "We're not talking about her."

"Then explain."

Everything rode on the next few minutes. On piquing Natalie's interest and getting her mind spinning. Jarrett depended on her shark instincts. He didn't trust people in government and pretty much despised anyone related to the CIA, but he believed he could count on *who* she was—someone who deserved to manage and delegate but ran into a wall of less intelligent good old boys.

It could turn out that she needed him as much as he needed her. Or she could be the CIA official who fucked everything up and called for the killings. If so, he was a dead man.

Jarrett hoped his gut read this one right. "I have information that could be vital to you."

"Hand it over and I'll decide."

"Because I'm that fucking dumb."

"What are you looking for?" She tapped her fingernails against the side of her glass in a steady rhythm.

"Some help."

It almost killed him to say it. He'd learned long ago never to look to anyone else for anything, even food and a roof over his head. He trusted few and confided in two. With Becca, three. He never imagined eight months ago that he'd be thinking of adding her to that short list.

"I'm going to need more information if you plan to negotiate with me," Natalie said as the clicking against the glass continued.

"You're not getting any details now."

"Why?"

"That's not important."

She gave a laugh, hollow and tense and not even a little genuine. "How exactly am I supposed to help then? I don't even know what the hell we're talking about."

That would come later. She had to know what type of intelligence he could bring to her. He had to entice her and get her thinking. By the time she craved the information, she wouldn't balk at handing him what he needed. "In return, you get to be the agent who brings in names and dates on the China issue."

"The property."

Sounded like she was a step behind. For some reason, that surprised him. "The weapons."

Her hand flattened against the table. "You lost me. Explain."

"Spare me the bullshit."

"You understand that by telling me this, even hypothetically—"

"I haven't told you anything."

"—I can bring a team of agents in this building and tear it apart board by board? I can get warrants and install listening devices, to the extent I haven't already."

"You haven't." And he knew because he swept the place all the time. Wade had many uses. His tech aptitude and training in detection were just two.

"My people could say anything about you and we could make it stick."

The comment sounded like a threat but her tone suggested something else. Damn if she wasn't warning him. Jarrett hadn't seen that coming. Still, he decided to give her a harsh reminder. "Again, you tried that and failed."

"This is the kind of issue that allows us to put you somewhere, locked away and quiet, where Sebastian would never find you."

"What version of the Constitution are you reading exactly?" But her bosses could and they would, which is why Jarrett kept the leverage in the first place. Now he toyed with the idea of turning some of it over and that risk could cost him everything.

"This isn't a game." She rolled the glass between her palms. The heavy bottom thudded against the wooden bar.

"No, Natalie. It isn't."

"Tell me what you have." She sent the glass spinning.

He grabbed it before it slid off the edge of the bar. "First, we figure out what you can do for me."

Becca stared at Elijah across the second-floor conference room. Jarrett wandered off downstairs to work. Wade had disappeared. This might be the best time to get some answers. Private ones.

She leaned back and eyed the man she once trusted to keep her alive. "Of all the places and all the safe houses, you came here."

Eli didn't look up from the pages of redacted files in front of him. "So did you."

"But I had less to lose."

"How do you figure?"

"I had a relationship with Jarrett once. There's a connection here for me." Talk about a loose definition of the word "connection."

Eli's head slowly rose. He pinned her with a furious stare that matched the red stain of anger on his cheeks. "You fucked him as part of a job then screwed him over. I'm not sure you had the high road here."

The harsh words hit their target. She felt the blows land but refused to flinch. Pushing her foot against the floor, she continued to rock her chair back and forth as if she didn't care about the barbs and how perfectly they landed. "At least I didn't have him arrested."

"You're the one who asked Todd to move up the timetable on the operation that led to Jarrett's arrest."

Seemed everyone had heard that story. Shame it was only partially true. "No."

"I was there, Becca. You can fool Jarrett long enough to get his pants off, but I remember."

"I told Todd to pull the plug on the operation and move on." Using all her hours of training, she forced her body to stay still. No fidgeting. No useless hand movements or twisting of hands. That all showed weakness and Eli would move in for the kill. "Something you should have done as senior officer in the field."

"There's no microphone in here. At least I don't know about it if there is." Elijah pointed around the room. Even yelled the last part of the sentence to the far corner. "No need to lie to impress your bed buddy."

And this was why people hated Elijah. He was relentless. He found a weakness, figured out the words that would hurt the most, and then poked until you broke. The win meant everything to him.

She understood it. Didn't mean she liked it. "I see getting shot and almost killed hasn't stopped you from being an asshole."

He rapped his fist against the table. "I'm a survivor."

"You can throw around whatever name you want."

A strange calm washed over him. The tension left his body and he slumped in his chair. "How about I throw one out for you."

He swung right back to the same topic. Approached it from a different angle, but was ready to cut her down with a verbal assault that would have her doubting.

If he expected her to sit back and take it—to weep—he had the wrong woman. She did some poking of her own. "Right, because I'm the only one of us sleeping with someone in the building. What's the endgame with that, Eli?"

"That's none of your fucking business." Except for the words he chose, he sounded bored.

"No double standard there. I'm the whore but you're innocent when you use Wade and sleep with him."

"It's nothing."

He said the words, but the slight break in eye contact told another story. They underwent the same training. She knew the signs. He had to know she'd push until he cracked.

"What does that mean?" she asked.

"I needed somewhere to go. This building made sense. Hell, I was bleeding right outside so crawling here was basically my one option. I had information and thought Jarrett and I could use each other."

"And Wade?"

"Wade was convenient."

That fit with Elijah's past practices. But it clashed with what she knew about Wade. He was gay. Didn't talk about it, but didn't hide it. She'd seen him with a man kind of steady right before she left. He wasn't the type she'd expect to welcome just anyone into his bed and life for an extended period of time. He was too private. Too careful. She guessed that stemmed from his difficult past.

"So, you're pretending to be gay?" She said it because she thought it was the only thing that made sense. Even then, just barely. "This is all some scheme to have a warm body—any body, male or female, whatever's handy—close while you wait out your potential death sentence?"

"Save the labels and your attempts at analyzing me."

She didn't know what to make of that nonanswer. Picking up a pen, she scribbled a circle in the blank spot at the top of the page. "Who are you lying to here, Wade or yourself?"

"No one. It's sex. It means nothing."

"Of course it means something."

"Bodies and getting off."

In the last few months he'd become even more detached from his humanity. When she waded through and figured out everything else, she'd try to get an answer to that, too. Until then she could work on his attitude so that he was at least tolerable to be around. "What's wrong with you?"

"Nothing."

"You're not very convincing."

He sat up, shifting to the front of his chair. "Not every roll on the sheets is a big deal. The sex I'm having now is fine, but it's about release and that's all. A body to satisfy me."

A blur moved behind Eli. The shadow grabbed her attention but she kept her focus on Eli, not wanting him to know there was someone else out there. She guessed Jarrett until she saw a flash of dark pants and bare arms sticking out from under a T-shirt.

A second later Wade stepped into the doorway. The grim line of his mouth and bleakness in his eyes were almost too much for her to witness.

She tried to steer the conversation somewhere else. Anywhere else. "Eli, I think you should—"

"No." Wade's rough words broke through her plea. "Let him talk."

All the blood drained from Eli's face. He stood as he turned. "Wade."

"I can leave." She rose to her feet as well, but what she wanted to do was close her eyes. The stark pain on Wade's face and shock on Eli's had her wishing she'd never engaged in this verbal battle. The moment struck her as too personal, too intimate for her to share.

And bullshit Eli wasn't involved with Wade. She recognized panic when she saw it and Eli was sporting a huge case of it right now.

"Don't move." Wade pointed at her but his gaze never left Eli's face. "You're fine where you are."

"I didn't know you were there." Each word sounded as if it were ripped right from Eli's gut.

"Obviously."

Eli shook his head. "It's not what you think."

"Sounded pretty fucking clear to me."

Tension pounded off of Eli. "No."

"The mindless release portion of your stay here is over." Wade brought his hand out from behind his back. "Move your things back into the crash pad."

For the first time, she noticed the gun. Looking at Wade's cold eyes, she didn't doubt he could use it, which was the last thing any of them needed. She also saw something else. Something that became clearer with every second. Through the layers of crushing pain radiating off Wade and the strain around Eli's mouth there was a connection. Eli might claim they only had sex, but whatever flew back and forth between these two went deeper than that.

"I'm not sure this is the best time for this." She preferred any-time she was not in the room.

"It's the only time." Wade tapped the gun's barrel against the outside of his thigh as he continued to stare at Elijah. "You have an hour. After that, I ask Jarrett to kick you out."

Wade's pain pulled at her. It filled the room until she choked on it. "I'm sorry."

He shook his head but didn't face her. "Don't be. There's no reason for us to pretend. Not really my style anyway."

After moments of stiff silence, Eli reacted. He shifted his weight and talked with his hands. "We were arguing. I got wound up."

"Let me guess, it was nothing."

"You need to listen to me." Eli reached a hand out to Wade. He shrugged it away. Didn't even blink. "Fifty-nine minutes."

Wade left the conference room in a stupor. Somehow his legs carried him downstairs. He didn't remember entering elevator codes or swiping his security card. Music thumped through the wall from the bar and a few members of the cooking staff wandered by. He blocked it all.

Disappointment and anger hit him in waves. He couldn't hold on to an emotion long enough to dwell on it. By the time he stood outside of Jarrett's office door, all he wanted to do was hand in his resignation and get out.

Forgoing his usual knock, he slid the card and walked in. "Jarrett."

"Did you get the financial reports on—" Jarrett glanced up and his eyes narrowed. "What happened?"

So much for thinking he could hide the bullshit bombarding his brain. Then again, Jarrett always knew. Wade realized early this man could read him. "Nothing."

"Not believable."

Wade dropped into the chair just inside the door. Didn't even make it over to Jarrett's desk. "I'm just going to hang out here a second." He leaned his head against the wall and closed his eyes.

Jarrett being Jarrett, he didn't cross-examine or insist on answers. He waited the moment out.

When the quiet stretched on, Wade filled it. "Eli is moving back into the crash pad."

"Any reason why?"

Because the man was a raging asshole who deserved to be alone. "It's time."

"How about I throw him off the building?"

The anger in Jarrett's voice had Wade opening his eyes. "Not tall enough to do enough damage."

Jarrett shrugged. "There are other buildings in D.C."

In the olden days, Jarrett would have meant they should consider the strategy. If Wade needed something handled, Jarrett would have listened and formulated a plan. He'd always been a businessman, but he never balked at getting his hands dirty. That willingness built trust between them immediately. Wade knew Jarrett wouldn't hide and save himself, letting his employees shoulder the burden.

Best thing Wade ever did was try to move in on Jarrett's territory all those years ago. He'd been young and cocky, and Jarrett should have killed him. He groomed him instead. Also insisted years later they go legitimate and refused to leave Wade behind on the streets, which at the moment seemed like a fucking shame because there was an old-school way to deal with Eli. But Wade didn't do that shit anymore . . . and he'd never be able to take Eli out.

So, that meant stewing in silence and hoping the pressure pounding on his chest would go away. "It's fine. No big deal."

"Is it?" Jarrett's voice was soft, concerned.

If it had been anyone but Jarrett, Wade would have let the subject drop. He wasn't the sharing type. No point in having a private life if you shot your mouth off about it all the time. But if there were a person in the metro area who would understand the joint beatings of betrayal and frustration and need to kick the ass of the person who meant something the day before, it would be Jarrett.

"It never should have started." Wade leaned forward with his elbows balanced on his knees and stared at the floor. "There's sex and then there's the other stuff, and I couldn't keep them separate."

"It's not easy to do that when you're living together."

Wade glanced up. "Are we talking about me or about you?"

"Just making conversation."

He held out his hands. Turned them over and stared at the nicks and old scars on the palms then the backs. "You don't need advice from me, but I'm going to give it to you anyway."

"I'm ready."

Which was good because Wade planned on saying it. "When you start out as one thing and try to change to another, the baggage from the past is still there."

Jarrett didn't move or cut off the conversation. He sat with his hands folded on the desk in front of him. "We overcame our pasts. It can be done."

"It's different when you're dragging someone else's baggage, too." And Elijah and Becca had tons of it. They carried crap from their pasts and their jobs. Now they were on the run and unsure of what would happen next. Death waited. All of that made them desperate, and desperate meant trust came hard.

Jarrett inhaled deep enough for his shoulders to move. "Go ahead and just say it."

Wade thought about putting this part off. He'd said it before but in shitty ways that made him sound like a dick. Now he'd say it with more respect because after stepping up to save Jarrett when she thought Eli would shoot him, she deserved some of that. "Let her go before her leaving shreds you."

"Too late." Jarrett rubbed his forehead.

Not a surprise, but still. "Shit."

"Yeah, I know. But we're talking about you and how I need to go upstairs and beat Elijah to death."

And Jarrett would probably land a few punches if Wade gave him the okay. "He's not worth it. Besides, I knew better."

"Amazing how that doesn't help, isn't it?"

Wade nodded. "Fucking right."

TWENTY-THREE

Jarrett headed up to the second floor to kick Eli out. Enough threats. This time it was happening. A punch to that smug face might do it.

The car came to a stop and Jarrett waited for the doors to open. The buzz of his phone stopped him from getting off and heading for Wade's condo door. Wade's text asked that he be the one to handle the situation. It was the one request with the power to stop Jarrett.

He swore under his breath as he thought about acting now and apologizing later. After replaying Wade's voice in his head, Jarrett turned toward the open conference room door instead of directly for Elijah. The all-out assault could wait. Jarrett would give Wade a chance and if he faltered, Jarrett would step in. He owed it to Wade to clean house.

Seeing Becca sitting there, right at the head of the long table, halted Jarrett's steps just outside the doorway. Hair in a ponytail and her usual tank top in place. This time a thin strip of a white bra peeked out from underneath.

She alternated between writing notes and typing on the computer. So serious. So dedicated to ferreting out the truth.

"You need to work on your undercover skills. I can hear you breathing." She didn't face him but a smile crossed her lips.

More than likely she knew he was on the same floor before the elevator opened. She didn't need cameras or an elaborate system of security cards that also tracked movements throughout the building. She had a sort of sense that told her things were about to happen or people were right behind her, which was part of what made her a good field agent. Also made her spooky as hell and hard to trick.

He took the seat to her right. "I wasn't trying to hide."

The smile faded as her gaze traveled over his face. She set the pen down. "You look awful."

"Thanks."

"I'm serious." Her eyes narrowed the longer she stared. "What's going on?"

Normally he'd shrug off the question and turn the conversation to something else. Something not about him or Wade or anything personal. But she had a right to know.

When she left here, she might throw in with Elijah and she needed a warning about what that would mean. Some days the guy acted like he lacked a conscience. "There's a problem in the building."

She nodded. "You talked to Wade."

Looked like, once again, she'd jumped ahead of him. Made him wonder if maybe she did plant a device in his office and live-streamed every conversation. Hard to do since she hadn't been on the main floor since her first day back in the building, but Becca was crafty.

"You did?" he asked, knowing the answer.

"I was there when Elijah gave the 'it's just sex' speech. He was talking to me and the message was loud and clear—Wade doesn't matter."

If possible, the truth of what happened was worse than Jarrett had imagined. A heated rage roared through him. Jarrett shoved back his chair and stood up, determined to do more than kick the asshole out. "I'm going to kill the bastard."

"Don't." Her hand landed on his arm. "From the look I saw on Wade's face, I think he might beat you to it. It's possible he needs to be the one to do it."

No matter how hard he tried to block it, Jarrett couldn't keep Wade's warning out of his head. Wade wasn't the only one walking a thin line.

"He's not in the position to do anything." Jarrett remembered Wade's blank expression. "Hell, right now he can't muster the energy to get out of the damn chair in my office."

"He wasn't detached. Eli meant something to him."

Jarrett blew out a long breath and sat back down. The chair creaked under the force of his grip on the armrests. "It was that way from day one."

"I didn't realize they were actually a couple."

Jarrett winced over the word. Instead of focusing on Wade, his mind flipped to his own living arrangements. He'd tried to make living with her mean nothing more than sex, but she threw out the word "couple" like it automatically applied to these types of situations.

He cleared his throat as he tried to clear every thought from his head. "I told you they were living together."

"I mean they were serious."

Jarrett turned around every word she uttered. Tried to make it fit into their situation and see how they could end up in a different place than Wade, but couldn't get there.

With his elbow on the armrest, Jarrett tapped his fingers against his temple. The thudding matched the boom of the headache inside. "Is that even possible with Eli?"

"You didn't see his face. He didn't expect Wade to overhear, and Wade's reaction in kicking him out stunned him. Honestly, I think Elijah was spewing and didn't mean most of the garbage he said, but I'm not sure he can un-ring that bell now."

Jarrett got a look at Wade downstairs, after the fact, and that was enough. Wade grew up poor and stole because that was the career path laid out by his father, taking other people's stuff. The upbringing made Wade tough, which Jarrett appreciated. It also made those rare times when Wade dropped the shield all the more excruciating to watch.

"I don't care if Eli went off or regrets his words or whatever. I've got Wade sitting in my office and . . ." The visual image popped back into Jarrett's head and the pain in his head shot down to his feet.

"What?"

"Nothing." But something.

Wade today. Jarrett wondered if he'd suffer the same fate tomorrow.

She reached across the table and put a hand over his. "Jarrett, don't shut me out."

He didn't move. "It's interesting, isn't it?"

"What are we talking about?"

He turned her hand over and traced a line down her palm. "How you try to make something work and you keep moving it around and shoving it on this side and ignoring how that side doesn't fit."

Her arm tensed. "Are we still talking about Eli and Wade?"

With a surge of willpower, he let go of her hand and sat back. "Sex is sex."

She didn't back off. If anything, she leaned in. "Jarrett, no."

"You don't give the orders. I do." He had to stand up, walk away. Sitting this close he could see deep into her eyes and smell her hair. If he let his mind wander for even a second, he'd replay the last few nights, her in his bed, everything back the way it was.

But everything had changed. Somehow her being there made him want to forget it all, the frustration, the seething anger, the heartbreaking disappointment. He'd been thinking about buying her a ring eight months ago, and she'd been meeting with her bosses about whether to keep him as an assignment.

He knew she'd been fed a line about the drugs. He got that now. Even understood how she tried to get Todd to call the whole thing off. He believed it all, but in the end the fact remained—when it came down to choosing between him and her job, he lost. He would always lose, just like Wade gambled and lost.

She might insist things had changed but he'd always be wondering when the day would come for her to make another stand and she'd pick someone else. Something else. A cause, a belief, a job.

The answer was simple. He needed to make the deal with Natalie. Save Becca because he fucking loved her and that's what a man did when he was dumb enough to fall in love with the one woman who could destroy him.

She'd go on. He'd rebuild. Probably move his living space out of the building. No way could he live up there after losing her a second time. There wasn't a choice and the clock kept ticking.

She dropped to her knees on the floor in front of him. Her hands skimmed up and down the top of his thighs. "Why are you acting like this? What happened downstairs?"

He clenched his back teeth together and kept his fingers wrapped around the armrests. "A dose of reality."

She sat back on her heels. "And now you've returned to being an ass."

"Returned? You made it clear before that I never stopped." He tried to swivel the chair so he could get out and step away from her.

She grabbed the armrests and held him steady. "You know who else does this type of crap?"

"I'm sure you're going to tell me."

"Eli."

At the comparison, Jarrett's heart hardened and his mind went blank. "Do not push me, Becca."

"What will you do?"

She made everything so fucking hard. Staying with her. Leaving her. No way would he physically hurt her, and she knew it, but this torture had to stop. The days of wanting her to pay had passed into oblivion along with his dreams of revenge. He didn't need any of that now that he understood her role.

"Just know that my goodwill only extends so far," he said when he couldn't think of a suitable threat.

"How far?" One hand brushed up the inside of his thighs.

Immediately, his cock jumped to life. He grabbed her hand, squeezing to make her stop. "What are you doing?"

She didn't pull away. "You have to ask that?"

Old habits died hard. She wanted something and used her body. He wanted to keep her in line and used sex. It was a sick cycle they couldn't seem to break when the tension rose.

"Know that if you go one inch farther it's just sex." He'd hold himself back like he had the first time in the guest room. Show her indifference and disdain in an attempt to make her believe she meant nothing.

"Maybe for you." Her fingers tightened against his thigh.

"No." He couldn't do it. The façade crumbled just looking at her. He scooted the chair back, rolling just a few inches away but enough to break her hold. "Stop."

Her hand fell to her lap. "You're saying no?"

"You're not that irresistible."

"And you're replaceable."

The verbal smack landed harder than he expected it could. "I'm sure I am."

She pushed to her feet and grabbed the laptop and notebook off the table. Her hands were constant movements as she made piles and loaded down her arms. When she spun around to face him again her skin had turned a chalky white. "When you're done being afraid and hiding behind old feuds and wasted anger, let me know."

He called up his last bit of fury, reaching for the one thing he fought to forgive and couldn't get there. "I went to jail because of you."

"Ever notice that's the one excuse you use when you don't have anything else?"

He hated that she spied his defenses and tried to rip those down, too. "I can give you a list of sins."

"I'll pass. Far as I can see, you're not offering anything I need."
She opened the door and walked out.

Just as he wanted her to.

Becca didn't exhale until the elevator doors closed in front
of her. The car sat there unmoving, waiting for her to enter a code.
She lifted a hand toward the keypad but tightened it into a fist when
the tremors shaking her body made standing still impossible.

Jarrett was running scared.

Something about the Wade and Eli situation had Jarrett stum-
bling. Reverting to his clipped voice commands and verbal bruising.
She accused him of being like Eli. Though they shared the same
instincts to strike out, Jarrett was different, but he had no trouble
hiding his decency under a thick layer of stubbornness and attitude.

In those moments when he dropped the barrier and let her in,
when he joked and even smiled once in a while, a sensation of pure
lightness moved through her. Buried under the gruffness and the
distrust beat something good. He wasn't perfect or even innocent,
but she'd never demanded either from him.

She messed up. She got lost in her pain. She'd lashed out and
hadn't stepped in to back him up. Hadn't saved him.

All the mistakes and missteps ran through her mind as she
stared at the keypad. Her fingers touched the number buttons. One
after the other, she entered the code for the third floor. By the time
she finished, exhaustion whipped through her.

She needed distance, so tonight she would stay in the guest
room. Say no to him for the first time. If he even tried to come in.

The elevator gave off a fine hum as it moved. The sound buzzed through her head and cleared away the cobwebs. She came to the club, or that's what she'd convinced herself. Really, she came for him to see if there was anything left since everything else in her life was gone. Now she knew the truth—she loved him and the feeling wasn't going away.

Tomorrow she'd figure out a way to convince him to stop pushing her away. The alternative was too bleak for her to lose this battle.

Wade walked into the quiet condo. He looked for signs of Elijah and spied them everywhere. His shoes by the couch. Paperwork on the kitchen counter. Looked like he wasn't going down without a fight.

Good thing Wade was in just the kind of shitty mood to give him one.

He walked to the bedroom because he somehow knew that's where he would find Eli. If the man was curled up in the sheets, waiting, Wade might have to call in Jarrett to keep from killing Elijah right there. He always resorted to sex and it always worked.

Except now.

Wade stepped into the doorway and glanced inside the room he let few people enter. Clearly he needed to tighten his standards even more.

Elijah sat on the edge of the bed in the jeans and T-shirt he wore earlier. When he looked, he stood. "Listen to me."

"You're down to thirteen minutes." The time had probably expired. Wade didn't even care anymore, so long as Eli got out.

He held up his hands. "Becca was meddling and I was trying to get her to shut up."

"Don't blame her for this one."

The excuse was too easy. Wade had used it to rationalize everything from Eli's declining mood to Jarrett's risk taking. Truth was, she stepped into the house and followed the rules and when Jarrett needed someone she stepped up. Wade wanted to hate her, but he owed her.

"Don't you see?" Eli pleading with his eyes and his voice. He talked with his hands and stepped in close. He used every weapon in his arsenal to make his argument. "She's the problem."

"For Jarrett." That much Wade had to admit. She walked in and Jarrett's common sense unraveled. It was one of the reasons Wade always looked at her with a skeptical eye. She was a danger to everything they'd ever worked for.

"She poisons everything," Eli said.

"Not between us. You did that." It actually set off an ache in Wade's stomach to say the simple word.

"No." Eli reached out.

Wade knocked his hand away. "Oh, that's right. There is no 'us,' there's just sex."

"It's more than that."

"Whatever it was, from now on I'll get it somewhere else." It felt good to say and see Eli's head snap back at the verbal blow. Carrying through with finding a warm body to fuck away Eli's memory was going to be a lot harder.

This time he made contact, put a palm right on Wade's chest. "Let me—"

Using both hands, Wade shoved Eli back before the caress could burn and confuse everything. "Do not fucking touch me."

"Wade, we can figure this out."

That was relationship talk, and Eli had made it clear they didn't have one of those.

Wade took another step back, out of touching range, and went to the closet. "I already did. You're leaving."

"Okay, look, I screwed up."

He could feel the heat of Eli's body right behind him and didn't turn around. "I'm guessing that's as close as I'll ever get to an apology from you."

"I'm trying to explain that I said the wrong thing at the wrong time, but this doesn't have to end."

Absolutely wrong. "It never should have started."

Before Eli could enter into a new argument Wade bent down and grabbed the khaki gym bag on the floor of his closet. Eli brought it but hadn't opened it in weeks. Wade threw it on the bed and shoved the edges open, unveiling the mostly empty inside.

Walking to the dresser, Wade yanked on the top drawer, nearly pulling the thing right out and sending it crashing to the floor. His vision faded and his mind flipped as the combined assault of Eli's closeness and pleading took their toll. Wade gathered up socks and shirts. He didn't know what belonged to whom, but he'd buy new. He'd rather dump it all than have Eli leave something behind.

Eli followed around after Wade, keeping up a steady stream of arguments and throwing clothes out of the bag as soon as Wade dumped them in. He finally came up for a breath. "Wade, look at me."

No fucking way. He shut it all down. His mind, his body. What kind of idiot fell for someone like Eli, and so fast. Desperate now, Wade balled up the sock pairs and threw them in the general direction of the bag.

Eli grabbed one in midair. "Okay, stop."

At the last minute, instead of slamming into him, Wade pivoted around him back to the closet. There had to be some sign of Eli in there, too. He'd throw out everything in the laundry basket, but he could take clothes off the hangers. "If you won't pack, I will."

"Forget all that." When Wade kept moving, Eli used his arm to sweep the bag off the bed. The move was dramatic and loud as the corner hit the alarm clock and sent it crashing to the floor with a crack.

Wade stood in the doorway to the closet, refusing to let any of this touch him. "Eleven minutes."

"Shut up with the goddamn countdown."

The more Eli yelled, the flatter Wade made his tone. "Elijah, you aren't getting this. You set the terms of what could happen between us. I'm saying no. Not interested."

Elijah dropped to the bed. "I was angry. Don't you think I have a right to be? Look at what's happening in my life right now."

Guilt. Another one of Eli's favorites. This time Wade wasn't buying that either. "None of that is about me."

"Becca said the wrong thing and I went off. It's that simple. My temper is not a surprise."

"It's one of the least attractive things about you." Wade could list so many flaws that he wondered what he ever saw in the guy. The second he thought it, he stumbled. He knew.

Eli believed the attraction came from sex. That was part of it, but there was something that drilled down so much deeper. In those quiet times when he would treat Wade to a random touch or stare at him with such longing. There was a part of this guy that wanted to be normal. Wade knew that to be true, but Eli fought it with the weighty strength of years of denial.

A strange calm washed over Elijah. "But there are things about me you find attractive."

Looked like they circled back to the seduction play. This time Wade shored up his resistance. "Not at the moment."

"Let me remind you." Eli's hand rested on the top of Wade's belt. His fingertips wandered lower.

Wade forced his body to remain still and his face to remain blank. "Move your hand."

"You're angry now, but—"

Wade stepped back and headed for the family room. "If you're not in the hall in one minute, I'm marching you to the street with a gun to your back. Your choice."

"You think with my training and experience I can't take a weapon from you?"

Not today. Not with the fury wrapping around him and squeezing him in its grip. "Try."

"You were a petty thief. I'm a goddamn agent."

There it was. Pushed into a corner, Elijah came out fighting. Wade recognized the defense mechanism. "You get one shot, then it's my turn and I won't fucking miss."

"Forget all that." Elijah sliced a hand through the air. "This, me leaving, this fight, it's all a mistake. You'll regret it."

Wade stared at the man he thought might one day mean something. "Mistake. Yeah, that's the conclusion I reached about us an hour ago."

"You're pissing me off."

Wade tapped his watch. "And you're out of time."

TWENTY-FOUR

The next morning Natalie sat in the chair across the desk from Jarrett. His head swam and his stomach grumbled from the combination of too much caffeine and no food. He didn't sleep for ten seconds the night before. Not that the cause was a big secret. Being alone in his bed while Becca slept down the hall did it. Fucked him up completely.

Natalie crossed one leg over the other as she glanced from Jarrett to Bast. "Are you ready to talk specifics?"

"Off the record and completely hypothetically." Bast set his briefcase on the floor but remained standing right next to Jarrett's chair. "This is definitely a conversation that never happened."

Natalie sighed. "If you insist."

"I do."

Ready to get to the basics, Jarrett jumped in. He didn't need to consult notes because the list was imprinted on his brain. He'd spent all evening mentally running through it. "Wade's record gets cleared and you leave him alone."

"Has he done something wrong?" Natalie brushed a piece of nonexistent lint off her dark skirt. "And here you've been insisting he's reformed."

Jarrett ignored the sarcasm because playing into it would mean sitting here for hours. And he was just too damn tired to engage. "Becca gets out and you leave her alone. She doesn't die in a home invasion or get hit by a car or taken out in a random hunting accident. She walks away and you pretend you've never heard of her."

He counted off only a few of the possibilities. Those were enough to make his brain shut off.

Natalie's smile fell. "I thought you didn't know where she was."

Apparently Natalie still wanted to play some games. Fine, he would comply. "You're smarter than that."

"Becca convinced you to do this for her?" Natalie's gaze went to Bast then back to Jarrett. "That must be some amazing sex."

He gritted his teeth because something about this woman always made Jarrett grit his teeth. He admired her, but he didn't like her. Most of the time he wanted her to either get out or shut up. Both applied now.

"She doesn't know," Jarrett said.

"Excuse me?"

"You heard him." Bast's deep voice boomed through the room.

"You're making the decision for her without asking her? How very 1950s of you."

Okay, that was fair, but Jarrett ignored it. "Can we keep going?"

"What if she wants to come back to the CIA?" Natalie acted like that would be everyone's choice. As if there were no other place to work.

"That's not going to happen." Because Jarrett was making it a condition of the deal.

They could send Becca out on medical leave, lie to her, he didn't care. She stayed out. He wasn't saving her so someone at the agency could turn around and take her out as a precaution or just for fun. Who knew what went through their collective minds when it came to secrecy.

"We spent a lot of money training her, preparing her for operations. I'd hate to see that go to waste. I doubt she's qualified for much else anyway," Natalie said, enjoying this far too much.

Bast clearly didn't share her enthusiasm. He finally moved. Unbuttoned his suit jacket, but it was enough to get Natalie's attention. "The provision is clear. Move on."

"I still don't understand why you gentlemen think she doesn't get a say. She's a grown-up." Natalie's eyes narrowed. "And how is she supposed to make a living?"

"I'll take care of that." Jarrett thought that should end the argument.

"You're going to give your girlfriend money to go away?"

He grabbed for his pen and smoothed it between his fingers. Anything to keep him from firing off like a rocket.

The woman was damn smart. A characteristic she shared with Becca. Jarrett thought for not the first time that the CIA would be wise to recognize the goldmine it had with the women working there. Comparing them to Elijah, Jarrett determined the women were definitely more stable.

"Again, not your concern." Out of the corner of his eye, Jarrett saw Bast shift his weight. It was small and barely perceptible, but Jarrett was looking for a sign from him. He'd hear about the account later, but for now Bast stayed quiet.

Natalie held up a hand. "Let me guess, it's going to be some mysterious account you tell her is for compensation for her CIA days."

"No, you'll tell her. Your job is to present it to her. Where it comes from, is my job and confidential." He'd set up the account and had the paperwork ready for Becca's signature. All Natalie had to do was get Becca to sign it. The funding would be private. Becca would never be able to trace it back to him.

"Oh, really?"

"You will help her disappear and make sure any record that could trace to her also disappears." He cleared his throat. "She is your main concern."

Natalie turned to Bast. "You're letting this happen?"

"To borrow your words, Jarrett is a grown man," Bast said in his usual even voice.

"He's acting like a lovesick schoolboy."

Since Jarrett could guess what was going through Bast's mind and knew he agreed with Natalie on this point, Jarrett cut off the conversation. "I'm taking Becca out of my life."

Natalie nodded. "And we both know why."

Jarrett refused to believe Natalie knew his true feelings. He prided himself on his control. No way was he that transparent to people who barely knew him.

Bast cleared his throat. "On to the next point."

"You stay away from my club, my employees and Bast." Jarrett ignored Bast standing right next to him and the tension choking the room. "Nonnegotiable."

Natalie made a face. "How are you going to make that enforceable?"

"That's my job," Bast pointed out.

"A bit self-serving, isn't it?" She looked back and forth between the men. When both stayed quiet, she nodded. "Fine, but you are taking away all my fun."

Only Natalie would see it that way. The whole thing made something deep and dark twist in Jarrett's gut. "You get the information you want. All the risk is mine."

"How so?"

"Eventually someone will wake up and trace this all back to me." Jarrett twisted the pen cap hard enough to flip it off.

Natalie's gaze bounced to his hands then back to his face. "Which is why you want Becca gone and Wade protected."

"If you do your job, this will stay quiet and that won't be a worry."

"But that's not his biggest concern. Is it, Jarrett?" Natalie leaned forward. "You think I'll come after you, or someone at the CIA will."

This was Jarrett's last card and he played it. "In addition to the China material, I'll be handing over some documents, just to you, about Spectrum and the removal of the team."

"I doubt you have more than I do."

Jarrett glanced at Bast, who nodded. "Which reminds me, there is one other person you need to protect."

Natalie made a face that telegraphed how unimportant she found this topic to be. "Who?"

"Elijah Sterling."

Her cool demeanor slipped for a second. Her foot stopped swinging and the corners of her mouth dipped down. As soon as the change came it left again. "Did you miss the news? He's dead."

"I guess you don't know more than I do."

Bast smiled. "Checkmate."

"Interesting." Natalie blew out a long breath. "I notice you're not asking for protection for yourself."

"You will protect him," Bast said. "Count on that."

"But that's the problem." Jarrett knew Bast hated this part.

Jarrett wasn't a fan either because he'd never been the martyr type. He didn't change his life around just to lose it in some faked accident or tragedy. "Natalie here can't promise to protect me because she doesn't know who destroyed Spectrum in the first place. That means she can't stop them from coming after me, too."

She shrugged. "Maybe I did it."

Jarrett no longer saw that as a possibility. Elijah found her digital footprints on some of the files he searched. They were recent and she tried to cover the trail, but Elijah was an expert and this was not her forte.

Jarrett had planted the seed in her head and she picked it up . . . just as he hoped. "You told me you didn't and on this one subject, I trust you."

She snorted. "Bad idea."

"That's what I was thinking," Bast said at the same time.

Time to wrap this up before Wade came snooping or Becca went searching for information. She stayed quiet in her room last night, but Jarrett knew that wouldn't last. She was a fighter and if he guessed right, she was gathering strength for her next battle with him. "Becca and Elijah will be long gone and there will be documents protecting the rest. That's going to happen."

"Why don't you run?" Natalie asked.

"Not my style." Since the question seemed genuine rather than sarcastic, Jarrett didn't take offense. "Do we have a deal?"

Her gaze went to Bast. "I'll wait to hear from you about finalizing the details."

Bast escorted Natalie to the building's front door and out onto the sidewalk. Jarrett knew because he watched it all on the security monitors. He saw the servers come in and head for the locker room. He watched Bast and Natalie stand outside for a good ten minutes, Natalie's head shaking the entire time. He heard Bast buzz to come back in and prepared for the fight.

The monitors switched and Jarrett scanned most of the inside of the building. Elijah sitting on the bed in the crash pad, not moving. The chef and his staff preparing for the evening's service. Only Becca and Wade stayed out of site. Stopped by privacy, which made Jarrett think he might need to add a few more rooms to his security system.

Before Jarrett could take the visual tour again, Bast walked through the open door and slammed it shut behind him. "I'm going to tell you one last time as the guy you pay to do this work for you, this is a mistake. No woman is worth this."

Jarrett anticipated the battle. They'd been having it for days. "This from the guy who lets his ex-wife walk all over him."

"I'm serious here. You can't back away from this. You are giving up most of your leverage. If anyone at the CIA decides you're a risk, you will be gone." Bast flattened his palms against the desk and loomed right across from Jarrett. "I'm not sure I can save you again."

"You underestimate your talents."

"*You* underestimate how serious this is."

Jarrett closed his eyes and counted to ten. Or tried. He didn't make it past six. When he opened them again he didn't feel any calmer. "Do you honestly believe that? You think I don't know what this means? I'm having my business lawyer put together the paperwork to place this building and all my assets in trust run by you."

Bast stood up straight. "What the fuck?"

"I'm depending on you to make sure Wade and my employees are taken care of. You'll watch over the account for Becca."

"An account you never told me about."

"You get the rest of the secrets and can decide how to handle them." Jarrett knew Bast would take care of everything. That's what he did. He fixed and streamlined. He would not ignore Jarrett's wishes.

"Christ, don't talk like that. I don't want your assets." Bast was yelling and the man rarely raised his voice.

"Tough shit."

"I'd rather have you alive and out of jail. You and Wade."

"Damn it, Bast. I know that." Jarrett's voice now matched Bast's in the yelling contest.

"Tell me why." He dropped into the chair across from Jarrett. "Make me understand how a man who has carefully rebuilt his life and his image, who has taken the shit hand he was dealt and spun it into gold, makes this decision."

Jarrett didn't need to think about it for a second. He could hide the truth but Bast knew, too. "I love her, man."

Bast blew out a long breath. "It can't be that simple."

"Nothing happens to her." That was Jarrett's goal. He moved everything around and risked everything for her.

"Would she make this kind of grand gesture for you?"

"I don't know. I don't really care." But he knew the answer to that one, too. She had the chance and she hadn't. She believed the worst and walked away.

He refused to let that matter.

"How can you say that?" Bast shook his head. "How can you do all of this if the feelings only run one way?"

But that was the point. They didn't run one way. She loved him back. Jarrett knew it to his soul. Felt it in her touch and heard it mirrored in the way she didn't back down in a verbal battle. He'd let that be enough. "My whole life I've tried to handle other people and make situations work for me, but the truth is the only thing I can truly control is me. How I act and my decisions."

Bast leaned forward. "Let her go. I'm begging you."

"I am, but to do that I have to know she's safe."

"She's a trained agent. She can handle her own safety."

"Tell that to the other members of her team." Jarrett shuffled files around in front of him then handed one to Bast. "Look at the photos. The one who had his head blown off from behind is especially compelling."

Bast took the paperwork then dropped it on the desk without looking at it. "I never imagined you'd be the type to sacrifice everything for love."

"Me either." Really, never. Not with his background. Not with his experience.

Bast sat back in his chair. "Tell me she's worth it."

"Without even knowing it, I waited my whole life for her."

Bast stared up at the ceiling. "Fine."

"What does that mean?"

He lowered his head again. "I'll go negotiate with Natalie."

The words set Jarrett on edge. "We've already set the terms."

"You're handling the love part, something I never thought I'd say." Bast stood up. "Now let me do my job."

"I appreciate that, but—"

"No." He pointed at Jarrett. "Shut the fuck up."

Between the furious tone and the anger flashing in Bast's eyes, Jarrett didn't say anything for a second. "Excuse me?"

"That's a good-bye and you are not over. You want to clear the board, let's do it, but I get the chance to help you win, too." Bast kept pointing. Kept yelling.

"It's not possible."

"You're the hopeless romantic all of a sudden. Let me be the lawyer and try to save your sorry ass."

Jarrett took that as the sacred vow it was. Bast even used the word "lawyer," which never happened. As usual, he was the most solid guy Jarrett knew. "Fair enough."

"Yeah, well, let's just hope I'm as good at this as I say I am." Bast grabbed his briefcase off the floor. "And then wait until you get my bill. You may need to sign the building over as collateral."

If Bast could pull this off, Jarrett just might. "No problem."

"Don't bargain anything else away while I'm gone."

TWENTY-FIVE

She should have refused to go with him until his attitude improved, but that could be decades at this rate. Becca came to that decision as she rode down the elevator with Jarrett in total silence.

He'd been impossible for more than a day. He stomped around, barely spoke and slept in his own bed. Then a half hour ago he rushed her around, even tried to hand her a shirt to put over her white tank top.

If he was trying to piss her off, he'd succeeded.

She crossed her arms and leaned against the back railing of the car. "Are you going to tell me what's going on?"

"Be patient." When the doors opened he put his hand in the open space and motioned for her to step onto the second floor.

She didn't move. "Do you have any idea how patronizing that sounds?"

"You could be more grateful."

For a smart man he was acting like a complete idiot.

Her gaze went past him to the open conference room door. She couldn't see inside, but she heard the low rumble of a man's voice. Still she leaned. She was happy to play this argument to an audience, if that's what he wanted, but she knew that would only shut Jarrett down further. As if that were even possible.

"Did you forget how we left this?" she asked. "You were being an ass and then you walked out."

"That's not how I remember it."

The voice inside the room cut off. Whoever lingered in there was now listening in. That was fine with Becca. If they wanted a show, she'd give them one. "Any chance you'll knock off the asshole behavior anytime soon?"

"Rest assured you won't have to put up with it much longer." He pointed into the empty hallway. "Right now we have a meeting."

More out of curiosity than anything else, she pushed off against the back wall and started moving. She avoided his hand and walked right past him. "Since when are you cryptic?"

She hit the doorway. Her gaze went to Bast where he stood by the far window.

Then a woman she thought she'd never see again opened her mouth. "Good question."

Becca felt the blood rush out of her head. "Natalie?"

The other woman stood up. "Becca Ford. I must say, you look good for a dead woman."

Becca whipped around so fast to face Jarrett that she got dizzy. Fear and disappointment rolled into a ball and clogged her throat.

He lied to her. Took her in, made love to her, assured her she was safe. He promised to keep her hidden and now he was handing her over to a woman who sat behind a desk at the agency and gave orders. One of which could have been the order to terminate Spectrum.

"What did you do?" The words sliced against the soft inside of her throat as she whispered them.

For a fraction of a second, Jarrett's stern expression slipped. Concern and an odd softness replaced the coldness in his eyes. Then the guard snapped up into place again. "Calm down."

The clipped phrase sent her panic spiraling into anger. "Don't talk to me like I'm a child."

"Don't act like one."

"Maybe we should all sit down," Bast said.

Jarrett talked right over his friend, his unblinking stare never moving from Becca's face. "Just listen."

"To you sell me out? Is this some sort of payback for eight months ago?" The reality crushed her. Drove a stake from the top of her head straight down her middle. She grabbed on to the back of a chair to keep from falling at his feet.

"Becca—"

"I messed up back then. Okay." Damn him. He was going to make her beg for her life. Rip away the last bit of pride she had when it came to him. "Is that what you need to hear?"

"You're not listening to me."

"I'll say it to you, to them, if that's what it takes." Her hearing muffled and a second wave of dizziness pummeled into her. "I didn't trust you and you got screwed. There is no one to blame but me. Are you happy now?"

"I would be if you settled down." Jarrett reached for her arm.

She shrugged out of his hold and turned to Natalie. "Give me your gun."

On the second try, Jarrett's hand connected. With a hold on Becca's upper arm, he turned her back to him. "What the hell are you doing?"

"That's what this is about, right? You want me to bleed."

"You're talking nonsense."

"Do not give anyone in this room a gun," Bast said to Natalie.

Becca heard Bast's voice and felt Natalie right next to her. Everything ran together. With Jarrett still holding her, she glanced over at Natalie. "Are you carrying?"

"Always."

With nothing left to lose, Becca spelled it out. He threw around comments about her betrayal months ago, but his was fresh. It threw her into a new hell, complete with danger and pain and a profound sense of loss over the man she loved more than anything. "We had a deal. Protection for sex."

Jarrett didn't even flinch at having the secret out there in front of Natalie, someone Becca didn't even know he'd met.

"Now you have a new deal," he said.

More secrets. They piled up and multiplied. She thought they could wiggle free and move on. She saw now that they shoveled some and more caved in around them.

Her chest ached when she looked at him, so she turned to Natalie. "Why are you really here?"

"To help."

"That has never been my experience."

Natalie picked up two sealed folders from the table. "Believe what you want but after talking with Bast and thinking it through, I'm trying to give you options."

"Option. Singular. She doesn't get a choice." Jarrett shifted until Natalie stood in his direct line of sight.

His yelling vibrated through Becca until she wanted to cover her ears. "Stop with that bullshit."

"Okay," Bast said in his usual reasonable lawyer voice. "Let's all sit down."

Jarrett turned on his best friend. "There is one option. Why is Natalie talking about two?"

Bast glared. "Maybe Becca isn't the only one who needs to sit down and listen."

Jarrett's eyes narrowed at his best friend. "What did you do?"

"My job."

She had no idea what was happening and didn't care. "And this is my life. I am not your client, Bast."

Bast's glare didn't falter. "So?"

She broke Jarrett's hold. The second the contact ended, the last bits of energy whooshed out of her. She made it to the chair but just barely. "I did not ask for anything."

Jarrett sat down next to her, almost on top of her. "You don't even know what's happening."

"That's my point. You can't control everything." She tried to shift the chair over to get a little breathing room, but the wheels wouldn't move.

He pounded a finger on the desk right in front of her. "You came to me for help and you're getting it."

"You are unbelievable. You think because we've been sleeping together you own me?"

His face turned to a mask of teeth-clenching fury. "Stop talking."

Bast cleared his throat. "Uh, Jarrett."

But Jarrett wasn't done. His anger spread through the room, falling over everything. "I'm not listening to you go off and blame me and assume I'm trying to hurt you. I am risking everything for you."

The man still didn't get it. He thought being a partner meant ordering her around. That worked when he told her she meant nothing, but not now. "I don't know what that means but whatever it is, I didn't ask for it."

"You don't have a choice."

She spun her chair around to face him instead of Natalie. "Why do you think it's okay to say that garbage to me?"

"Because I love you and I want you safe." The words pinged off every wall and wiped every other noise from the room. "There, are you fucking satisfied?" His shoulders fell and some of the intensity ran out of him. "I love you."

Natalie rolled her eyes as she took her seat. "What woman wouldn't find being screamed at romantic?"

"The delivery does need work," Bast said.

Becca struggled to take it all in. Relief and happiness battled with a well-earned wariness. The feelings conflicted and battled until all she could do was sit there with her mouth hanging open.

He declared his love, and not in the privacy of their bedroom. Out in the open with other people there. It was sweet and charming and so unlike him, but as with everything else Jarrett did, the message came wrapped in this confusing mixture of fury and desperation. He loved her, but she got the distinct impression he didn't want to.

"You think this is the way to tell me something so important?" she asked in a harsh whisper.

The stress lines around his mouth deepened. "I need it done."

She didn't know what the "it" was in the sentence. The meeting, their relationship, his feelings for her. The "it" could be anything, and most of the alternatives sucked for her.

She needed space and a minute to think. She had to pull herself together before she grabbed him and told him to say the words the right way.

She turned to Natalie. "Let me hear this supposed deal. That way I can say no and get the hell out of here."

"You don't get to say no."

Becca didn't even spare Jarrett a glance that time. "You would be wise to not talk right now."

"She is a trained killer," Bast said as he sat in the chair across from them.

Jarrett waved him off. "She can kill me for all I care. I'll survive."

Bast laughed. "How do you survive death?"

Becca closed her eyes for a second. She was sick of male talking. They could sit together and figure out whatever was bugging them later. They were talking about her life and she wanted to get to it. "Natalie, tell me why you're here."

"We've arranged for you to disappear." Natalie put a hand on top of one folder. Her shiny gold watch caught the light. "You get a new identity, a healthy bank account from the agency for your trouble, one that means you'll never have to work, and I guarantee your safety."

Becca knew the drill. Not many got the offer, but it happened. "So, I go away forever."

The words made her mouth numb. The rest of her followed.

"Yes. Gone, but alive and not hounded. That's the point. You have your freedom, to a certain extent. You'll always need to be careful, but I'd expect that from you anyway."

Never seeing Jarrett again. Never coming back to the area. More years without a home. "And what do I give up in return?"

"Jarrett handled most of that, but you would lose your identity."

"It's simple and you stop running." Jarrett put his hand over hers. "For the first time in your life, you're not looking over your shoulder to see who's chasing you."

Becca tried to take it all in. Tried and failed.

Natalie slid the second folder closer to Becca. "Or you can—"

"There is no 'or' here." Jarrett reached out to snag the folder. "That's the only deal."

Natalie pulled it back and out of his reach. She kept her focus on Becca as she held the first folder up. "This is the information on the disappearance. You leave, you break all ties, and no one comes after you. Since this is through back channels, there's room for one. You go alone."

The words tumbled in Becca's head. She felt frozen, as if all of this was happening around her but she couldn't move or dive in. She finally forced her throat to move. The words that came out were not the ones she meant to say. "You're okay with never seeing me again, Jarrett?"

He nodded. "If it keeps you alive."

Her body went limp. She barely had the energy to lift her arm. She looked to Natalie for an explanation of all of it. "Why would you agree to that?"

"It's a good deal and I get to be the agent who brings in some much-needed information."

That could only mean one thing. Becca's gaze shifted to Jarrett. "What exactly does the agency get from you?"

"That doesn't matter."

"It does to me."

"To me, too," Bast mumbled.

Instead of getting answers, the room remained quiet. Natalie broke the silence when she held up the second envelope. "Or you can keep your identity under this scenario."

Jarrett stood up so suddenly his chair spun behind him then crashed to the floor. "What the hell are you doing?"

"As I told you before, she's a grown-up," Natalie said. "She gets a choice."

Jarrett turned on Bast. "Is this your doing? I told you only Becca's safety mattered."

If the anger thumping through the room had an impact on Bast, he didn't show it. "And I told you to let me do my job."

Becca blocked it all and stared at the second envelope. "What happens in this scenario?"

"You choose it, you'll get to open it and see."

No explanation. "Blind?"

"Right." Natalie waved the envelope. "You get your freedom and walk away clean or you get this."

"Absolutely not." Jarrett lunged for it again but missed when Natalie pulled back.

And her scowl suggested she was not happy with his behavior. "I will pull that gun if you don't sit down."

Bast leaned in. "Jarrett, give it a second."

He shook his head. "Why would she pick something without knowing the terms? How can you let this happen?"

"I negotiated this option," Bast said. "And that should tell you this option is a good one."

Becca thought about the wariness in Bast's eyes when he looked at her. About the way he protected Jarrett at all costs, something she loved for Jarrett but could mean death for her. "Why does the idea of you guiding my future scare me?"

Natalie waved the envelope again. "In this scenario she keeps her name and her life, her job if she wants it—"

"No." Jarrett's voice rose even louder the second time.

But factors in the second one appealed to her. Not the job, but the rest. Becca thought about walking away from everything, including him, and she had to know what was in the second envelope. Whatever it was couldn't rip through her with the same force as the idea of leaving him again did.

Much more of this and she'd be bleeding on the floor.

She took a long and steady inhale. "You don't decide for me, Jarrett."

"I want you safe."

"She's relatively safe in the second. Well, safe from an arranged accident." Natalie tapped the folder against her open palm on the opposite hand. "The difference is she doesn't leave. She picks whether to stay or go."

"No sane person would take a deal without reading it first," Jarrett said as his gaze focused on the envelope's movements.

Becca almost laughed over the irony. "Yet you want me to take the deal you made without me ever seeing the fine print."

"The lady has you there." Natalie picked up both envelopes and held them. She looked straight at Becca, ignoring the men in the room. "Your choice."

Jarrett let out a string of profanity that would have made his old associates proud. "Natalie, shut the hell up."

Becca made the decision and reached for the envelope before Jarrett stopped talking. "I'll take number two."

She was up and out of her chair with Jarrett behind her. He didn't touch her, but his presence loomed all around her and the intensity of his stare burned into her back.

"Becca, listen to me." He put his hands over hers. "I love you and I want you safe."

"I know." Right then, standing there, seeing the pain in his eyes, she did know. His execution was totally messed up, but he was trying to do the right thing. What *he* thought was right, not what she wanted.

Natalie nodded to Becca. "Open it."

She ripped the seal and pulled out a memo with a familiar heading. She'd been reading them for years. This one provided the details of an internal investigation.

One word stuck out. "Todd."

Jarrett stopped fidgeting. "What?"

"It's an intel report." She scanned the paragraphs. "Todd set up the sting at the club based on faked intel."

Jarrett's breath blew across her cheek as he read over her shoulder. "I already know that."

"This didn't come from above or from an informant. Todd sought information for his own use. So he could sell it and profit from it." Natalie smacked her lips together. "Apparently Todd is working for someone other than us, and you were a way for him to stockpile cash."

Becca reached the paragraph near the bottom of the first page that explained it all. "He got the CIA to poke around in your club based on one set of details while he searched for the real info he wanted about one of your members."

Jarrett leaned in closer. "Who?"

Her finger traveled over the line, highlighting it for him. "A senator on the Intelligence Committee. Todd got what he needed and planted the drugs to put the spotlight on you. It gave him cover to get out and ruin your reputation."

"How did he get in here to handle the drugs?" Jarrett asked, in a voice filled with confusion.

"That was me." Natalie raised her hand. "I approved a plan for him to plant microphones and cameras in your place as part of the real operation but that's not how he used it. Your security wasn't as strong back then. I know because I've tried to break it since."

"What?" Full-fledged fury replaced the confusion in Jarrett's voice now.

Natalie nodded in Bast's direction. "Then he saved you from a prison term with his negotiations and the spotlight shifted again."

"Everything would have been fine because the CIA got legitimate information, which covered Todd's tracks at the agency," Bast said, filling in the blanks.

Natalie turned back to Jarrett. "While you and Wade were sitting in jail, we removed the surveillance equipment."

"It all worked." Bast held up a finger. "But Todd had one problem."

"Becca," Natalie said.

It was like some sort of rehearsed routine. Bast and Natalie tag-teamed. Whatever Bast had been negotiating, he'd done it directly with Natalie. As far as Becca was concerned, they qualified as the strangest bedfellows ever.

But there was one fact that didn't fit. Probably more than one, but even through Becca's muddled state, one jumped out at her. "How do you figure that? I was a mess when Jarrett went to jail."

"True, but it was too neat. Jarrett got off and I poked around a bit. The assault on Spectrum started right after." Natalie shook her head. "It smelled wrong. Too perfect and tied up too neatly."

"When you put it all together, the only answer is Todd took out the other Spectrum agents to cover his tracks. If he was a victim but the only one left, there would be no one around to piece the information together or question him. The higher-ups at the CIA were satisfied Becca turned and tried to fake her own death with the condo bombing she escaped. Jarrett had his deal and wasn't poking around." Bast touched his tie. "At my suggestion."

Jarrett nodded. "I didn't want anything to do with Spectrum at that point."

"Exactly, you'd decided what happened—you got set up and Becca helped do it—and you were looking for revenge, but not poking around in exactly what happened. That's not where your head was." Natalie smiled. "But I was. That's the part Todd didn't see at first."

All the behind-the-scenes work and Natalie stayed quiet. Becca didn't know whether to be furious or to go with the sensation of relief pouring through her. They knew who started it all and who tried to end her.

When it came to Todd, only one thing went through Becca's head. "That son of a bitch."

"He's confined to a desk job, thanks to his injuries, but is clearly just laying low," Natalie said. "Since he thinks Elijah is dead, Todd is probably using his time tracking you, Becca, so he can finish framing you, then get out of town with his money."

"It's genius really." When Jarrett glared, Bast held up a hand. "What? It is. He's hiding at his desk, with access to information right in front of him."

"I put it all together when Jarrett handed me some of the information you compiled over the last few days. Until then I didn't know you provided a coded message about a lack of evidence at the club," Natalie explained to Becca.

She remembered the message and her fight with Elijah over it in this very room. She tried to explain but he insisted he'd never seen it. Looked like she owed one more apology. "Nothing happened with it."

"Todd buried it at our end so he could go ahead with the arrest as planned. You just moved up his timetable."

"But you saved the document, which told Natalie where to look in the system," Bast said, filling in the final piece.

The weight that had been smashing Becca into the ground lifted. For the first time in months, she didn't have the pricking sensation on the back of her neck. "So, what happens now?"

Natalie nodded at the two folders. "That's for you to decide."

They acted like there was a question. Becca knew the answer. There really only was one answer.

"I keep my life. I make my own decisions." Becca glanced over her shoulder at Jarrett when she said the last part.

He was a mess she couldn't untangle now. Not on top of all the other blows from today. She'd crawl off and try to heal. Part of her wanted to tuck away her love for him somewhere safe and never look at it. That way, it couldn't disappear or die. The other, bigger part of her wanted to shake him until that hard shell covering him smashed into pieces.

But first, she owed a debt. "Natalie, I'm not sure what to say."

"She made it happen," Bast said. "Without her agreeing to listen and be open to options other than those Jarrett proposed this wouldn't be happening."

"'Thank you' is sufficient." Natalie's gaze bounced to Jarrett before landing on Becca again. "I'd also like you to come back to work and help us sort out this mess and see what else Todd might have done, but that's up to you."

"I'll think about it." Becca heard Jarrett start to say something and slowly turned to look at him. "Yeah, Jarrett. Me. I decide, and right now I'm deciding to leave."

Jarrett watched her go. His feet were frozen to the spot. He'd run through every scenario on how this meeting would work. He prepared for angry Becca and hurt Becca. He never thought to look out for the joint power of Bast and Natalie.

Bast folded his arms behind his head. "You're welcome."

It was possible Jarrett's head would explode. He could feel the rage boiling in there right now. "Are you kidding?"

"Natalie knows the identity of the mole and reason for the operation. She gets to be the superstar, Becca's name gets cleared and you hold on to most of the information you thought you'd have to hand over, but you agree to provide Natalie with intelligence from time to time." Bast ticked off the pieces and highlighted each one with a thump of his pen against his pad.

Natalie shook her head. "I reluctantly agreed to the last part."

"This was the negotiation?" Jarrett still wasn't sure what had happened. Somehow they talked about sex and he declared his love for Becca, in between offhanded references to national security breaches. It was the damn oddest fifteen minutes of his life.

And he noticed Becca didn't respond to his comment about loving her, except to get angrier. He had no idea how to take that.

Bast smiled. "I guess I really am as good as I say I am."

"I don't like being conned and that's exactly what Todd did, so I agreed to work with your negotiator," Natalie said.

"Are you sure it's not because you're a romantic at heart? The thing with the two files where Jarrett could see what Becca really wanted." Bast winked at her. "Brilliant."

"Romantic?" Natalie gave one of her eye rolls, only this one didn't convey her usual level of boredom. "That's ridiculous."

Bast lowered his arms to the table. "I'm not so sure."

"I owed Becca this," Natalie said. "Becca wanted to call off the operation. She had the good sense to send up a red flag and to double back. Unfortunately she went to Todd with her concerns and not someone else."

Jarrett finally broke out of his haze long enough to catch up. "You?"

Natalie nodded. "I would have listened."

"What happens to Todd now?" Jarrett hoped the answer included a firing squad.

"Please don't tell him the answer to that." Bast held up a hand. "We're looking for plausible deniability here."

Natalie gathered up the remainder of her files and folders. "The agency needs more people like Becca."

Jarrett snapped right back into fighting mode. "Never going to happen."

There was no way he'd watch Becca walk into danger again. She did it once and nearly got killed. She spent a lifetime running and hiding when it was obvious from how easily she settled into life with him both times that she craved a family and stability. He could give her those.

"You still think you decide?" Natalie ignored Jarrett and spoke directly to Bast. "He acts as if he's already won her back."

Those two working together scared Jarrett. It was hard enough fighting with one of them and coming out the winner. Getting double-teamed made him want to throw up the white flag. "What?"

Bast shook his head. "Sorry, man, but you're skipping a step."

"What are you two talking about?"

"Becca referenced your 'asshole behavior' and leaving, or did you miss those parts?" Natalie asked with a grin that spelled trouble.

"I wouldn't be surprised if she's rappelling down the side of your building right now to get away from you." Bast leaned back and looked at the window behind him. "For the record, I'm not negotiating the reconciliation of your love life."

And she would do it, too. If she got sick of his heavy-handedness, she'd tell him off and go. She made that much clear.

Jarrett remembered her face and her words, and panic flowed through every vein. He was in the hall a second later. "You can see yourselves out."

TWENTY-SIX

Becca stepped into the huge closet in Jarrett's bedroom. Breaking this rule felt right. He could stick his juvenile "keep out" crap.

Hangers jangled as she skipped slipping clothes off and folding them. She went with grabbing them by the armful and dumping them in the suitcase she took off the top shelf of his side of the closet. It sat in the middle of his bed and was already overflowing.

Once she finished here, she'd move on to the guestroom. If he didn't have another bag she could steal, she'd use trash bags. Anything to get finished and get out of there.

She turned for another clothing run and Jarrett stepped in front of her. He was the last thing she could handle right now. "Move."

"What are you doing?"

He had to be clueless not to know, but she filled him in anyway. "Packing."

She spun around him and headed back to the racks. This time

she tugged on her pants, yanking them loose and sending the hangers flying.

Jarrett leaned against the doorframe and watched her. "Why?"

"Because you're an idiot."

"Not sure that's a change. It was true when you got here."

She stood in front of him with pants hanging over her arms. "This isn't funny, Jarrett."

His gaze slipped to her haul then back to her face. "You're not going anywhere."

There it was. The one phrase guaranteed to get her to raise her fighting instincts. "Why do you continue to think you own me?"

"I don't."

"Could have fooled me." She tried to move around him but he shifted his weight. Rather than play the game, she stood there. She could call on all her stamina reserves and outwait him. This was too important to just drop. "I mean, what was with that ridiculous scene downstairs? You turned me over to Natalie so she could rush me out of town in secret."

He frowned at her. "Is that what you think that was?"

"Wasn't it?"

He put his hands on her elbows in a light touch that couldn't hold her if she shifted. "I turned over everything. Every piece of information about the China deal. Every piece of leverage I had been holding back to stay out of the clutches of the CIA to buy your freedom." He shook his head as he swore. "Hell, I would have given her the deed to the fucking building if that was what it took to keep you safe."

The enormity of what he was saying crashed down on Becca. A man who built an empire on his own was willing to give it away, to forfeit his freedom, for her. The cost was so enormous. And the idea of a world without him in it threatened to double her over. Even when they were apart, she at least knew he was in his house and safe, but with the sacrifice he tried to make, he would have lost all that.

Her muscles turned to jelly and the clothing dropped out of her hold, piece by piece, right to the floor. "You could have been arrested. Or worse."

His expression didn't change. "I didn't care. I still don't."

What was he saying? "I want you to care."

"Why?"

She shook her head. She would have turned away but his hand slipped under her chin, forcing her to look at him. She wanted to evade, but the words came stammering out. "Because I love you."

There, she'd said it. She'd felt it for so long and with such intensity, it was probably right that it came out during a fight. That summed up who they were. Two people yelling about their love while they argued.

He smiled as his thumb brushed over her cheek. "You do."

Not a question. A statement. "That's it? That's how you respond?"

"I'm pretty fucking thrilled."

"But you knew. How?"

"You wouldn't have come here if you didn't." He cupped her face in his palms. "I know the bullshit about limited resources and needing my access, but we both know you had other options. You could have turned to someone else and you came to me."

"I never thought about anyone else." That was the truth. Even in the beginning when she fought back doubts and worried he might send her away, she knew she had to try.

"I had to believe you seeking me out meant something."

The memory of his words from that first time in his office bounced back at her. "You acted like you hated me."

He claimed he wanted to humiliate her and use her for sex but his touch said otherwise. Oh, he fought it for days. Almost two weeks in, he still acted like an ass sometimes and stole her breath in others.

"I tried. I really did." Pain echoed in his voice. "I can't lie about that, but I couldn't make the anger stick."

That was the before. They could forgive those moments and explain them away. But they needed to tackle the now. "Why send me away? You were sitting down there with Natalie, wrapping up my life without ever talking to me."

His hold moved to her shoulders and he brought her in closer to his body. They kicked at the clothes at their feet until her hand rested against his chest.

"I couldn't take the risk you'd think you could take on the entire CIA by yourself," he said as his gaze searched her face.

Some of the painful sternness had disappeared. Stress lines still pulled on his mouth and eyes, but she saw something else there. Something lighter, freer. Maybe hope. She recognized the sensation because it fluttered to life within her.

"With you." She spread her fingers out, covering as much of him as possible. "Not by myself. I wanted to be with you."

He leaned in and kissed her. A lovely touch that lingered before falling away.

"I love you," he said in a whisper against her mouth.

It was so easy to fall back into this warm feeling. He finally declared his love and he stood there with his eyes glowing and a smile tugging on his lips. It was normal and healthy. But it wasn't everything. It wasn't enough.

When he lowered his mouth again, she caught him with a touch of her hand against his cheek. "I want more."

"Anything."

She hoped that was true. The anxiety bouncing around in her stomach suggested it might not be. "I've turned this around and looked at it a million ways and I've come to some conclusions. I think we've loved each other stretching back to eight months ago."

He turned his head and kissed the inside of her wrist in that sensitive spot that drove her wild. "God, yes."

"We settle into patterns, it all gets comfortable. You tone down the controlling crap and become tolerable." When he started to talk she placed a finger over his warm lips. "But none of that counts if we don't trust each other. If you can't open up to me and we can't communicate, it won't matter what deal I have with the agency."

He pulled her hand away and threaded his fingers through hers. "I trust you."

That was too easy. It came too fast. "Since when?"

"Maybe always. Do you really think I would have let you in the building, in my condo, if I didn't have a spark of trust?"

Not that she thought he was lying. She knew he believed it, but this was a time when actions spoke louder. "Jarrett, you just proved downstairs that you don't. You didn't let me make the decisions about my life."

He started shaking his head before she finished the sentence. "That was about me being so desperate to keep you safe that I would have done anything, including drugging you and putting you in a crate and sending you away."

"Your controlling side."

"Guilty."

"Is it that easy to separate from me?" Her breath caught in her

throat as she waited for an answer. Actually held there until she
wondered if her lungs had shut down.

The darkness that sometimes overwhelmed him moved through
his eyes now. "You can't believe that."

"What am I supposed to think?"

He leaned back against the wall and brought her body between
his thighs. "I need you to hear this." When she nodded, he continued. "Losing you the first time broke me into pieces. The idea
of getting you back only to lose you again shattered me. Ripped
me the fuck in two. I've been sick with it."

She touched his face then. His mouth and lips. "Jarrett."

"I love you. I trust you. I want to spend my life with you. I don't
know how else to say it. It sounds simple but the emotions behind
the words are complicated and huge." His hands tensed against
her. "You know my history. You know how difficult it was for
me to get it this place with anyone, and it's only ever happened
with you."

"You deserve it."

"We both deserve a family and forever love. We can have it
together."

Her head dropped and her cheek rubbed against his. "I don't
want to be coddled or sent away. I want to be with you, as an equal.
We talk, we work things out. We figure out if we have a future."

He lifted her head and stared down into her eyes. His intense
will thrummed into her, as if he silently pleaded with her to believe.
"We do."

Her doubts fell away, crashing on the floor around her. The
lightness filling her head didn't have anything to do with panic or
fear. Or even anger. It spun with a kind of relief that made her
giddy. "I want that."

"Then believe me when I say I trust you. A part of me always did, but then you stuck the gun in the back of Elijah's head and I was a goner."

She smiled at the memory. It wasn't funny at the time and it might take another ten years to get there, but at least it no longer made her tremble with rage. "I would have shot him."

"So fucking hot."

And the man knew a thing or two about hot. "Having a man risk everything to give me a white picket fence in Kansas was pretty sexy, too."

"You want to live in Kansas, we'll go to Kansas."

Maybe not the best proposition for some women, but for Becca it sounded perfect. He was giving her a choice and a life. Handing her back the power. The willingness to follow her anywhere made her love him even more.

She kissed a line across his throat and loved the way his Adam's apple bobbed under her mouth. "I'll settle for moving into your bedroom."

"On the condition we make a new agreement."

With deliberate slowness, she lifted her head. If he said the wrong thing, she just might punch him. She held her forefinger and thumb an inch apart. "You are so close to not messing this up."

"Trust me."

Those were the magic words. When she heard them, her body relaxed and her arms slipped around his neck. "Go ahead."

"We forgive all the times we didn't talk to each other when we should have. We stop keeping secrets." His hands rubbed up and down her back. "And we forget how we met and got together. Instead, we focus on how we stay together."

No wonder she loved him. Through all the gruffness and snapping lay this. "That was a pretty romantic statement right there."

"You know I want to add that you don't work for Natalie again, but I'm trying not to be a douche."

Poor baby.

But now came the biggest leap of all. Moving in a second time was big because it meant diving in and not holding back. This would be the real thing and not part of an assignment. And she wanted to be all in. "I was thinking."

"Uh-oh."

She tugged on his hair. "You might need someone to help out with membership. Maybe look into security and intelligence. After all, if there are congressmen in here with national security info someone might steal in a moment of ill-advised drunkenness, I can handle that."

His eyebrow lifted, but he couldn't hide that smile. "Really?"

"I think Wade and I could work well together. In time he might even grow to like me." Probably way in the future.

"I feel safer already."

"And from now on if someone wants to set you up, they have to go through me." She planned to hang up her guns, except for a few. But for him she would bring out all the weapons. Her rule still stood—no one touched Jarrett but her.

His hands slid down to her ass. "Right now I want to be in you."

The man was predictable and she was not complaining.

She ran her hands over his head and into his hair. "I love you."

"Show me."

He ended the words by kissing her. This one wasn't sweet. It carried a naughty edge, complete with tongue and a bit of nipping.

When she felt him shift toward the bedroom, she lifted her head. "No, I think we should try the closet."

"I love when you're a dirty girl."

Her hands went to his belt. "Then the next half hour is going to be pretty amazing for you."

Wade waited at the door while Elijah stood at the head of the conference room table. He read a memo Bast said Natalie had provided. Wade knew what it contained because Bast knocked on the condo door and briefed him before he asked to talk with Eli.

Wade only hovered because of security concerns. The sooner all the extra people were out of the top two floors of the building, the better.

Eli got to the end and dropped it on the table. "So, this is over."

Sitting there with the briefcase open and sitting in front of him, Bast nodded. "Natalie cleared the slate. Once we get the final signal, you're free to return to your old job."

"Like hell." Wade didn't even try to whisper it.

"Okay," Bast said. "I don't actually think that would be wise either."

"Where's Todd now?" Wade asked.

Bast cleared his throat. "I get the distinct impression he won't be an issue by the end of the day."

Eli stared at both of them, his gaze traveling between them. But he didn't say anything. The hunted look hadn't left his eyes and his shoulders still bunched with tension.

To diffuse, Wade stated the obvious. "By tomorrow you should be safe on the streets again."

Eli shot him a blank look. "What happens if I want to stay here?"

That was easy. In those moments when Wade thought about giving in, he just had to call up the memory of walking into that conference room. Eli's words played like a horrible tape in his head. "No."

That door closed when Eli announced that his time in the building was about sex. Not even memorable sex. Just a release. Like something he could do with his fucking hand but had Wade do instead because he was *right there*.

"We need to talk about this." If Eli cared about having a witness, he didn't show it.

But it didn't matter if fifty people hung around. The answer was the same for Wade. "You said everything already. I heard it."

"Give me another chance."

Wade ignored the request. When the pleading moved to Eli's face, Wade looked away. "Take a few days to figure out where you're going and get the final okay from Natalie, then move out. The crash pad is yours until the beginning of next week."

Locks clicked as Bast shut his briefcase. "On that topic, I have an offer for you."

Elijah blinked. "What?"

"A job offer."

Elijah scoffed. "Your law firm needs an assassin on the payroll?"

"Interesting thought." Bast smiled as he stood up. "But not to my knowledge."

"Then, no offense, but I'm not exactly the civilized office type."

Maybe that was a sign of growth. Wade hadn't realized Eli even knew that about himself.

"That's not what I need." Bast set his business card down on the table in front of Elijah. "I'm looking for your tech skills. You locate and recover devices, collect and analyze details, and you can work around a firewall. Maybe some protection, bodyguard work."

Elijah looked at the card but didn't pick it up. "Is this work you're barely describing legal?"

"I'm a lawyer."

"Is that an answer?" Wade asked because, well, he kind of had to.

"Take the card." Bast slid it closer to Elijah's closed fist. "Call me tomorrow."

This time he picked it up. Flipped it over, read it, then flipped again. "Can you guarantee no one will try to kill me on the job?"

"'Guarantee' is a strong word." Bast shook both of their hands. "I'll talk to you tomorrow, Eli."

Bast walked out and the resulting silence was like a living thing. It crawled and swirled. Wade had to get out. He grabbed the keys out of his pocket and got as far as the doorway.

"Wade—"

"Eli, look." Wade turned around again. This part had to be said and once it was it never had to be said again. "You wanted some fun and a release. I get that, but I'm not your guy."

"We can try to fix this."

He nodded at the card in Elijah's hand. "Take the job."

"I don't care about that."

"Bast is a good man. Take the offer and give up black-ops before the next Todd waiting in line out there or going through training actually succeeds and kills you."

Elijah's smile didn't reach his eyes. "You don't think I can take care of myself?"

"I don't think you can outrun a bullet." And the idea of reading about Eli's death in the paper under the guise of a strange accident made Wade want to heave.

"And you would care if something happened to me."

Wade hesitated, debating. The truth wouldn't change anything, so . . . "I would care. Good-bye, Eli."

TWENTY-SEVEN

Jarrett was almost afraid to be too happy the next morning. Luck rarely worked on his side. He hustled his butt off for everything he owned and accomplished. He'd made millions, but not without backbreaking hours and a few choices he'd rather not discuss, and couldn't in some counties.

But this might be the best perk of his job. He sat in his office chair and watched Becca bend across his desk with that fine ass on full display at mouth level. She cycled through the security monitor views. She had already declared they needed an overhaul because of blind spots. He had no idea what the hell she was talking about. He'd write her a check for anything, agree to almost anything, if it kept the smile on her face.

Now she watched as their guest walked through the back hall toward the office. "You should have people escorted in. There's no need for anyone to be wandering around in the back offices."

He started to wonder if Becca would run an even tighter ship than he did. "This one is safe."

Kyra poked her head around the corner and into the open doorway. "Hello."

Jarrett waved her inside. He also thought about grabbing Becca and sitting her on his lap, but he guessed she'd find that to be a private activity. And she stood up too fast for him to catch her.

"Becca, this is Kyra."

With a bright smile on her face, Becca reached across the desk and shook the younger woman's hand. "Hi, Kyra."

"It's about time we met. I've heard all about you."

Becca sent him a "we'll talk later" glare. "Depending on when that conversation happened, I dread what you've heard."

"This morning on the phone." Kyra fluttered her eyelashes like something out of a cartoon. "He used the word 'love.' "

"Isn't that cute?" Becca smiled down at him as she brushed her hand over his hair.

"That's enough of that talk." But not the touching. She was free to do that anytime. To let her know, he caught her hand and brought her around until she stood beside his chair. His palm went wandering behind her.

"What's going on?" Becca asked.

"Jarrett asked me to come in."

Becca glanced down at him again. "Why?"

"To offer her a job."

Kyra's mouth dropped open. When she closed it again she looked at Becca, not him. "Did you know about this?"

Becca shrugged. "News to me."

"Because I just came up with the idea." He rushed to add that, trying to stave off a lecture about communication that might be headed his way later.

The excitement vanished as quickly as it came. Kyra frowned at him. "What's up with the change in position?"

"Oh, I see what you're doing." Becca made a humming sound. "The change is Wade."

"Becca." Jarrett used her name as a warning. He had no idea how much Wade wanted his baby sister to know about his love life.

"She deserves to know what's going on. I would want to know."

He trailed a hand down the back of her thigh. "You're an only child."

"Is that the point?"

"Wait." Kyra shifted to the front of her chair. "Is Wade okay?"

"He had a falling out with someone he was dating." Jarrett thought that was as vague as he could be without resorting to hand signals.

"You mean a guy." Kyra rolled her eyes. "Really, Jarrett. It's not a secret he's gay. He announced that to me years ago. Not the rest of the family, of course, but I know."

Jarrett decided to skip the tiptoeing. "In that case, he had a shitty breakup."

"I didn't even know he was seriously dating someone."

"I think he was stunned, too. Point is, it might be good for you to hang around for a few months." More careful word choices, but telling her every detail wouldn't solve anything. "A familiar face. You can always make him smile."

Becca snorted. "I'd like to see that."

"And when he kills me for even suggesting this, you can both come to my funeral." Because Wade would be pissed. At this point Jarrett would take anything over the quiet moping.

"I won't let that happen." Becca patted Jarrett's shoulder as she said it.

Kyra laughed. "You really must love him."

"Most days."

He pinched Becca's butt and smiled when she jerked in reaction.

Kyra must have missed the byplay because she launched into a new round of questions. "How bad was it?"

No way was Jarrett answering that. "Maybe you should start training right away."

Becca pulled hard on both ends of the scarf. Jarrett had looped the long length of silk around the bedpost of the headboard. She wrapped the ends around her wrists and now held on as if letting go would end everything.

The bed creaked and a small tear ripped through the air a second ago. Still, she didn't let go.

This was round two of the morning. She woke to him spooning her. What started as heat and warm skin turned into something so much better. His palm found her breasts as he pulled her ass higher and tighter against his cock.

Her eyes had barely opened before he pushed her forward. Her hand slapped against the mattress for leverage as he fitted his cock against her. He rubbed and caressed until her wetness had her opening her thighs to make room for him. Her fingers grabbed the sheets as she stretched out and let him do whatever he wanted with her.

After, she checked the clock and drifted back to sleep only to wake to him sliding down her body an hour later. She started on her stomach this morning, but she was on her back now. Looking down, she could see his dark hair between her legs. His head bobbed and his tongue flicked. Her body already tense and sensitive from the morning lovemaking ached for release now.

And he was relentless. He pushed her right to the edge with the pumping of his fingers and lick of his tongue. When her hips started to move and her shoulders shifted, he pulled back and blew a warm puff of air over her. When he did it the second time, she broke out in a sweat.

Her forearms shook from the strain of pulling on the scarf. The tense coiling inside her begged for release. She wanted to scream and tell him to finish it, but she knew that would promise an extension to the sensual torture.

He'd always liked going down on her, which made her just about the luckiest woman ever. The sensations he stirred could make her scream. But if he didn't finish this now, she was going to pass out.

She squeezed her thighs against his shoulders. When that didn't change his pace, she tugged on his hair.

He glanced up with hazy eyes and wet lips. "Good morning."

"Finish it."

The smile he gave her was positively wicked. "Not yet."

His tongue swiped against her in a long, luscious lick. Her breath caught and her heartbeat hiccupped.

The man was going to kill her.

"Jarrett, now." She threaded her fingers through his hair and pressed his mouth tighter against her.

He moaned and the sound vibrated against her. "Soon."

"Paybacks are hell."

He peeked up at her. She could see his tongue work its way in and out of her. Those sexy eyes focused on her as his fingers pressed in deeper. The combination of his face and his hands . . . and that tongue. It was a wonder she didn't have a heart attack.

She closed her eyes and let her head fall back against the pillow. Sensations washed over her. She went from ready to near explosion. Excitement welled inside her and her lower body left the bed.

Still he licked.

One heel dug into the mattress and the other slid up his back. She was wrapped around him and his mouth was on her. Those arm muscles flexed one more time and she pulled down hard on the scarf. The orgasm ripped through her a second later. Started at her center and radiated out until every inch of her caught fire.

"Yes." She breathed the word into the air.

The licking continued as the tremors rumbled through her. Lying there, her chest convulsing as she tried to draw in air, she noticed the weight of his body on her and the sweet intimacy of being naked with him and comfortable. She might never put on clothes again. She didn't dare suggest it or he would insist on it.

"What has you smiling?"

One eye popped open and his face swam before her. With his body balanced on his elbow, he hung over her. His fingers caressed her nipple as he leaned in for a kiss. She tasted herself on his tongue and smelled her scent all over him. She thought that was the sexiest thing ever.

When they finally came up for air, her body trembled. "You can do that anytime."

"It was amazing."

Her hands opened and the scarf lay against her palms. "I may never move again."

"That has my vote." He sprinkled kisses over her breasts as his cock pressed against her thigh. "Stay right here and I'll come in every fifteen minutes and satisfy you."

"Then I'll never walk again."

Looked like he was ready for another round. Right. As soon as her heart started beating again, she'd join in.

The phone buzzed on the nightstand. The vibrating moved it a few inches until it traveled to the edge.

The thing went off all the time. She wanted to throw it in the toilet. "Who is that?"

He chuckled. "Someone with a terrible sense of text timing."

"Two minutes ago would have been terrible. This is merely annoying."

He picked up the phone and blinked a few times while he read the screen. "Okay. Huh."

At that response she came fully awake. "What is it?"

"It's from Natalie."

A topic sure to kill the mood. "That's never good."

Jarrett sank back into the pillows as he read. "Seems an economist named Todd Rivers died in a house fire at his home in Maryland."

"Are you kidding?"

Jarrett scrolled down with his thumb. "The authorities think it was a—"

"Gas leak."

He glanced at her. "How did you know?"

"Trade secret." She thought about the man she once knew and tried to figure out how he'd gone so far off course. Taking the job too seriously was one thing. Fighting for promotions she could see. Selling out his team and his country? There was no excuse she could muster. No way she could make that right.

She'd been through a lot, but there was never a question about which side she would pick. Flaws and all, her work with the agency had meaning and she refused to apologize for it.

Jarrett dumped the phone back on the table as he yawned and stretched. "Remind me to stay on Natalie's good side."

But Becca's mind wasn't on Natalie. "I guess I should feel bad for him."

"I wanted to do it myself. Take Todd right out of the game and make sure he knew who was twisting the blade." Jarrett pulled her over him until his arms wrapped around her and her hand rested on the middle of his chest.

"Not a good idea."

"He tried to kill you." Jarrett's body shook as he spoke. "There's no way I forgive that."

She decided they'd had enough agency-related excitement. They'd also spent more time on Todd than he was worth. Tomorrow at some point she'd mourn the man she thought he was. Until then, she'd enjoy the one and only man who had come to mean everything to her.

She kissed his chest, then did it again, letting her hair brush over his skin. Just the way he liked it.

"What was that for?"

She could hear the smile in his voice. She lifted her head to see it because every one of them still blinded her with happiness. "I love you."

"Don't stop."

His serious tone stopped her. She ran a finger over his bottom lip. "Never."

"I love you, too." He kissed her head. After a few beats of silence, he spoke again. "Since we're up . . ."

Her eyes popped open. So much for drifting back to sleep.

And she couldn't help but chuckle over the eagerness in his voice. "Good grief, man."

"Well, you did say something about me getting a turn."

She slid on top of him. "And you can always trust me to follow through with my promises."

"Always."

ABOUT THE AUTHOR

Bestselling and award-winning author **HelenKay Dimon** spent twelve years in the most unromantic career ever—divorce lawyer. After dedicating all that time and effort to helping people terminate relationships, she is thrilled to write romance novels full time. Her books have been featured at *E! Online* and in the *Chicago Tribune*, and she has had two of her books named "Red-Hot Reads" in *Cosmopolitan* magazine. When not writing, she teaches fiction and romance writing at MiraCosta College and UCSD and generally wastes a lot of time watching bad Syfy channel movies.

HelenKay loves to talk with her readers and can be reached through her website, helenkaydimon.com, or her Facebook page, facebook .com/HelenKayDimon.